THE SEA GOD TO THE RESCUE!

The pirates leaped to their feet and came running after Jason. Then they halted, screamed, and drew back in obvious terror. Jason turned and looked behind him and saw the being that was emerging from the water.

It was a biped, somewhat larger than a man and it stood with a forward-leaning posture balanced by a long thick tail that ended in flukes. What it stood on were webbed feet, and the two arms ended in clusters of four long claws connected by thick webbing. The body was bulky but lithe, with what looked like gills to the side. The eyes were large and dark.

It wasn't until later that Jason took in all these details. In that first instant, he could absorb the overall impression . . . and feel a tantalizing sense of familiarity, as though he ought to recognize the being. He was thinking about it when the mouth opened and the alien spoke in a strange Achaean: indescribably accented as a result of [illegible]ced by nonhuman vocal appara[illegible]f long, long practice.

"Come with m[illegible]ed at the water.

Jason could on[illegible]commotion among the pirates. [illegible], beside the idol, there was a wavering in the air, not at all like that caused by rising heat, but rather a disturbance of something more fundamental, of reality itself.

"Quickly!" said the alien. "Follow me if you wish to live!" Without another word, the being turned with a sinuous twist of its entire body and dived smoothly into the water.

BAEN BOOKS by STEVE WHITE

Blood of the Heroes

The Prometheus Project

Demon's Gate

Forge of the Titans

Eagle Against the Stars

Prince of Sunset

The Disinherited
Legacy
Debt of Ages

with David Weber:
Crusade
In Death Ground
The Stars At War
Insurrection
The Shiva Option
The Stars at War II

with Shirley Meier:
Exodus

BLOOD OF THE HEROES

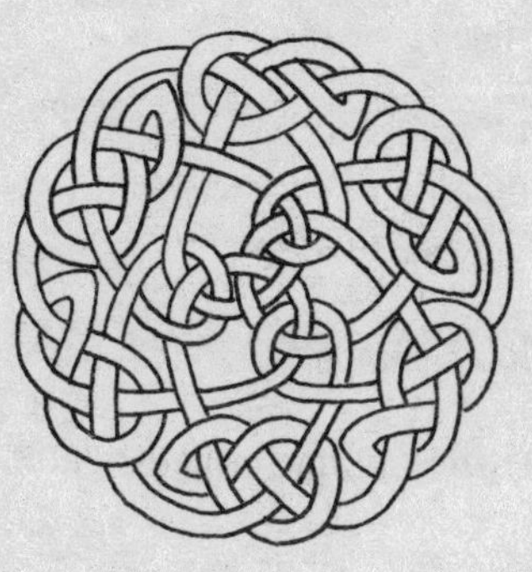

STEVE WHITE

BLOOD OF THE HEROES

A Baen Book

Baen Publishing Enterprises
P.O. Box 1403
Riverdale, NY 10471
www.baen.com

ISBN 10: 1-4165-2143-7
ISBN 13: 978-1-4165-2143-3

Cover art by Bob Eggleton

First Baen paperback printing, August 2007

Distributed by Simon & Schuster
1230 Avenue of the Americas
New York, NY 10020

Printed in the United States of America

10 9 8 7 6 5 4 3 2 1

To Sandy,
who is almost as indispensable
as she is loved.

CHAPTER ONE

Jason Thanou had never really cared for Earth all that much. Now, watching the blue-white-and-buff globe wax in the observation lounge's wraparound viewscreen, he saw nothing in the spectacle to make him forget his dislike.

So, he wondered, *why am I reacting this way?*

He knew he had no reason to be surprised. It was always the same, aboard a ship approaching Earth—no other planet had the same effect, not even the planet of his birth. It came at the indefinable moment when the mother planet, as sentimentalists called it, ceased to be *away* and became *down*—a world and not an astronomical object. Nor did the feeling fade with familiarity; he still felt the excited apprehension that caused the heart to race and the skin to tingle and the bowels to loosen. It never changed. Nor was it unique to him. Most outworlders admitted to the same strange exhilaration, and Jason had never found the others' denials convincing.

Still, he wondered why. Especially on this occasion, when he was here against his will and should by rights have felt nothing but cold distaste.

He decided the animus and the shivers both had the same cause: the sheer, psychologically oppressive ancientness of the place. It was a world—no, *the* world—that humans had not molded from barrenness over the past few centuries (to use the Earth-standard units of time everyone still used, which was yet another irritant). Here, the memory of billions of human lives across thousands of years permeated every acre. History had soaked into the soil like blood—an apt simile, from what Jason knew of Earth's past, which was quite a lot thanks to the job he'd once had. . . .

And to which he was now returning involuntarily. The resentment that had been simmering within him for the entire voyage boiled up anew, banishing his philosophical musings and leaving only a flat dislike of everything about this trip, especially this overripe fruit of a planet.

Jason heard a soft murmuring behind him as stewards moved among the passengers in the lounge. No blaring announcement from an intercom—this was a pricey spaceline. That, at least, was one way he'd been able to exact revenge. He had booked passage normally beyond his means, knowing he would have to be reimbursed.

"Excuse me, Commander Thanou," said one of the stewards diffidently. "We are entering our final approach pattern for Pontic Spaceport."

Jason smiled inwardly at the name of Eastern Europe's

central spaceport on the steppes north of the Black Sea, so typical of the Earth fad for reviving place names of archaic flavor. "Thank you. Has my planetside transportation been arranged as I requested?"

"It has, Commander. You have a reservation on an aircoach departing two hours after our arrival. We have made certain that you will arrive in Athens by midafternoon local time." The steward's courtesy, verging on obsequiousness, went beyond the requirements of his job.

"Excellent," Jason said absently, most of his attention on the viewscreen. The north coastline of the Mediterranean was beginning to scroll beneath the ship.

Why Athens? Jason wondered, not for the first time. *Why does Rutherford want me to report to him at his office there, and not at Service headquarters in Australia? Is it just another of his little ways of irritating me?*

Well, two can play at that game. . . .

"Thank the purser for me," he said. "And now, I think I'll return to my stateroom. I believe I have time to change clothes before we land."

"Most certainly, Commander." The steward's attitude was reflected in the stares from Jason's fellow passengers as he left the lounge. He'd grown used to that attitude, and those stares, since the nature of his business on Earth had become general shipboard knowledge.

Time travelers had that effect on people.

"I assume you're trying to irritate me," said Kyle Rutherford coldly.

"Whatever do you mean?" asked Jason with an air of innocence whose bogusness was insultingly obvious.

Rutherford merely continued to glare from behind his desk, to the left of the door which had just slid silently shut behind Jason. Opposite the door, a virtual window provided a view of Athens from a higher level than the office in fact occupied. The location was about right, though, peering over the Philopappos Hill toward the Acropolis, serene in its ruined perfection, timeless . . . literally timeless as well as figuratively so, in the temporal stasis bubble that enclosed it. The technology had come too late to protect it from the atmospheric pollution that had almost eaten it away in the Hydrocarbon Era. But now, with that gone, what was left stood in the unique, eerie clarity of motionless air, to be gazed at from without rather than suffering the unintended vandalism of millions of tramping feet.

Elsewhere, the office held memorabilia. To the right, the wall opposite Rutherford's desk was covered with photographs at which a visitor from a couple of generations back would have peered in deepening puzzlement. Behind his desk, a display case contained various ordinary-seeming if very old-fashioned objects . . . which, Jason decided with an inner chuckle, made it a fitting backdrop for Rutherford.

"You *know* what I mean!" Rutherford finally blurted. He nearly forgot to speak in the pedantic accent affected by Earth's intelligentsia when addressing outworlders and other vulgarians.

"Oh, this." Jason pretended to finally notice the target of Rutherford's glare. He glanced down at the uniform he was wearing—field gray, with facings of silver-edged dark green, very much in a traditional quasi-military style. "I *am* entitled to wear it, you know, being an active-duty officer of the Hesperian Colonial Rangers."

The irony was that he hadn't worn it in . . . he'd forgotten how long. The difficulty of getting the Rangers into uniforms was so proverbial that it had become a point of pride with them. They even added their own flamboyant individual touches to the starkly utilitarian and unmilitary-looking field versions. Only on very special occasions, and under extreme duress, could they be induced to put on the service dress kit in which Jason now stood, and on which he had lavished a hitherto well-concealed capacity for spit and polish.

"I must beg to correct you," said Rutherford in a voice as frosty as his thinning hair and neatly trimmed Vandyke beard. "You're in the Temporal Service."

"Not any more!"

"I call your attention to the agreement by which you were permitted to take extremely early retirement from the Service—specifically to Part VI, Article D, Paragraph 15, Subparagraph—"

"Yes, yes, I know! The errand boy you sent to Hesperia explained it to me in great and loving detail." In fact, Jason had known about the deliberately inconspicuous clause all along. He had just never dreamed it would actually be invoked.

Rutherford permitted himself a tight little smile of constipated triumph. "Well, then, you understand that the Temporal Regulatory Authority has the right to reactivate you under certain special circumstances. Those circumstances have now arisen, and the right has been exercised. The Hesperian planetary government has placed you on temporary detached duty with the Service."

"Not of my own free will!"

Rutherford sighed theatrically. "Let us have done with this nonsense. I recall very well that you quit the Service five years ago in some childish fit of pique, and returned to your homeworld in the . . . oh, what system is it?"

"Psi 5 Aurigae," Jason ground out between gritted teeth. Pretended inability to remember which colonial system was which was yet another grating affectation of Rutherford's type of Earthman.

"But of course. At any rate, you rejoined that system's paramilitary constabulary, from which the Service had previously recruited you for your—" Rutherford looked like he had bitten into a bad pickle "—undeniable talents. Evidently you had decided that nursemaiding terraformers and tracking down smugglers of forbidden nanotechnology and rescuing thrill-seekers were more rewarding than the opportunity you had previously been afforded to do something *important*."

Jason thought of his homeworld, on the outer fringes of the human diaspora, as yet raw and unfinished and needing so much, especially law and order. There—in contrast to this fossilized world—human effort could still make a difference for the future. But he chopped off an angry retort and put on the insolent smile he knew was expected of him.

"Hey, some of those thrill-seekers are young and female . . . and you'd be amazed how grateful they can be for getting rescued! Besides, if memory serves, quitting the Service wasn't purely my idea. Come to think of it, you were the one who pointed that out to me. I seem to recall words like 'disrespect' and 'flippancy.' "

"True enough. I wasn't too terribly devastated to see you go, nor were certain others in the Authority whose age and learning and experience you were apt to disparage."

"Then why inflict my bad attitude on yourselves by hauling me back now?"

"I'll not insult your intelligence by claiming to be overjoyed to see you. Indeed, I would not have agreed to reactivating you had there been any alternative. Oh, and please do take a chair."

"I'd prefer to stand. And *why* is there no alternative to me?" Jason leaned over Rutherford's desk and made himself be reasonable and even ingratiating, for he thought he glimpsed a possibility of talking his way out of this. "Come on, Kyle! What can I possibly contribute that would outweigh the disadvantage of having someone on the team whose heart isn't in it? You know how I feel about—"

"Yes, I remember your vehemence about the oppressive weight of history that presses down on Earth." Rutherford took on a look of smug vindication. "Well, then, this is just the mission for you! You're going to see Earth before most of that history had happened—Earth when it was young. Slightly more than four thousand years younger than it is at present, in fact."

Without recalling having done it, Jason found that he had sat down. "Would you care to explain that statement?"

"Certainly." Rutherford leaned forward, and his eyes glowed with an avidity that made him almost sympathetic. "We want you to lead an expedition to observe the volcanic explosion of Santorini in 1628 B.C. and its aftermath."

All at once, Jason's resentment was forgotten. "*What?* But . . . how?"

"Yes, I know, it is incomparably further back than we have ever sent humans before. But there have never been any absolute, theoretical objections to a temporal displacement of this magnitude . . . or any magnitude, for that matter. The limiting factors have been political and economic. We have, with great difficulty, obtained authorization for this expedition. It helps that this project lacks the . . . sensitive aspects of some of our other proposals involving the distant past."

"Right. I remember how you had to quietly drop the idea of an expedition to Jerusalem in the spring of 30 A.D."

"Indeed." Rutherford shuddered at the recollection. "At the same time, the event in question is one of the most important in human history, and one whose effects are still very much in dispute."

Jason nodded unconsciously. One of the justifications for time travel's hideous expense was the resolution of historical controversies and mysteries. Written records tended to be incomplete, biased, self-serving or downright mendacious. Only direct observation could reveal the truth behind the veil of lies, myths, defamation and propaganda. Already, only half a century after its invention, the Fujiwara-Weintraub Temporal Displacer had forced historians to rethink much of what they had thought they'd known. And, in the process, the investigators had been able to establish a trade in items from the past that was so lucrative it helped defray the cost.

Of course, Jason reflected, *they often keep some of the choicest items for themselves.* He glanced at the display case behind Rutherford's desk. A sword caught his eye: a standard-issue early nineteenth century dragoon saber, somewhat the worse for wear and utterly undistinguished save for the fact that on a March day in 1836 a certain William Barrett Travis, colonel by dubious virtue of a commission from an arguably illegal insurrectionist government, had used it to draw a line in the dust of an old Spanish mission's courtyard in San Antonio, Texas, North America. . . .

Jason dragged his mind back to the matter at hand. "You still haven't explained why you need me, in particular. I'm not the only one with my qualifications. Almost," he added, because it seemed a shame not to live down to Rutherford's expectations, "but not quite."

"Two reasons. The first is the perennial problem of physical inconspicuousness. Of all the available persons with your qualifications—fairly rare ones, as you have indicated with your characteristic modesty—we feel you are the one with the best chance of passing unremarked in the target milieu."

"Probably true," Jason grudgingly conceded. Most of Earth, for most of its history, had not been as ethnically cosmopolitan as it had become since the Industrial Revolution. A blond, blue-eyed European in Ming Dynasty China, or an obvious African in Peter the Great's Russia, would have some explaining to do. In theory, the capability to alter physical appearances by nanotechnological resequencing of the genetic code had existed for centuries. But the crazy excesses of the Transhuman movement before its bloody suppression had placed that sort of thing beyond the pale of acceptability. The Service had to make do with what it had. For this part of the world, what it had were people like Jason, who looked as Greek as his name sounded, even though he was—like most living humans, and practically all the outworld ones—a walking bouillabaisse of national origins.

"Secondly," Rutherford continued, "the sheer, unprecedented magnitude of this temporal displacement—more than three times as far back as we have ever attempted to send humans, in fact—limits the mass which can be displaced, and therefore restricts us to a numerically small expedition."

Jason gave another nod of unconscious agreement. The tradeoff was axiomatic.

"In point of fact, we are limited to three people. The matters we wish to observe involve at least two entirely separate fields of knowledge. Therefore two members of the team must be specialists. This leaves only one position—that of mission leader—for a generalist. So that person must be a recognized expert in survival under unique and sometimes unanticipated conditions, with a proven record of resourcefulness." Rutherford paused, then resumed with an obvious effort. "Doubtless it was for these very qualities that the Hesperian Rangers found you valuable."

Jason didn't even notice Rutherford's inept best effort at flattery. His mind was too busy running through the difficulties. "But . . . this is crazy! What about language? Do we even know what they were speaking then, much less how it sounded?"

"That problem has, of course, been taken into account. I will go into more detail later, for you and the other members of the team." Rutherford's eyes took on a shrewd twinkle. "Aren't you interested in knowing who they are?"

"Not particularly."

Taking the absence of outright refusal as emphatic agreement, Rutherford manipulated controls on his desk. A holographically projected three-dimensional viewscreen appeared in the middle of the air. It showed a woman's face—a high-cheekboned face of classical regularity framed by long straight hair of a very dark auburn. Large green eyes gazed out from beneath straight dark brows. The nose was a graceful aquiline curve. The wide, rather full-lipped mouth wore an expression that was cool almost to the point of severity.

Jason sat up straight and stared. All at once, this job seemed more interesting.

"Deirdre Sadaka-Ramirez," said Rutherford. "A recognized expert in geology and vulcanology. And very experienced in fieldwork on her homeworld of Mithras."

Jason's pleasurable speculations hit a bump. *Well, now I understand the severity*, he thought.

The third planet of Zeta Tucanae had been settled early, during the era of slower-than-light colonization before the invention of the negative-mass drive. The colonists had been very much on their own when they'd discovered that the planet held unsuspected autochthones. Whether or not the nightmarish beings had been truly intelligent was still a subject of learned debate. What was beyond debate was the insensate ferocity with which they had sought the extirpation of the bipedal invaders from space. (The fact that the terraforming project was making their world uninhabitable for them might have had something to do with it.) The human species' survival on Mithras had hung by a thread, and women had not been expendable. An entire ethos had grown up around the necessity for protecting them, leading to a resurrection of nearly forgotten social attitudes. That had been a couple of centuries ago, and Mithras was now part of the general cosmopolitan culture. But even today, women from that world still had a reputation for aggressively—sometimes abrasively—asserting an equality that, in the larger human society, had long ago passed beyond the need for assertion.

Well, thought Jason with an inward sigh, *I always did like a challenge.*

Rutherford fiddled with the controls again, and a new face appeared—a far less interesting one, from Jason's standpoint. Male, gaunt-featured . . . and definitely middle-aged.

"Wait a minute—" Jason began.

Rutherford overrode him. "Dr. Sidney Nagel—quite possibly Earth's premier living authority on the history and archaeology of the Aegean Bronze Age, despite his relative youth."

" 'Relative youth'? He's—"

"I am aware that he is somewhat older than most people we send back in time to primitive milieus. But we have assured ourselves that he will be up to the hardships involved. He met all our health and fitness requirements." Rutherford smiled. "He had incentive to do so, after a career spent trying to resolve mysteries by educated guesswork and inferences from a heartbreakingly few hard facts. Offered an opportunity to actually see the era . . . well, he would have been willing to sell his soul to the Devil for it, in an age when such things were thought possible. Nowadays, he was willing to undergo a hard regimen of physical conditioning, and pass our standard training course in low-technology survival."

Jason studied the image. There was something to be said for that kind of motivation. And yet, as he looked at the professorial face with its humorless mouth and dark-brown eyes flanking a substantial beak of a nose, he found himself thinking: *A Rutherford in training.*

"I suppose," he said aloud, "that neither of them knows anything about time travel."

"Well, I imagine they know what the average well-informed layman knows, from the popular literature on the subject."

"Which means they know nothing," said Jason dourly.

"I am counting on you to repair that lack."

"Me? But you've got all the top experts working for you." Jason shifted in his chair.

"Experts tend to stupefy the listener with technical jargon and unnecessary detail. Certain unkind persons have even accused *me* of this sort of behavior. An introduction from someone whose knowledge is of a practical nature, acquired in the field, might be more useful."

"Some sense in that." Agreeing with Rutherford caused Jason physical pain.

"In fact," Rutherford continued, on a rising note of self-satisfaction, "you can begin their orientation at once."

"What? You mean they're here in Athens?"

"I thought it well to bring them here, in anticipation that you would wish to meet your team members without delay." Rutherford stood up. "Shall I send for them?"

For an instant, Jason's resentment came roaring back in full force. His mouth almost opened to tell Rutherford where to put this mission, to declare that he would legally contest the Service's right to order him into the past. . . .

The past when—how did Rutherford put it?—Earth was young. Jason's eyes strayed to the Acropolis. *I wonder what was there then?*

And besides, Deirdre Sadaka-Ramirez did look awfully

intriguing. . . .

"Well, I don't suppose it could hurt to talk to them."

Rutherford smiled and spoke into a grille on his desktop. "Please ask them to come in."

CHAPTER TWO

"Please be seated," Rutherford told them as they entered. "Permit me to introduce Commander Jason Thanou, your mission leader." He was on his best behavior, giving Jason his Rangers rank and even pronouncing his surname correctly. ("Thane-oh," not "Than-ooh.") He then proceeded to introduce the new arrivals, which was redundant but which gave Jason a chance to study them.

Deirdre Sadaka-Ramirez wasn't quite as tall as he'd imagined from her face, which was probably just as well from the standpoint of blending into the Bronze Age population. She wasn't short, though, and her figure was a solidly constructed hourglass. The latter was obvious even in the no-nonsense jumpsuit she was wearing—maroon, which complemented her coloring. She gave Jason a brief smile of measured cordiality.

Dr. Nagel was very much as per expectations, aside from being somewhat stockier than his sharp features suggested. His consciously old-fashioned, expensively fusty clothing was the uniform of academia. Jason noted a tightening of his thin lips at Rutherford's use of the term "mission leader." As soon after the introductions as politeness permitted—or perhaps just slightly sooner than that—he turned to Rutherford, ignoring Jason.

"I say, Kyle, given my credentials in Aegean Bronze Age studies, surely it should be myself who—"

"No, Sidney. I remind you of the Articles of Agreement you signed with the Temporal Regulatory Authority."

"Well, er, yes, I seem to recall some legalistic boilerplate. But I naturally assumed that it didn't apply in *my* case."

"Revise your assumptions." Rutherford's brusqueness with a kindred spirit was almost shocking, until Jason recalled how the old bastard could be when it came to defending his administrative turf. "The Authority has exclusive jurisdiction of all extratemporal activities. That has been settled beyond dispute for a generation. And the Temporal Service is the Authority's enforcement arm. Every expedition into the past is required to be under the supervision of a Service representative whose legal powers are comparable to those of a ship's captain in the age of sail—and for much the same reasons. If you find you are unable in good conscience to abide by these terms, your only honorable course is to withdraw from the expedition." Rutherford took on a crafty look. "I daresay we could probably find a willing replacement from among the ranks of your colleagues."

Nagel's face darkened with emotion. "You mean that

impudent puppy Boudreau! Or Markova, with her asinine, unacceptable theory that—" He got himself under control with a comically visible effort. "Of course not, Kyle. I have every intention of following the Authority's guidelines to the letter. I never meant to imply otherwise. And I have no doubt that Mr. Thanou's competence is of a high order."

"The Authority has the fullest confidence in him," said Rutherford pointedly.

"I'm sure we all do, regardless of . . . er, that is . . ." Nagel's *we*, addressed to Rutherford, had held a certain near-imperceptible intonation that Jason had learned to recognize. It meant "we *Earthmen*." But now Nagel trailed off to a miserable halt, having belatedly realized that making his meaning explicit might not be advisable. What brought him to that realization was a glare from Deirdre Sadaka-Ramirez—another outworlder—under which he now wilted.

Oh, yes, Jason sighed inwardly. *This trip is going to be lots of fun.*

"And now," said Rutherford after letting Nagel suffer for a few seconds, "I've asked Commander Thanou to give you the benefit of his extensive experience by answering any questions you may have about the theory and practice of time travel."

Deirdre Sadaka-Ramirez broke the awkward pause. "Actually, Commander, it might be better if you would simply run through the basics for us. I probably don't know enough about the subject to be able to frame questions."

At least she admits it, thought Jason. Nagel, now himself again, sat back with the superior smile of the overspecialized academic, secure in the certainty that his expertise in his particular field qualified him as an expert in *every* field.

"Surely, Ms. Sadaka-Ramirez," said Jason, giving her the look of undivided attention that he'd always found got the best results with women, "you must have *some* questions in your mind about it. Most people seem to, even though we've been doing it for a while now."

"Well, yes. I'm just afraid they'll seem foolish. I've read something of the history of time travel as a concept. It used to be a common fictional device, but one which was clearly understood to be impossible in the real world."

"So was beating the limiting velocity of light," Jason pointed out. "Until someone actually found a way around it. *Around*, not *through*. That's a crucial distinction."

"Understood," she nodded. "But time travel was regarded as a fundamental philosophical impossibility, because of the paradoxes it allowed for. As somebody once put it, if you could travel into the past, then what was to prevent you from killing your grandfather before he met your grandmother? In which case, you would never have been born . . . and so how could you have traveled back in time and killed him?"

"The 'Grandfather Paradox,' it was called," Jason nodded. "The classic response to it was: 'Why should I want to kill him? I think he's a wonderful old fellow.' " He held up a forestalling hand. "Yes, of course I'm being facetious. The possibility still exists, even if only for doing it by accident. And, in the entire scope of the future, there are bound to be people with good reasons for wanting to change history—killing Hitler while he was still just a bum in pre-World War I Vienna, for example, or similar cases in the early stages of the Transhuman movement. But please continue."

"The other problem was perhaps not as immediately obvious. If you could travel into the future and come back with, say, next week's racing results, it would mean information was being transmitted at more-than-infinite velocity, violating the relativistic lightspeed limit—which, as you've indicated, can't be violated, just evaded in certain mathematically limited ways. In fact, it would violate causality itself." She looked at Jason levelly and spoke in a challenging tone which was clearly habitual with her. "As far as I can see, those arguments are still as valid as they ever were. But they can't be, can they? After all, time travel is now so well established that it needs a bureaucracy to regulate it. So please help me with this."

"As a matter of fact," said Jason, "you haven't begun to exhaust the philosophical objections to time travel. Actually, I think you may have had the right idea the first time; I'll just start at the beginning, and hopefully the answers to your questions will become apparent." He turned to Nagel with a smile. "I apologize in advance if I seem to be patronizing you by lecturing you on what you may already know." *Thus giving you a taste of being patronized, you pompous, conceited jackass!* he loudly did not add. Without giving Rutherford a chance to summon up a warning glare, he started in.

"About seventy years ago, Weintraub made the crucial discovery that all matter possesses what he termed 'temporal energy potential,' an 'anchor' holding it in time. He confirmed this experimentally by manipulating it so as to displace objects in time. Those first experiments involved subatomic particles, and the displacement was of infinitesimal duration. Only with the most sensitive of measuring instruments was it possible to observe that the particles appeared a few microseconds *before* the experiment, remaining for a period measured in nanoseconds—the same period for which they vanished *after* the power was turned on—and then 'snapping back' to their proper time. Temporal energy potential is very stubborn stuff. It also exists only up to the constantly advancing 'present.' This, by the way, answers the second objection you raised, Ms. Sadaka-Ramirez. The future is, in an absolute sense, nonexistent until it happens. There can be no travel into it.

"At first Weintraub's discovery, however revolutionary in theoretical terms, had no practical application. Nobody, it seemed, had to worry about murdered grandfathers. But then, twenty years later, Fujiwara discovered an all-or-nothing process by which the temporal energy potential of objects could be cancelled entirely."

Rutherford, who had been doing an admirable job of holding his tongue, could no longer contain himself. "The mathematical underpinning of this process is one which—"

"—you don't want to hear about," Jason finished for him firmly. "Believe me, you really don't." Rutherford subsided unhappily, and Jason resumed. "All you need to know is that the process is controllable, so that matter can be sent back in time to a desired date in the past—and will remain in the past until its temporal energy potential is restored by use of a 'temporal retrieval device' or TRD, whereupon it 'snaps back' to the linear present."

"Uh . . . excuse me," Deirdre ventured. "'Linear present' . . . ?"

"Sorry. That's a convenience label we use for the fact that time passes at the same rate for a temporally displaced object as it does in the 'present' from which the object was displaced. This became apparent in

Weintraub's pioneering experiments, as I indicated earlier. And it proved to hold true for living beings as well, contrary to some earlier theoretical speculations that living matter constituted a 'reverse state of entropy' or something like that." Jason saw from his listeners' expressions that he was starting to lose them. Even Nagel's know-it-all look was wavering. "Let me put it this way. Suppose you were sent back in time from the Authority's displacer stage in Australia at 10:00 A.M. on June 1, and spent five days and one hour in the past before your TRD activated. You would then reappear on the stage at 11:00 A.M. on June 6. That's flat. Remember what I said before about the constantly advancing wave front between the past and the future that we call the 'present'? Well, you're wedded to it. You can't just pick a date and time you're going to return to. This is an immutable fact that the Service has to live with. It's fundamental to our operating procedures.

"Now, the displacement of matter back into the past requires a massive physical installation and a tremendous expenditure of energy. The actual energy requirement is tied to two factors: the mass being displaced, and how far back that mass is being sent. For *this* displacement, it's going to cost a lot to send even the three of us." From Rutherford's direction came a grunt of sad accord. "Furthermore, for objects of significant mass an initial energy surge is required—an 'oomph' if you will." Jason pretended not to notice Rutherford's wince of pain. "This sends the object in question back about three hundred years before the effect becomes controllable. Therefore you can't be sent to a time any more recent than that. Incidentally, this disposes of another theoretical difficulty with time travel; there is no possibility of going back and meeting your own younger self.

"Anyway, there is only one such installation. It's here on Earth—"

"Naturally," Nagel interjected.

Jason gritted his mental teeth. But Nagel, however insufferable, was right. Only on this planet was there a past—a human past, anyway—to be explored.

"—in Western Australia," Jason finished, proud of himself for his level tone of voice. "It had to be built in a relatively empty country, as far as possible from large population centers, because the energy requirements could only be met by an antimatter power plant. It's the only such power plant on the surface of Earth—or of any other inhabited planet—rather than in orbit like all the others. There are elaborate fail-safe systems in place, and the chances of an accident are considered vanishingly remote. But . . ." Jason let the thought trail off.

Nagel momentarily let his guard slip, and his expression showed that he'd never considered this issue. "Then why isn't this installation placed in space as well?"

"A reasonable question, Dr. Nagel." Jason decided he might as well be conciliatory, especially inasmuch as it really *was* a reasonable question. "In fact, for reasons which are too technical to go into just now, time travel will only work within, and in relation to, a substantial gravity field. If you think about it, this *has* to be the case. Otherwise . . . well, someone who traveled into the past would find himself watching Earth recede at roughly eighteen miles a second as it revolves around the Sun, and wishing he'd thought to wear a space suit." Actually, it was worse than that, given the Sun's orbital velocity around the center of the galaxy . . . and that was just for starters. But Jason decided to keep it simple. "Another fortunate consequence: it doesn't matter where the displacer is located on the surface of the planet producing the gravity field. The displacer stage can whisk you anywhere on Earth at the same time it's displacing you into the past. We won't have to make our way across the ancient world from Australia to Greece."

Nagel leaned forward, now openly intrigued. "But why hasn't this made all forms of public transportation on Earth obsolete? World-wide teleportation—"

"It doesn't work that way. Remember the three-hundred-year minimum trip into the past? You have to go at least that far back. And when your TRD activates and you regain your temporal energy potential, you snap back to exactly the same location you were displaced from, due to conservation-of-energy considerations. Anyway, even if it was possible to flick people around in the present, the expense would limit it to being a toy for the super rich."

Deirdre Sadaka-Ramirez spoke up. "You keep talking about this 'TRD.' . . ."

"Right—the temporal retrieval device. As I've explained, it takes a huge, expensive, energy-intensive installation we call the 'displacer' to cancel an object's temporal energy potential and send it into the past. But restoring that temporal energy potential so that the object returns to the linear present is almost unbelievably easy. For a human-sized object—with its clothing and as much mass as a human can conveniently carry—all it takes is a device that can be miniaturized to the size of a small pea, drawing an insignificant amount of energy. Good thing, too; this makes time travel practical."

"Yes, I can see that," she nodded her dark-auburn head. "I recall being told that we're going to have to have this device implanted. . . ." A cloud shadow seemed to cross her features. Nagel looked equally troubled. Jason understood their queasiness, which practically all of society shared. It was another hangover from the Transhuman madness.

"That's correct," he said quietly. "It's a very minor surgical operation, which will be performed after we get to Australia."

"Is that really necessary?" asked Nagel peevishly. "Can't we just carry the things?"

"Standard Temporal Service procedure dictates that—" Rutherford began. Jason motioned him to silence. He subsided huffily and let the younger man answer Nagel.

"Yes, I suppose so," Jason conceded. "You could carry an obviously advanced device which would take a lot of explaining in the past—and which you might lose. Or it could be miniaturized as I've said—in which case you'd almost certainly lose it. And if you lose it, you're stranded in the past *permanently*." Jason paused to let that sink in, then put on a reassuring smile. "Anyway, this doesn't involve any proscribed bionics. The TRD isn't neurally interfaced with your brain in any way."

"Then how do you activate the thing?" Nagel demanded.

"You don't. It activates automatically, at a predetermined moment, timed by atomic decay—and you're back on the displacer stage in Australia, in the linear present."

A look of alarm began to awaken on Nagel's features. "But what if we should need to return to the present before that?"

"You can't," said Jason with finality. "This accounts for the provision in the Articles of Agreement you signed releasing the Temporal Regulatory Authority from liability." *More "legalistic boilerplate" you couldn't be bothered with reading*, he guessed. "If anything happens to you, you can't be rushed back to a modern hospital; you're stuck in the past for a fixed duration, with all that implies about medical care or the lack of it." Jason decided he'd better accentuate the positive. "This way, the Authority knows exactly when to expect you back, and can make sure the stage is clear at that time. Otherwise, you might find yourself occupying the same volume as another object." Jason didn't elaborate on that. His listeners' expressions showed he didn't need to.

"Yes," Deirdre said thoughtfully. "With only the one displacer stage in existence, I can see how 'traffic control' might be a problem. But what about our initial displacement into the past? There's not going to be anybody back then making sure our arrival location is clear."

"Yes!" exclaimed Nagel, to whom these problems had clearly never occurred. "And what about the air itself, in the space where we're going to occupy when we, uh, materialize?"

"Let me address those points in reverse order. We don't need to worry about the air, or any other matter in gaseous state; the energy release involved in the displacement suffices to shove it out of our way. And the displacement process involves a feedback feature which makes it impossible to send an object to time/space coordinates which are occupied by another solid object. If there's anything there, it will simply default to the nearest unoccupied location. Unfortunately, this does *not* work for the snapping-back process when the temporal energy potential is restored. Hence our concern with 'traffic control.' "

"All right," Deirdre nodded. "Understood. But isn't it a little unsettling to suddenly find yourself back in the present, without warning?"

"Oh, it won't be without warning," Jason assured her. "I'll let you know when to expect it."

"And how will *you* know?" Nagel inquired archly. "Do I gather you'll be wearing a wristwatch in the Bronze Age?"

"Scarcely, Dr. Nagel." Jason's voice was level and unapologetic. "In point of fact, I *do* have an actual, neurally interfaced computer implant."

For a moment, there was the kind of awkward silence that always prevails when people are too polite to pronounce a bigot word that has entered unbidden into their well-bred minds—in this case, *cyborg*.

"The Service enjoys a special, limited exemption from the Human Integrity Act," Jason explained, "as do certain law enforcement agencies like the Hesperian Colonial Rangers, from which I'm on temporary detached duty, in case you've wondered about this uniform. The implant has its uses for us. It enables us to carry around a lot of useful information. And I can use it to record whatever I see and hear—within limits, of course, since the storage capacity isn't infinite, but it's the only recording capability we'll have."

"That last feature is uniquely useful on this mission," Rutherford interjected. "In more recent eras, paper and ink would be locally obtainable; you would be able to take notes and conveniently bring them back with you. In the Bronze Age, that is not going to be the case." He took on a look of annoyance. "We really *do* need a new set of tenses for time travel, don't we?"

"Absolutely," Jason agreed, forestalling a digression. "But at any rate, another advantage of my implant is that I'll always know the actual time in the linear present."

Deirdre Sadaka-Ramirez spoke briskly, as though eager to move on to another subject. "Well, then, that's one thing we won't have to worry about. And this is all very interesting. But you still haven't answered my most basic question: how is it that we can travel back in time despite the paradoxes it seems to allow for? I suppose you're going to tell me the past can't be changed, but—"

"Oh, but the past *can* be changed," said Jason blandly. "We do it all the time."

They simply stared at him.

"In fact," he continued, enjoying the effect he was creating, "changing the past is the basis for our one, very unsatisfactory means of communicating with the present. You see, there is no such thing as a 'temporal radio' or anything like that."

"We're not totally ignorant, you know!" snapped Nagel.

"Of *course* not, Doctor," said Jason, in as soothing a tone as he could manage while snickering inwardly. "So you understand that time travelers are on their own. They can, however, leave a message—in some durable form, and well hidden—at a prearranged place and time. After that point in time rolls around in the linear present, the Authority sends somebody to that location to find it. And to answer your question before you even ask it: yes, we've thought of looking in such a location in advance. The message wasn't there. After the moment in the linear present when the plan called for the message to be deposited, the location was visited again . . . and the message *was* there."

There was an interval of uncomfortable silence.

"I was not aware of this . . . experiment," Nagel finally said.

"We don't go out of our way to publicize it," Rutherford admitted.

Deirdre Sadaka-Ramirez shook herself, and spoke almost defiantly. "Have you ever tried going to one of these locations before that 'point in the linear present' and staying there, watching, *through* that moment?"

Jason and Rutherford exchanged a look. Rutherford nodded.

"Naturally that's been thought of," Jason told her. "In fact, it's been done twice. In the first case, an expedition had been sent back to 1953 to clear up the details of Stalin's death. They were to leave a message at a particular location outside Moscow, Russia. A team was sent there to perform precisely the kind of observation you've suggested."

"And . . . ?" she breathed with a mixture of eagerness and apprehension.

"On the way from Australia, the team's aircar developed a malfunction. They were stuck in Calcutta until the moment was past. Then they went on to Moscow and found the message."

Deirdre Sadaka-Ramirez sat back, looking deflated and vaguely resentful.

"It was tried again when a team went back to 2021, a crucial time during the Chinese breakup. You can be sure every member of that team was required to be combat-trained! Anyway, that time the Authority made certain to have the observers in place at the message site outside the ruins of Beijing before the team even departed, and kept them there through the prearranged linear-present moment. The message never appeared."

"And what conclusions were drawn from that?" Deirdre asked eagerly.

"None. When the team returned—mostly in the form of corpses—the two survivors explained that they'd gotten caught up in a fire fight and had never been able to leave the message."

This time her look of resentment was not vague. Jason's smile only intensified it.

"I'm really not trying to be difficult." *Well, maybe just a little*, he mentally hedged. "I'm leading up to the real answer to your question about paradoxes. The past can be changed, yes—but only in small ways. Ways that don't create paradoxes. And don't ask me why. The incidence of alcoholism among physicists and philosophers has risen since they've started trying to figure it out. It seems to be related to the Observer Effect—Schrödinger's Cat, and all that. What it boils down to is that a time traveler can't change the observed world. Nobody ever had any reason to check those message sites before, so that's all right. But you can't go back and kill one of your own ancestors, simply because we know he *didn't* get killed."

"But," Nagel spluttered, "as a practical matter, what prevents you from killing him?"

"I have no idea, Dr. Nagel. But *something* will, if you try to. And the same goes for anything that will preclude the existence of your society. The *past* can be changed, but *history* can't."

Deirdre looked thoughtful. "You try to shoot Hitler in

Vienna before World War I, and the gun will jam."

"That's one possibility. But the way these things more typically work, you'd find out later that you had shot some *other* bum by mistake."

Nagel, obviously uncomfortable with this entire discussion, made a blustering effort to assert control. "Shall we turn our attention to practicalities? One thing I *do* know—" a withering glare at Jason "—is that we are to be supplied with the local spoken language by direct neural induction."

"That is correct," Rutherford nodded. "It is one of the Authority's obligations, specified in the Articles of Agreement."

"Well and good. But how can this be possible for the era in question? Granted, my definitive study of the subject has established beyond *reasonable* question—not to be confused with the questions raised by upstarts like Boudreau and Markova!—that an early form of Greek was already being spoken on the mainland, while one or more languages of the Hittite-Luwian family still prevailed on Crete and the Cyclades islands, including Santorini. But even I do not pretend to be able to provide a pronouncing gazetteer for these languages!"

Rutherford, back in his element, smiled a smile that exceeded even his usual capacity for oozing complacency. "Please rest assured that this has been taken into account, Sidney. The very fact that this expedition is being dispatched should tell you that we know. . . ." He let the sentence hang.

"You *know?*" Nagel leaned forward with an avidity that seemed odd in one who claimed to *know* already. *Perhaps,* Jason thought, *he wasn't quite as certain of his conclusions as he pretended.* "But how . . . ? Oh, tell me—!"

"All in good time, Sidney." Rutherford wasn't really a sadist, Jason reflected, but he did love his little secrets. "This will come out in the briefings you will receive in Australia. For now, I've asked you all to meet here in Greece so that we can examine the landscapes in question first-hand. I realize, Sidney, that this will be somewhat redundant for you. I also caution you that those landscapes will be quite different in the seventeenth century B.C. For one thing, Greece was much more extensively forested then. Still, this type of familiarization is not without value. I have an itinerary planned for tomorrow. I suggest we all make an early night of it."

They took the hint and began filing out. As they departed, Deirdre Sadaka-Ramirez gave Jason a coolly appraising look, and a challenging smile lifted the corners of her full lips.

" 'A ship's captain in the age of sail,' eh? I hope you don't plan to flog us."

Jason returned her smile in kind. "Only when necessary."

CHAPTER THREE

Jason had visited Greece before—modern Greece where Rutherford had his office, and the Greece of the past where he could so easily pass for a local. But he hadn't really spent as much time in either as one might have thought. His Service base of operations was in Australia, and temporal expeditions had—until now—ventured back only as far as the High Middle Ages, when the Byzantine Empire was still fitfully alive but Greece proper had already become an impoverished beachcomber by the shore of history. Neither in the present century nor in any other had he ever been to the places Rutherford now took them.

First they went southwest by aircar, over the Saronic Gulf with Salamis to the right, as the morning sun lay a dazzling trail on the watery grave of Xerxes' fleets. Then they were over dry land again—very dry, for this was the austere Peloponnesus. Specifically, Rutherford informed them, they traversed the Argolid. Jason stared down, brooding, at a landscape that epitomized Earth to him, for it has been shaped by human habitation so long that the terracing of the hillsides was practically as much a natural feature as the rock formations wrought by blind geological processes.

Presently, the gleam of sunlit water appeared again, ahead and to the left—the Gulf of Argos. Their destination was short of that, not far from the mouth of a river straggling through a plain covered with olive groves and orchards and crisscrossed with eucalyptus-lined roads. They landed beside such a road, where the trees shaded the riverbed—more gravel and alluvial silt than water, at least at this early-summer time of year. A town was just visible in the distance, at the base of a mountain—Argos, according to Rutherford.

Nagel's impatience could no longer be contained. "Kyle, why have you brought us here?"

"Because, Sidney, this is where you are going to appear in the seventeenth century B.C." Rutherford gave a frowning headshake.

"But why here?" Nagel asked. "Why not Santorini—safely before the explosion, of course!—or Crete or one of the Cyclades islands?"

"All in good time, Sidney." Rutherford's serenity was as sublime as it was infuriating. Jason, knowing the futility of trying to extract information before the old boy was good and ready, held his tongue. Deirdre Sadaka-Ramirez ignored the whole byplay, and simply stared at a vista utterly foreign to her experience.

"I caution you all," Rutherford resumed, "that things will be different in the target milieu. For one thing, Greece was far more well-watered then. This river—the Inachos, by the way—was capacious. Indeed, it must have often flooded."

"The least of these people's worries now," Jason commented.

"Nevertheless," Rutherford continued, ignoring him, "the basic contours of the land are not believed to have changed fundamentally. Our time is somewhat limited, but we will familiarize ourselves with this area before departing for Crete."

They spent most of the day doing hops around the valley, pausing for lunch at a waterfront *taverna* Rutherford knew at Nauplia, by the sea at the base of a cliff crowned by a fortress built by the Venetians in the medieval times to which Jason had traveled. It was a surprisingly good lunch, Jason thought—although, admittedly, he was very hungry. Deirdre, looking askance at the contents of the kitchen pots, satisfied herself with a basic Greek salad—mostly black olives, feta cheese and slices of startlingly red tomato, practically afloat in olive oil on a minimal bed of lettuce—accompanied by a *peponi* melon. Jason considered steering her away from resinated wine, but then suggested she try it, which she did gamely enough. He had a feeling it was probably closer to what would be available in the Bronze Age, before there were tourist palates to consider.

Afterwards they resumed their stops, pausing at each for a walk through territory of whose relevance Rutherford assured them in his usual uninformative way. Nagel made no attempt to conceal his above-it-all disdain. Deirdre was just as open in her fascination. Jason stored away topographical data with a methodical eye, untroubled by any stirrings of ancestral memories; he didn't think of himself as particularly Greek, nor as anything at all except Hesperian.

They didn't stop at the sinister cyclopean ruins at Mycenae and Tiryns, merely glimpsing them from the air. Rutherford assured them that those massive fortifications hadn't existed as such in the target era. Then they left Tiryns and nearby Nauplia behind and headed south over the sea.

At first they hugged the eastern coast of the Peloponnesus, where the Gibraltar-like mass of Monemvasia rose from the sea, before passing Cape Malea and turning southeastward across the Aegean. The sun was low in the sky when Crete—looking almost like a continent after so many diminutive islands—appeared ahead and to the right, occluding the darkening sky with its brooding, mountainous mass. By the time they grounded at Herakleion, the sun was setting behind Mount Juktas, the "Head of Zeus."

After dinner they once again "made an early night of it" at Rutherford's insistence. He also insisted, shortly after dawn the following morning, that they take a ground car up the valley from Herakleion to Knossos. The road was a winding, twisting one, but at least they only had to traverse a few miles—and listen to a limited amount of Nagel's grumbling—before stopping at the screen of cypresses behind which lay the mound of Knossos. Rutherford had called ahead, and the stasis field that protected the ruins from the ages had been lifted. It was still early, and they were alone as they walked through the trees and emerged to see the Palace of Minos.

Five hundred years after Sir Arthur Evans' excavation of this site, no one except specialists remembered the controversy that had once raged over his decision to reconstruct what he had unearthed, lest it collapse into rubble in the absence of the soil that had held it up for more than three thousand years. Nagel was such a specialist, and he muttered ritualistically about reinforced concrete columns, and frescoes that owed as much to late nineteenth century *art nouveau* as to the Minoan Bronze Age.

"Well, Sidney," Rutherford reminded him, "you may have the opportunity to see how close Sir Arthur actually came."

That silenced Nagel, and he looked around with new eyes at what he'd seen so many times before. Jason and Deirdre ignored him, for as far as the world at large was concerned, Evans had long ago triumphed over his detractors—or at least outlasted them. The passage of centuries had made his reconstructions a part of history in themselves, so that what he and his architect Christian Doll had wrought was now as legitimate a feature of Knossos as the works of the nameless builders of millennia before.

Like all Service members, Jason had gotten an extensive familiarization with Earth's history. Deirdre didn't have that depth and breadth of background knowledge, but as part of her preparation for this expedition she had learned something of this particular milieu. So, whatever Nagel may have thought, they both had some inkling of where they were and what it meant. As they walked through the northwest entrance and the propylaeum hall with its copied frescoes, Jason began to feel oppressed by the sheer, inconceivable ancientness of this haunted place. This was the concentrated and distilled essence of old Earth.

They proceeded through the dark, cavernous storerooms and walked up a flight of steps into the central courtyard. "Is this where they did the bull-leaping?" asked Deirdre, gesturing back in the direction of the frescoes they'd seen.

"That's what many popularizations would have us believe," said Nagel smugly. "But a moment's thought should convince anyone of the unlikelihood that it was ever done on a stone-paved surface."

"Hard enough to believe they ever did it *anywhere*," Jason mused, rubbing his itchy, bristly jaw. Rutherford had ordered him and Nagel to stop shaving.

"You are not the first to have that reaction," Nagel acknowledged with a kind of condescending graciousness. "When the frescoes first came to light, experts in rodeo-type sports flatly denied the possibility. But there is no room for doubt that it did occur."

They continued on, across the courtyard and down the restored grand staircase to the private apartments, with their appealing light airiness and their startlingly sophisticated plumbing. Then it was back to the west side of the courtyard and down a short flight of steps into what was called the throne room, although there was no proof that it had really been anything of the sort. Here, the ghosts clustered thickly around the high-backed alabaster chair that had given the chamber its name. Stealing a glance at Deirdre's face, Jason could tell that she felt their presence as well.

The psychological atmosphere lightened again when

they went above to a gallery of restored frescoes. Here again were the boys and girls vaulting over the backs of charging bulls, and portraits glowing with that blend of innocence and sophistication that the world of Evans' day had seen in them, and found so appealing.

"And it's never died down," Nagel pontificated. "The fascination is rooted in the mystery, of course. Even after the Minoan scripts were deciphered—the Linear B in the twentieth century, the Linear A somewhat later—the surviving tablets revealed no more about the society's inner life than a random day's worth of emptied bureaucratic wastebaskets would reveal about us. So we can read whatever we want into these people's art, and see whatever we want to see. To paraphrase what someone once said about the Neanderthals, each generation gets the Minoans it deserves."

"Not like the later Classical Greeks, who *did* put themselves on record," Jason remarked. "Admire them all you want, but you keep on bumping up against slavery and purdah and suicidal political stupidity."

Nagel gave him a sharp glace, as though really noticing him for the first time. "Very astute, Mr. Thanou." His *very* held an unmistakable connotation of *surprisingly*. "Evans' post-Victorian sentimentalism—he seems to have thought of the Minoans as children quivering on the verge of exquisite decadence—is something from which we still haven't altogether freed ourselves. Not too surprising. Evans was fairly imperious in his views, as though Knossos was his private estate. Come to think of it, Knossos *was* his private estate; he had bought the place. No one was apt to argue with him. So his influence lives on, despite everything that was discovered subsequently—clear evidence of human sacrifice, for example, and undeniable indications of ritual cannibalism."

On that somewhat chilling note, they reemerged into the warm Cretan sun, now at midmorning. After the initial tour, Rutherford had a series of in-depth studies he wanted them to do, in conjunction with reconstructions of the palace's layout, including the upper stories, holographically projected by his portable computer. Jason continued to note spatial relationships and distances, and store them away—not just in his memory, but also in the cybernetic memory of the implant in his skull, which recorded that which his eyes saw and could play it back through direct connection to his optic nerve. He saw nothing to be gained by reminding his companions of this capability, grateful though they might be for it later on.

Nagel found it necessary to quibble about the relevance of what they were seeing to what had existed in 1628 B.C., when the palace had already been half a millennium old. "It grew over time you know, almost like a living organism. At first it was isolated blocks of buildings grouped around the central court. Over the centuries, connections were built, open lanes became passageways and corridors, whole courtyards were roofed over and became rooms containing older structures, and the whole complex acquired an indescribable complexity, like . . . like . . ."

"Gormenghast," Jason supplied. Deirdre shot him an appreciative grin—evidently her reading of classic fantasy hadn't been limited to time-travel stories.

Nagel, on the other hand, gave him a glare of annoyed incomprehension. "At any rate, Kyle," he said, ostentatiously ignoring Jason, "it would be useful if we could make several visits to it, at intervals of a few centuries each, to confirm the stages by which the structure evolved."

Rutherford looked like he was having difficulty breathing—probably going into a kind of budgetary shock, Jason thought. "Well, at any rate, Sidney," he finally managed, still wheezing a bit, "the general outline had assumed more or less its final form by our target period, had it not?"

"Probably," Nagel grudgingly admitted. "After all these centuries, the exact dividing line between the Middle Minoan and Late Minoan periods is still a vexed question. We may find it still in its Middle Minoan III stage." The thought seemed to cheer him.

It was night before they returned to Herakleion. The next morning and early afternoon were spent in a series of brief visits to other sites in Crete—Phaestos, Gournia, Triada. Rutherford didn't let them stay in any one place very long, because they needed to depart from Athens for Australia the following evening, and he had one more stop he wanted them to make: Santorini.

"Needless to say," he told them, "the landscape there is even more changed than all the others you've seen. Indeed, most of the landscape simply doesn't exist anymore. Still, it can't hurt to have a look, and it's almost directly on our route back to Athens."

So they flew north from Herakleion over the blue Aegean for seventy miles. The mountains of Crete were still visible behind them in the afternoon sun when the islands of the Santorini group appeared ahead.

Their aircar swung around to the west in a near half-circle, to approach from the northwest, through the gap between the big crescent-shaped island of Thera to the left, and smaller, barren Therasia to the right, to pass over the deep waters of the Santorini caldera. They flew at an altitude of a thousand feet, which put them about level with the tops of the sheer cliffs that walled the caldera in strata of gray, black, rust-red and, at the top, dazzling white. Ahead, in the center of the caldera, the volcanic cone of Nea Kameni rose from the water.

Jason looked down at that water, almost as deep as the surrounding cliffs were high, too deep for any anchor chain to reach bottom. He tried, and failed, to imagine the event—"eruption" was a banality—which had obliterated the center of a large circular island, leaving this thirty-two-square-mile sea-filled crater ringed by shattered fragments of the original island. Here, very clearly, was a place where the Earth had vomited its guts out.

Jason stole a look at Deirdre. The touristlike fascination she'd shown up till now was gone, replaced by a look of intense, focused concentration. It was, Jason realized, the look of one who was finally seeing at first hand a place previously studied in great depth but only from a distance.

They followed the cliffs of Thera southward. Presently a brilliantly whitewashed town appeared, sprawling along the white cliff crest of which it seemed an outgrowth.

"In the old days," Rutherford told them, "the only access was by boat. You had to tie up at a jetty at the base of the cliffs, and go up nine hundred feet by foot or muleback. The adventurous, and those in search of authentic ambience, still do so." He pointed downward at the ramps and steps, cut into the cliff face in a crazy series of zigzags and switchbacks. Jason took one look and decided he was grateful for the aircar that wafted them to the top of the cliff and down onto a small landing area on the outskirts of the town.

They walked through narrow, winding, multilevel streets—alleys, really—to the hotel where Rutherford had arranged accommodations. Rutherford himself was fidgeting to use what remained of the daylight, but they were all tired after their series of excursions on Crete earlier in the day. He grudgingly agreed that they could afford an evening of relaxation.

Jason settled into his room—small, austere, immaculate—and then, restless, walked up to a rooftop terrace where a few people sat at small tables. The hotel was perched at the very edge of the vertiginous cliff, and the terrace overlooked the caldera. Jason leaned on the rough-textured balustrade and peered down at the crazy mule trail and the jetty far below. Then he gazed outward, west over waters that the sun, setting behind Nea Kameni, had turned to a trail of molten bronze, rippling out to that dark mass of solidified lava.

"Hard to imagine, isn't it?"

Jason turned at the sound of the familiar voice behind him. "Oh, hi, Ms. Sadaka-Ramirez."

"Deirdre, please." She had changed into a lightweight pale-blue dress whose translucent material would, Jason thought mischievously, have shown to best advantage with the low-lying sun behind her. "We may as well be on first-name terms, since we're going to be spending quite a lot of time in each other's company. *Subjective* time, I suppose I should say."

"So we are. I'm Jason. Let me buy you a drink."

For an instant, her face wore a defensive look—but only for an instant, before she smoothed it out. "Sure. Let's try the local wine."

Jason made no protest. They seated themselves at a

tiny table in an angle formed by the balustrade and an equally rough wall with a tiny stand-up bar—a pass-through, really—where Jason procured a carafe of wine.

"Not bad," he said after sipping it. "A little fizzy, but not bad. You say it's local? I'm surprised they can grow grapes here."

"Actually, they grow quite a few things here—tomatoes, barley and beans, as well as grapes. Volcanic soil is very fertile."

"Yes, but it needs water. This island can't possibly have any streams, and there's hardly any rain."

"It's due to something we got here too late in the day to see. Because of the way the cliffs overshadow the caldera, the sun doesn't hit the water until almost noon. And the water is very cold, being so deep. So the sudden heat causes lots of water vapor to rise up the cliffs and then pour down the slopes. So there's a high level of humidity."

Jason gave her a sharp look. "You really *have* made a study of this place, haven't you? By the way, what did you mean earlier? What is it that's hard to imagine?"

"What happened here four thousand years ago." She swept her arm around in a gesture that took in the entire volcanically sculpted panorama, and her face wore the same look he'd seen earlier when she had gotten her first look at Santorini from the air. "At that time a circular island—called, we believe, Kalliste—took in this whole semicircle of islets. And at the center of it was a mountain a mile high. These cliffs are just the remnants of that mountain's foothills!" She pointed to the cliffside where it curved away from them into the distance. "See that light-colored stratum? It's the pumice and general ejecta of that mountain, which blew out to cover the island. And it's a hundred to a hundred and fifty feet thick! Most of that cloud of ash and acidic gas—hot enough to vaporize people and other living things—expanded outward, covering the seabed and the islands to the southeast. Eventually, the ash and dust spread as far as Egypt.

"In the meantime, for a single unimaginable instant, towering walls of water must have hesitated above the cavity that had been blasted out. Then they crashed into it, striking that furnace-hot bottom and recoiling back outward in tsunamis—waves hundreds of feet high that must have devastated every coastal settlement in the Aegean that didn't have some kind of geographical shelter.

"It was the greatest natural disaster in Earth's history of which we have direct knowledge. The Krakatoa explosion in the early sixth century A.D., which started the dominoes of the Dark Ages falling, *may* have been bigger, but that's speculation. When Krakatoa blew its top again in 1883 A.D., in the full light of history, it depopulated the adjacent areas of the Indonesian archipelago and created visible effects literally around the world . . . and on that occasion it released only about a *third* of the energy that was released here where we're sitting, one autumn day in 1628 B.C."

Jason looked around at the peaceful, picturesque scene, with unfamiliar but appealing music making a counterpoint to the low murmur of conversations at the other tables. A shiver ran through him.

"And the volcano has been quiescent ever since?" he asked.

"Not altogether." Deirdre pointed outward at the Kameni islands in the middle of the caldera. "Those islands are fusions of volcanic cones resulting from a number of lesser eruptions since then. Palea Kameni had assumed its present form by the sixteenth century, when Nea Kameni appeared following a further eruption. Subsequent eruptions—including one in 1867 which was the first to be photographed—have been minor, and the configuration of the islands hasn't appreciably changed." She smiled. "Eventually, a new island will be built up, the same stresses will accumulate . . . and it will all happen again."

" 'World without end, amen,' " Jason quoted. He took a fortifying pull on his wine. "I repeat what I said earlier: you've obviously studied this place in depth. So maybe you can answer a question that's been bothering me. There seems to be no doubt in anybody's mind that the explosion took place in autumn of the year 1628 B.C. But how do we know that? It seems suspiciously exact."

"Oh, that's been known since around the turn of the twenty-first century, although it was controversial then. The 'autumn' part is an inference from the prevailing winds, as shown by the seabed deposits. And the year is a matter of dendrochronology."

"Uh . . . dendro . . . ?"

"Tree-ring dating. Trees grow a new ring every year, so their growth rates can be measured. And some very old ones like bristlecone pines, and certain others preserved in northern European bogs, date back to the Bronze Age. So we know there were a couple of very bad growth years—indicating very severe, prolonged winters such as would be produced by a world-girdling cloud of volcanic ash—between 1628 and 1626 B.C." She chuckled. "From what I've read, the archaeological establishment of that day went into deep denial when this came to light. It overturned some of their cherished theories, only a few years after they'd finally adjusted to radiocarbon dating."

"Nagel's ancestors," Jason remarked drily. He couldn't bring himself to worry about the crack's appropriateness—at least not as much as he knew he should.

Deirdre looked startled for a second, then laughed nervously. "Well," she temporized, not wanting to become a full accomplice in Jason's naughtiness, "they've come around by now, of course. They had to revise a lot of their assumptions to accommodate it. Or so I've read. I don't know the details, of course. History's not my field."

"No, it isn't. As much as I hate to admit it, I'm closer to Nagel than I am to you in terms of my areas of expertise. I had to soak up some background knowledge of Earth's history in the course of my job with the Service. Not that I have any academic credentials in the field, you understand," he added hastily.

"No," she smiled, "you don't seem the type. In fact, I can't avoid a certain curiosity. What led you into the Temporal Service in the first place?"

Jason felt an unaccustomed and unwelcome awkwardness. "Well, the pay is good," he offered. "Especially when you include the extratemporal duty bonus. And it all accumulates in a trust fund while you're displaced in time." This was true. After his separation from the Service there had been nothing to prevent him from retiring, except fear of an early death from boredom.

"No doubt. And I imagine that what you and Rutherford were telling us about the immutability of observed history must help. Otherwise it might be intolerable."

"What do you mean?" Actually, Jason was fairly sure he knew.

"Well, if it weren't that way you'd probably feel like you were walking on eggshells whenever you're in the past, afraid to do anything that might have unintended consequences. But as it is, if you *can* do something then it must be all right." She laughed. "I'm not expressing myself very well."

"Yes, you are. And you're right. There are circumstances in which you find you *must* do something." Jason's eyes seemed to focus on memory. "I was in Constantinople in 1204 when it was sacked by the Fourth Crusade."

"Uh, I'm afraid history—"

"—Isn't your field. I know. So just take my word that you wouldn't have wanted to be there to see it. Anyway, I found myself on a back street, and saw a Frankish soldier getting ready to rape a girl of no more than six. Judging from what was going on everywhere else in Constantinople that night, he probably would have killed her afterwards. Now, according to the kind of theories those old fiction writers played with, saving her life might have had imponderable consequences; she might have grown up and gotten married and given birth to a conqueror or inventor or religious reformer who changed subsequent history, or something like that. But, as you've pointed out, we now know that's not the case."

"Oh. So you saved her." Deirdre seemed to have an afterthought. "And, uh, what about the Frankish soldier?"

"Well," Jason replied obliquely, "there's no rule that says I can't enjoy my work."

Deirdre stared at him for a perceptible instant of silence, then hurried on. "Still, though, I can't help thinking there must be more to it. Surely you must feel awe at the knowledge of what you're seeing—and sheer curiosity. Especially what *we're* about to see. I've read some of the speculations—"

"Right. This island's volcanic history came to light in the late twentieth century, when revived, half-baked mysticism was fashionable. They used the term 'New Age' for anything that was particularly retrograde. George Orwell would have loved that, if he'd still been alive!" Jason laughed. "They decided that Santorini was the lost world of Atlantis. Or that the side effects caused the Plagues of Egypt, and the tsunami drowned Pharaoh's army in the Red Sea!"

"Yes, yes. But not all the ideas were that wild. Wasn't there a fairly respectable theory that the eruption wiped out or at least crippled the Minoan civilization?" Deirdre gestured southward, toward Crete from whence they'd come. "It seems plausible. After all, Crete was less than seventy miles from this cataclysm."

"It does seem that way, doesn't it? But the evidence is that Minoan society wasn't destroyed. In fact, they've discovered Minoan remains right here on Santorini on *top* of the ash deposits; those people came back. Oh, yes, there's still a strong probability—I'd say a near certainty—that the disaster got the Minoans started downhill. In fact, that's something we hope to confirm." Jason paused, and looked pensive. "I think it goes back to what Nagel was telling us at Knossos: every generation reads its own ideals, its own dreams, into those innocent-seeming faces that gaze out at us from those charming frescoes. So there's something deliciously tragic about the thought of them being abruptly blotted out by blind natural forces." He gave a scornful laugh and pressed on, unaware that he had let himself slip out of character. "For example, people looked at the lack of fortifications at Knossos and said, 'Oh, wonderful! The Minoans were high-minded pacifists just like us!' More likely, it was a case of fatheaded overconfidence in the ability of their fleets to keep any possible enemies away from Crete. Likewise, there used to be a theory that the Minoans were feminists four thousand years ahead of their times—"

"I've heard that last one," Deirdre said expressionlessly.

"Yes, but what's the evidence for it? Sculptures of female goddesses—something not unknown in ancient societies that we know were male-dominated. And frescoes of some really gorgeous women with expensive-looking clothes and elaborate hairdos and attitudes that suggest to us—though not necessarily to the original painters—sophistication and social status. For all we know, they could have been high-priced whores! No, it's just another case of looking at the Minoans and seeing what we want to see, without any real written records to burst our bubbles. Now, though, maybe we'll learn what they were *really* like."

"Maybe." The sun had set, and the first stars had appeared, but that couldn't account for a sudden seeming drop in temperature. Deirdre drained her wine and set the glass down with an unnecessarily loud click. "I think I'll turn in. Thanks for the wine."

Nice going, Jason chided himself as he watched her depart. He stood up, got another wine, and went to lean on the balustrade. The moon had peeked over the cliff tops, and it glistened on the caldera's unthinkably deep waters.

CHAPTER FOUR

Current hypersonic suborbital transports didn't use any form of reaction engines, of course. But the term "jet lag" was still in use . . . and altogether too damned appropriate, Jason thought, after their three-hour flight from Greece to Australia.

Rutherford gave them little time to recover. He had their schedule planned out to his usual degree of regimentation. After landing at the town-sized installation in the Great Sandy Desert not far northwest of Lake Mackay—about as close to the middle of nowhere as it was possible to get on today's Earth, as Jason had intimated—they barely had time to get settled into their quarters. Deirdre and Nagel were pleasantly surprised, for as viewed from the outside, the facilities looked almost as bleak as their surroundings. Inside, the accommodations were as comfortable as late-twenty-fourth-century technology and fairly lavish funding could make them. Their biological clocks told them it was time to retire to those luxury-hotel-like quarters . . . but it was still business hours for the laboratories to which Rutherford took them.

He had decided the implantation of their temporal retrieval devices should take place at once. This way, the two novices wouldn't have time to brood about it and let their cultural prejudices simmer. For it was as Jason had told them: a very trivial in/out surgery, after which it was a *fait accompli.* Since any part of the body would do as well as any other, the out-of-the-way and easy-to-forget inner side of the left arm, not far below the armpit, was used. Jason himself had had so many of the tiny TRDs put into and taken out of himself that he'd long ago stopped worrying about it, if indeed he ever had.

After that, Rutherford let them rest. But soon it was back to the labs for a procedure that was more elaborate and time-consuming . . . and which came as a surprise to Deirdre and Nagel. Deirdre in particular was taken aback. "They never mentioned this problem in any of the old fictional treatments of time travel I've read," she remarked.

"No," Rutherford smiled at her. "I've sampled some of those works myself. They were full of unscrupulous people doing things like selling automatic rifles to the Confederate States of America. But those authors never seem to have considered the *real* threat that even the most well-meaning of time travelers would pose to the people of the past, without ever intending to do so."

"I've often wondered why they didn't think of it," said

Jason. "Their own history told them all about the impact Europeans, with their millennia of exposure to the Old World disease pool, had had on isolated societies in Polynesia and the Americas."

"True. But you must remember that those writers lived during the early part of the Age of Antibiotics, before the consequences of that period's irresponsibility were appreciated. Today, of course, we know that excessive dispensing and inept use of penicillin and the other 'wonder drugs' over a period of generations put disease microorganisms through an extraordinary course of forced-draft evolution. Only the most resistant strains survived . . . and proceeded to give rise to super-resistant ones. During the twenty-first century, it became a race between those strains and ever more highly developed antibiotics."

"But," Nagel protested, "nowadays we all get broad spectrum immunization as a matter of routine public health."

"You're forgetting the Immunity Gap, Sidney."

Nagel fell silent. Actually, no one could forget that nightmare time when humanity had seemed on the verge of losing its race with the microbes, for those years' social chaos and apocalyptic panic had provided the soil from which the poisonous growth of the Transhuman movement had sprouted.

"During that period," Rutherford continued, "the human immune system had to undergo a bit of forced-draft evolution itself. So now we all harbor organisms against which the humans of earlier eras have no defenses. The further back one goes, the worse the problem becomes—and you are going very much further back than anyone ever has. Each of you would be a veritable 'Typhoid

Mary' in the Bronze Age. Fortunately, we are aware of the danger, and can prevent it."

"But," said Nagel, his face a shade paler, "what if the discoverers of time travel hadn't thought of this problem, and simply gone blundering ahead into the past?"

"But they *didn't*, Sidney," Rutherford told him soothingly. "That's the whole point of what Commander Thanou was explaining to you about time travel back in Athens. There are no paradoxes."

Nagel didn't look altogether satisfied. But like his companions, he proceeded to submit to a series of treatments involving injections alternating with spells of lying down strapped into vaguely alarming-looking and -sounding machinery. The technicians who processed them were far too busy to explain it all. But Rutherford assured them that their bodies were being cleansed of all microorganisms that would endanger the population of the seventeenth century B.C., by processes which spared those organisms that served a purpose. They had little choice but to accept his word.

After that it was time for a three-week orientation period, which gave Jason and Nagel more time to grow the beards whose lack would have been conspicuous where they were going. Rutherford's brief tour in Greece had given them a basic familiarity with the region. Now they were force-fed detailed information about it, and about the material culture in which they would find themselves. For most of the curriculum, relatively traditional teaching techniques, reinforced by neuro-electronic stimulation of the appropriate brain centers while sleeping or in a state of induced unconsciousness, sufficed. But in the matter of language . . .

“It would make no sense to send people into a past milieu without giving them the means of communicating there,” Jason explained when they met to discuss the subject. He ignored Nagel’s fidgeting. “Now, it doesn’t have to be exact. You don’t have to pass for a native of the locality where you find yourself; you can always claim to be from somewhere else where everybody knows the people talk funny. But accent or not, you have to be reasonably fluent in the language.”

“And,” Rutherford put in, “it would take too long to acquire such fluency by conventional means. Therefore, the Authority was able to successfully make a case for another exemption from the Human Integrity Act. We are permitted to use direct neural induction to impose a language’s patterns on the speech centers. It is somewhat disorienting, and requires a period of rest under antidepressant drugs afterwards. In fact, you may have noted a waiver clause in the Articles of Agreement concerning long-term effects. I should emphasize, however, that this is strictly precautionary. Be assured that we have never had an actual incidence of such problems.”

Nagel was clearly uninterested in any possible side effects. In fact, he could no longer contain himself. “Blast it, Kyle, I know all this! But *how* can you possibly have these ‘language patterns’ for the Aegean Bronze Age?”

Rutherford evidently decided that Nagel had suffered enough. “We have been planning this expedition for some time, Sidney. It is, after all, by far the most ambitious temporal displacement we have ever undertaken—*involving humans*. The risks involved justified the expense of preceding it with an unmanned probe.”

"An unmanned probe?" Deirdre echoed, too intrigued to take offense at the phraseology.

"Yes—using a unique approach." Rutherford's look of sublime self-satisfaction left no doubt in anyone's mind as to the identity of that approach's originator. "The probe was encased in a synthetic material which—to any low-technology tools of analysis, at any rate—appeared to be rough-hewn stone, in a crudely anthropomorphic shape. It was sent back to 1710 B.C., in the Inachos valley—which we visited on our outing from Athens, as you may recall."

"Why there?" Jason asked.

"The entire operation was somewhat controversial. After all, we were flinging an instrumentality into the past without any on-the-scene human oversight. In order to get approval, we had to agree to use an out-of-the-way locale where the risk of impacting observed history was minimized. But it was still within the same cultural—and, almost certainly, ethnolinguistic—zone as the more important centers."

Nagel, Jason thought, must have sensed where this was headed. He was practically panting.

"The experiment succeeded," Rutherford resumed. "The local people did precisely as we'd hoped: they found the probe, and made a god of it—or, if not a god, at least an object of worship. There are instances from recorded Greek history of objects that the immortals were believed to have flung to Earth—the Omphalos at the Oracle of Delphi, or the Palladium that the Greeks were supposed to have stolen from Troy. We counted on this particular kind of susceptibility already existing in protohistorical times."

Deirdre spoke with uncharacteristic hesitancy, as

though frightened of what she was saying. "Is it possible that, by your experiment, you *created* this 'susceptibility'?"

"I suppose that is within the realm of possibility," Rutherford allowed with chilling casualness. "At any rate, the locals took it to their village—which was later to grow into the town of Argos—and set it up in a shrine . . . and did a great deal of talking in its presence. Now, the probe was designed for ruggedness and durability above all else, for obvious reasons. It had no sophisticated cybernetic features—just basic audio and video pickups, which ran continuously for the entire duration of the mission, since we were able to give it a far higher recording capacity than Commander Thanou will have."

Yes, Jason thought. *I have other things taking up space. A heart, lungs, kidneys, a GI tract . . . and, whatever Nagel thinks, a brain.*

"The probe's TRD was set to activate at a local time in the small hours of the morning, when we hoped no one would be present to see it vanish. After we had retrieved it, we were able to study its recorded pictures and sound. We subjected them to computer analysis using universal translation programs."

Deirdre and Nagel didn't look as though this meant anything in particular to them. It did to Jason. He was familiar with the devices that were used in establishing communication with newly discovered alien races. With only a few minutes' exposure, it was possible to begin analyzing an entirely unknown language.

"But," Rutherford continued, "that turned out to be unnecessary in this case. The language proved to be an early form of Achaean Greek—essentially, the language of the Linear B tablets."

"*Yes!*" Nagel leaped to his feet with an enthusiasm of which Jason would never have dreamed him capable. "I *knew* it! *That* for Markova and her introduction of proto-Greek by the charioteers of the Grave Circle dynasties at Mycenae! Ha! And villagers wouldn't have been addressing their gods in the language of a caste of recent conquerors. The ancestral Graeco-Thracian speech must have entered the region as far back as the twenty-third century B.C. as I have theorized—probably just before the Centum-Satem rift started to occur within East Indo-European." He turned to Rutherford, voice charged with urgency. "Kyle, you *must* postpone our expedition! As soon as I have had a chance to examine these findings, it is *important* that I prepare a monograph immediately."

"Now wait just a damned minute—!" Deirdre began.

Rutherford laughed. "Do calm down, everyone! Sidney, the schedule for the expedition is set in stone, as these things tend to be. Remember Commander Thanou's remarks about 'traffic control'? There'll be plenty of time to demolish Markova after you return, armed with the unique prestige of having seen the era personally."

"Hmm . . . there *is* that." Nagel subsided with, for him, fairly good grace. "You won't allow this to become general knowledge until my return, will you?"

"Of course not. The probe's data is included in the overall body of the expedition's findings, for which you and Dr. Sadaka-Ramirez have exclusive publication rights, as specified in the Articles of Agreement. So put your mind at ease while we proceed to transfer some of that data to your brain."

Nagel immediately perked up at the reminder that he was going to actually learn the language whose identity was a question over which oceans of ink had been spilled for half a millennium. They went back to the labs, and a new set of machines.

For Jason, it was fairly old hat. He had acquired other tongues in the same way—including his own ancestral Demotic Greek. His initial impression was that you probably had to be a linguist to recognize *this* harsh language as related to it. On reflection, though, as the newly acquired patterns settled into his mind, he could glimpse occasional haunting similarities and recognize structural analogs.

He had ample opportunity to make such connections, for Rutherford drilled them in the language mercilessly, making sure their voice boxes could implement the speech patterns their brains now held. They also spent much time studying the video record the probe had brought back. It was difficult to know how to react to those images; their gritty, grubby, unscripted reality was hard to reconcile with the realization that these entirely natural-looking people's bones had been dust for over four thousand years.

Most of the footage was of minute-by-minute, hour-by-hour ordinariness. But the sense of peering through a window into the distant past gave those recordings a mesmerizing quality which Rutherford—had they only known—was counting on. It kept them staring at those images, and soaking up useful impressions of how the people of that era moved, gestured and even wore their clothes. The last became relevant when they got issued their own.

Those outfits were of a woolen fabric that was only moderately rough, and dyed in the bright colors they had seen in the recordings. Deirdre had expressed a certain surprise at that, having assumed that people impoverished, by modern standards, would dress drably. Jason knew from experience the fallacy of this common assumption; primitive people love bright primary colors. Naturally, these clothes had been left out in the weather long enough to acquire an authentic faded look. They consisted of tunics and cloaks for the men and something not too different, though longer, for Deirdre. Again, she expressed surprise, having expected something like the himation of Classical Greek times, or perhaps like the breast-exposing ankle-length flounced dresses of the Minoan ladies of the frescoes. Rutherford explained that the former was a mark of a domestic seclusion, while the latter was the particular fashion statement of a narrow class—quite possibly a class of priestesses, although this wasn't certain. Either way, Deirdre was clearly relieved. She was less happy about the footwear; hers consisted of light sandals, while the men both had openwork high-quarter shoes with curled toes.

They also received their equipment. With it came a lecture from Rutherford.

"There is a fixed policy against sending back anachronistically advanced items," he explained. "First of all, the time travelers would be put in an awkward position, having to explain such things. Secondly, there is the danger of contaminating the local culture, and thus altering observed history."

"But Kyle," said Nagel, "I thought that couldn't be done in any case. Didn't you and Mr. Thanou say that something would prevent it?"

"To the best of our knowledge, that is true," said Rutherford judiciously. "But one never knows just *what* is going to happen to prevent it. You might not want to be standing nearby when whatever it is occurs. So it's best if the problem never arises at all."

"But surely," Nagel wheedled, "in such a primitive era, we'll need—"

"Remember the Articles of Agreement, Sidney," Rutherford told him sternly. "You are going to be living on the local technological level. That is precisely why we were obligated to satisfy ourselves of your ability to endure it. And as a general rule you're not going to be expected to practice wilderness survival. Your *real* survival tools are these." He indicated their rough hempen traveling sacks, compatible with what the probe had observed . . . but with false bottoms into which those "survival tools" were woven for safekeeping. He withdrew a few of them: bronze and gold ornaments, copied from archaeological finds. "You're going to be in relatively well-populated areas where you can use these trade goods to purchase food and shelter. Pity that money hadn't been invented then; it would be far more convenient to carry . . . which, come to think of it, is precisely why money *did* eventually get invented."

There were other items, of course. They would carry sturdy five-foot walking sticks, an essential in an age when almost all traveling was by foot. There were horses in Greece, but they were seldom ridden, and chariots were only for the nobility. In addition, Jason was issued a bronze sword-dagger. Its blade was a beautifully tapering thing, designed for thrusting although it had a double edge and a fuller to strengthen it. Its tang flared out and back and then forward again to form a guard for the hand that grasped the ivory-encased hilt. The longer thrusting swords of the period would have been inappropriate—like chariots, they were for the aristocratic warriors, and Jason wasn't going to be posing as a member of *that* social set. Anyway, he decided while practicing with it, he liked this blade better.

Nagel watched him with a hint of nervousness "I say, do you know how to use that thing?"

"I think I can probably get by with it, Dr. Nagel." In fact, he was an expert with a number of similar weapons, using fighting styles millennia in advance of what they were doing in the Aegean Bronze Age. He didn't plan to start any fights, but he was confident he could finish any.

Along with the rest of their gear, they received names. Rutherford was puckishly pleased to let Jason keep his own. ("Even if it isn't a commonly used name at the time, it at least won't sound outlandish.") For the others, he'd come as close as possible to their actual given names: Deianeira for Deirdre and Synon for Nagel. Both were names that had been recorded on the probe's sound track.

At last, the time came for their final briefing by Rutherford. "You will arrive in the Inachos valley, a couple of miles north of Argos, on August 15, 1628 B.C.—not that they were using our dating system then, of course. That date was chosen to allow you time to position yourselves in a locale from which you can observe the effects of the volcano at reasonably close range, though at a safe remove. One of the Cyclades, or northern Crete, would be best; in either case, you should stay in the higher elevations."

"Can't we go to Santorini itself—or Kalliste, as it was originally called—first?" Deirdre asked. "Study it as it was before?"

"I leave that to Commander Thanou's discretion. It will

depend on how promptly you can make your way there. The problem is, we have no way of knowing the exact date. It could be early or late in the autumn. If the latter, you should have time for a visit."

"I hope so," she said earnestly, with a meaningful glance at Jason. "We could settle the question of the original size and shape of the island, and I could make some important geological observations even without advanced equipment."

"No doubt. But safety comes first. I cannot overemphasize that if you are on the island at the time of the explosion, you will assuredly die." Rutherford paused for effect, then resumed. "Your TRDs will activate on November 15. This will give you time to observe the aftereffects of the event. The extent to which it crippled the Minoan economy and created the conditions for the later conquest of Crete by mainland Greeks is a subject of unending controversy—which is one of the reasons we were able to get funding for this expedition. So you will be in the Bronze Age for three months. For the last part of that period, you will need to have established yourself in a secure locale, for the sailing season ends in mid-October, before the autumn gales begin. Commander Thanou, do you have anything to add?"

"I'd just like to reemphasize something that both of you have already been told. After the temporal displacement, there will be a moment of disorientation. It's worse if you arrive in darkness—in fact, it has been known to cause emotional collapse under those conditions. So we don't time our arrivals for midnight, as much as we would like to in the interest of minimizing the chance of anyone actually seeing time travelers appear out of nowhere.

Instead, we compromise by arriving just after daybreak. Still, it's disconcerting—and it will almost certainly affect you more than me, since this is your first time. Don't be alarmed; the effect is only temporary."

They proceeded to the great central dome which held the displacer stage: a circular platform about thirty feet in diameter, surrounded by masses of supporting equipment and ranks of control panels whose personnel ignored them in their Bronze Age clothing. Even odder-looking outfits were common here—like those of a passing group who were obviously returning from the Elizabethan era. Deirdre and Nagel tried not to stare, since no one else in the dome was. Jason glanced at the sacks those returnees were carrying and wondered how many first editions of Shakespeare they held, in addition to copious notes on the paper that was so fortuitously available in that age.

They swung their own sacks over the edge as they climbed onto the stage with the aid of their walking sticks. Rutherford solemnly shook hands with each of them, then withdrew to the glassed-in control center that overlooked the stage. They waited, watching a large digital clock count down.

When the moment came, it was as Jason remembered so well. There were no flashy visual effects. As viewed by outside observers like Rutherford, they simply vanished. They themselves felt a sensation outside normal human experience. It could only be compared to coming out of a deep and very convincing dream. But the comparison was not close, for there was a wavering of reality, leaving in its wake no sense of transition and no impression of time having passed. Afterwards, the displacer stage and everything around it were gone, though their minds held no recollection of it disappearing.

They were standing on a narrow, rutted road, with the morning sun peeking over the hills of Argolis to the east.

CHAPTER FIVE

As Jason had predicted, he was the first to recover from displacement sickness. Deirdre was next to reestablish her sense of reality after a disorientation foreign to normal human experience. She stopped trembling in a surprisingly short time. In fact, Jason wouldn't have objected if she'd continued to need assistance just a little longer.

"All right," he said after Nagel had finally regained his composure. "Let's get started for Argos." The town to which Rutherford's probe had been taken in 1710 B.C., as the yet-unborn twenty-fourth century measured time, was the obvious place for them to make their initial appearance in this world.

As they walked, the rising sun revealed a landscape disconcertingly different from everything the word

"Greece" called to mind. The hills to either side were darkly forested, and along the roadside the olive groves were generally surrounded by oak and poplar. Soon the two hills of Argos—the Apsis and the higher Larissa—became visible up ahead. The place had grown from the village of the recordings they had seen, spreading around the base of two hills. A wood-stockaded fort crowned the Larissa. Around its base clustered a town whose buildings were basically of wood construction in this well-forested milieu, though well plastered. The few early risers they passed looked no different from the ones they had viewed on film, and the looks they gave the new arrivals held no more curiosity than unfamiliar faces would normally occasion.

Security at the fort was not particularly tight, but a guard stood outside. Although the sun hadn't yet warmed the air to the heat to be expected later in this August day, he wore only a kilt and leg guards of linen. But he had a helmet constructed of overlapping hide thongs and covered with rows of boars' tusks, and carried a large, oxhide-covered, figure-eight-shaped shield. The only weapon he carried was a spear, which he hefted importantly as the strangers approached.

"Rejoice," said Jason, giving the general-purpose greeting. "We have come far, all the way from Aetolia, and ask your lord's hospitality." It was his first attempt to speak the language to a local, and he was sure he must sound heavily accented. But he had been given the correct, aristocratic idiom, so the favor he was asking was one to which he was presumptively entitled as a gentleman.

"Very well," said the guard. "Enter. You can tell your story to the *wanax* Acrisius."

Behind him, Jason could sense Nagel's excitement. It intensified as they crossed the compound toward a building which was larger than others they'd seen but apparently of the same kind of construction.

"That hall," Nagel whispered to him, all a-titter, "is a small-scale but inarguable ancestor of the royal megarons that will grow to sumptuous proportions in the later Mycenaean era."

"Well," Jason whispered back, "we've already learned that this Acrisius is entitled to call himself a *wanax*, or king." Of course, Acrisius wasn't in the same class as the proud rulers who, as he knew from his orientation, would soon establish themselves at Mycenae. Those rulers would accumulate so much treasure that they could afford to take with them into the afterlife the hoard of gold that Heinrich Schliemann would dig out of Grave Circle A thirty-four centuries from now. But most of their treasure would go as gifts to vassal warlords, in return for which they were obliged to fight for the high king on call. On his own modest scale, Acrisius doubtless assured the loyalty of his own vassals the same way. Thus were such things done in this moneyless economy. "Is that what surprised you—hearing that title?"

"No! It was his name! It is the name of one of the mythological dynasties that supposedly ruled the city-state of Argos—and this is far earlier than the fourteenth and thirteenth centuries B.C. to which learned speculation has assigned the actual originals of the Greek heroes. I hadn't dreamed we would encounter any identifiable individuals this far back!"

"Maybe it's just a coincidence," Deirdre suggested. "An accidental similarity of names."

"Right," Jason agreed. "Maybe scholars have taken those mythic genealogies too literally. They must be a grab bag of dimly remembered names, strung together in whatever way was politically useful to the rulers under whose patronage the myths were compiled."

"There must be something to that." The admission clearly took a lot out of Nagel, for it meant paying respectful attention to an observation about his field from someone lacking the proper academic credentials. But he accepted the theory the way a shipwreck survivor accepts a floating piece of wreckage. "For example, the myths will give Acrisius a quasi-divine ancestry, making him a descendant of a refugee Egyptian prince named Danaos."

The warlord who greeted them beside the central hearth of the central hall was, of course, nothing of the kind. He seemed an affable enough semibarbarian, though, as he listened to Jason recite their well-prepared story. He was even enlightened enough to give "Deianeira" a gesture of respect on the strength of Jason's declaration that she was a princess from Aetolia, far enough to the north that they could safely be vague about details. She was, the story went, niece to a very important Cretan whose sister had been politically married to a mainland chieftain. Deianeira's own husband had died, and now she was traveling to Crete to rejoin her mother's family. She was carrying that portion of her late husband's treasure which, in accordance with her mother's original marriage contract, belonged to her under Cretan inheritance laws.

Deirdre had been delighted to have that last part confirmed in the course of their orientation. Less delightful from her standpoint was the fact that Cretan society, while matrilineal, was *not* matriarchal. It was as male-dominated as every other known Bronze Age society. *Big surprise*, Jason had carefully refrained from saying. His own persona was that of a relative on her father's side who was escorting her to Crete—a middle-ranking landless warrior. "Synon" had been harder to account for. The nit-picking bureaucracy revealed by the Linear B tablets—for which Nagel would have been a natural—was still several centuries in the future of this pristinely illiterate society. They'd decided to pass him off as a Cretan-trained steward or seneschal or something, along to manage the property transfer—and related to the family, hence socially acceptable. Acrisius seemed to buy it.

Finally that worthy leaned back and scratched the thick salt-and-pepper beard that made him seem impressively mature among the mostly late-teens-to-early-twenties bravos who otherwise filled the hall. (He was probably about fifty, but in a kind of physical condition that Jason found surprising for someone of his age in this era.) "Be welcome. I must spend most of the day inspecting the outlying holdings. But rest from your travels, and eat with me later. We will talk at greater length."

"Thank you, lord."

As a slave led them to their rooms, Jason congratulated himself on how smoothly things had gone so far. Admittedly, he hadn't had a chance to broach the topic of Rutherford's disguised probe. But there would be time for that after the feast.

"Ah, yes, the image of Hyperion." Acrisius nodded and belched solemnly. "So you have heard of it?"

"Indeed we have," Jason assured him. "Even in Aetolia."

"It appeared in the time of our grandfathers' fathers. It might well have been eighty-two winters ago, as you say." Acrisius peered curiously at his guests, clearly intrigued by people who claimed to count time to such an unheard-of degree of precision. "Yes. My grandfather Lynkeos told me about the image of Hyperion. He was only a small boy at the time. But his own father told him about the way it vanished as suddenly as it had appeared. Everyone thought Hyperion had taken it back. But that was before the god himself came to ask about it."

Jason came suddenly alert. "The god himself came?"

"Oh, yes. That often happened in those days, you know. That was when the gods were still begetting Heroes on mortal women. My grandfather's father Danaos was a Hero, you know," he added parenthetically. Out of the corner of his eye, Jason saw Nagel stiffen. "But this was different," Acrisius continued. "Hyperion came demanding an accounting of our stewardship of his image. According to my grandfather, he almost seemed angry at first, on hearing it had vanished. It was puzzling. But then he assured everyone that he had, indeed, taken it back and that now it burns at the heart of the sun, an eternal offering. So everything was all right after all."

Jason made a sign of respect to the gods, as he had learned from the probe's recording. With a fraction of his consciousness, he made certain his companions were doing likewise.

It had come as no surprise to Nagel—in fact, it had been something of a vindication—that these people worshipped gods whose names, at least, corresponded to those of the Titans of classical Greek mythology: the generation of gods (six couples, or maybe seven, depending on which account you read) that had preceded the Olympians. Not that the distinction was entirely clear. In fact, there was a lot of overlap, with many of the Olympians also appearing in the rather incoherent local pantheon. Partway up the slopes of Larissa was a grotto sacred to Hera. Some of them were missing, though—like Apollo, an Asiatic deity whose worship wouldn't enter Greece until Iron Age times. At present, the job of sun god was handled by Hyperion . . . to whom the locals had decided Rutherford's bogus idol bore a resemblance.

And who, according to Acrisius, had come to look in on it.

Jason's eyes met Nagel's briefly. The historian looked as puzzled as Jason felt. He leaned forward in the flickering firelight. "We have never heard this part of the tale, Lord Acrisius. Did your grandfather tell you anything else about the god?"

"Well, he was barely walking at the time, you understand. But he got a glimpse of Hyperion. He never forgot it." Acrisius took on an expression foreign to his listeners, who came from a time when literal belief in the supernatural was no longer possible. "He had the look of the gods: very tall, with hair that was almost the color of silver, but with a golden shimmer. And he had the face of the gods: like that of men but more beautiful . . . and yet not like that of men, for its beauty is of another kind." He shivered, although the temperature was what one would expect in Greece in August, and took a deep drink. "Ah, well, that was long ago. The gods don't come among men nearly as much anymore. Let's talk about your plans, instead. Are you sure you want to go to Nauplia? Granted, you'll have no trouble getting passage there, but . . ." His voice trailed off, as though from an awkward subject.

"No, lord," Deirdre answered. Acrisius had proven enlightened enough to include "Deianeira" in the drinking. "We'll go to Lerna instead. It's no further, and a cousin of my late husband lives there." In fact, they had chosen the small seaside town on the western coast of the Gulf of Argos, across from Nauplia, for its inconspicuousness. Nauplia was literally in the shadow of Tiryns, where they'd learned a formidable warlord had established himself. Lerna, of immemorial antiquity even in this age, was a backwater whose only claim to mythological fame in later times was the Lernean Hydra that Hercules killed as one of his twelve labors. Come to think of it, Jason reflected, they would be passing the swamp on whose outskirts that nine-headed monster was supposed to have inhabited a rock outcropping that Rutherford had shown them. . . .

"Well," Acrisius said heartily, "I wish you a safe journey. You can walk it in a day." It was about ten miles, Jason thought, summoning up a map that, to him, seemed to float translucently in midair about a foot from his face. "You'll probably want to get an early start, to arrive in Lerna before nightfall. There are bandits at large in the swamps. In fact, I've heard some odd stories. . . ." Acrisius shook his head. "No. Never mind. Just be alert. Would you like me to send some men with you?"

"Thank you, lord, but that won't be necessary." Jason would have liked to ask about those "odd stories," but Acrisius was obviously disinclined to discuss the subject. They soon made their goodnights and made their way to their guest quarters. When the only reasonably safe artificial light-source was oil lamps, there were only four things to do after dark. Two—drinking and talking—they had already done. As for the third, Deirdre was still being discouragingly professional. That left sleeping.

Jason could tell from Nagel's body language that the historian wanted to talk in private. But there was no privacy in Acrisius' "palace" (at which the most impoverished resident of twenty-fourth century Earth would have turned up his nose), and standard Service procedure dictated that they use the local language at all times; paranoia was apt to rear its ugly head when strangers were overheard conversing among themselves in an unknown tongue. So he gave Nagel a cautionary gesture. It would have to wait until they were on the road.

"Something is not right," Nagel muttered the next morning, when they were out of sight of Argos.

The countryside through which they followed the road—more accurately, the well-traveled trail—to Lerna was no longer strange to them, after their earlier walk to Argos. Ahead, though, lay the swamps. From a distance, at least, it didn't look all that different from what Rutherford had showed them.

"What do you mean?" Deirdre asked Nagel. "What's not right?"

"A number of things—for example, that business about the Heroes being born of gods, as though it was something of relatively recent date. I'm still not sure what to make of that. We've always assumed that the ruling houses of much later historical times simply gave themselves divine genealogies. Now, it seems the idea of heroic demigods goes back much further than we'd imagined. Indeed, it's turning out that a good many things go back further than we'd imagined. But what really disturbs me is Acrisius' description of the god Hyperion."

"Why? He was just talking about something purely imaginary."

"Was he?" Jason inquired absently, while most of his attention was absorbed by his computer implant.

"Why, of *course* he was!" exclaimed Deirdre indignantly. "What do you even *mean* by that?"

"Well, he said he heard about it from his grandfather—"

"The unreliability of early childhood memories is well established. And why are we even talking about this . . . this—?"

"That's not the point," said Nagel. His tone stopped them by its very quietness, for he was too puzzled to summon up his usual asperity. "The point is that what Acrisius heard simply confirmed his preconceptions of what gods are supposed to look like. And it is *not* how the Greeks of historical times visualized their gods."

"Uh . . . you mean the platinum-blond hair? But didn't the Classical Greeks often describe the gods, and also their mortal offspring, that way?"

"In some cases." Nagel smiled tightly. "Certain racist ideologues of the early twentieth century read a great deal into that. But in fact, it merely reflected an enduring aesthetic bias. The Greeks in all eras tended to idealize the occasional blond among them. In this, as in everything else, the Greek gods were simply humans writ large. *Humans*—that's the operative word. Nowhere is there any suggestion that they thought of the gods as having the aspect of alienness to which Acrisius alluded. Bigger than humans, yes, and more beautiful than humans—but beautiful in a human way." Nagel frowned disapprovingly.

"These people's visualizations simply don't have the right . . . flavor."

Damned disobliging of them, Jason thought. *Don't they know it's their job to conform to your preconceptions?* "Isn't it possible," he asked aloud, "that it wasn't until later times that they changed their beliefs, and started thinking of the gods as idealized humans?"

"Yes," Deirdre chimed in. "Didn't early civilizations tend to picture their gods as weird-looking? Sometimes even half man and half animal?"

"Yes—the Egyptians, for example," Nagel conceded. "I would have no trouble with monstrous-looking deities. But I know of no early society whose gods looked like tall, beautiful humans *but not quite*. Furthermore, most religious systems—for reasons too obvious for discussion—place direct physical manifestations by the gods in a safely remote past. From what we've heard, these people have no problem believing that the gods have walked among them, begetting demigods, in the last few generations . . . and still do, although with less frequency."

"So what's the answer?" asked Deirdre with a mixture of impatience and grudging interest.

"I don't know," Nagel admitted. "Oh, by the way, on the subject of mythological genealogies . . . remember Acrisius' mention of his great-grandfather Danaos, who was a 'Hero,' or demigod? Well, according to those genealogies, that *was* Acrisius' great-grandfather." Nagel subsided into frowning preoccupation.

As it turned out, he was so preoccupied he forgot he was not walking on a paved road. He stepped into a hole and twisted his ankle. So they had to stop by the roadside for a while and await his whining convalescence, while

Jason mentally composed the piece of his mind he was going to give Rutherford on the subject of the Authority's standards of fitness for low-tech survival. Finally they were able to resume their walk, but only at Nagel's limping pace.

It will be dark before we get to Lerna, Jason muttered to himself. Already, the sun was setting, and they had only reached the swamp.

It was, he thought, the one area they had seen that would be more or less unchanged in the late twenty-fourth century: the same spur of red rock jutting out over a miasma of reedy marsh crossed by winding streams—fuller now than in Jason's lifetime—overlooked by weeping willows. The rock outcropping supported a stretch of solid ground for the road to traverse, even as Jason recalled from Rutherford's whirlwind tour.

"Come on," he called out in the twilight, unable to keep an edge of impatience out of his voice. "We've got to reach Lerna before nightfall. If we're still on the road, we'll have to make camp, and you heard what Acrisius said about—"

Naturally, the bandits attacked at that moment.

They charged out from under the rock outcropping where they'd lain concealed: half a dozen of them, ragged and shaggy-maned, wielding clubs and knives and screaming so as to paralyze their victims with fear.

In Nagel's case, at least, it worked. He froze up. Jason ran between him and the oncoming bandits, bringing up his walking stick. It wasn't long enough to be a proper quarterstaff such as he had learned to use in the Middle Ages, but he gripped it that way: left hand in the middle, right hand about a quarter of its length from one end. He spun it this way and that, forcing the bandits to step back momentarily before rushing him. One of them lifted his club high while another came in from the side with his knife. Jason slid his left hand down the shaft from the middle to meet the right hand, and smashed his staff down on top of knife-man's head. There was a sickening thud and a crack of snapping teeth as the bandit's jaws were driven together by the force of the blow. He hadn't even hit the ground before Jason recovered and brought his staff around and into the belly of the club-wielder. The latter's wind whooshed out and he doubled over. As his face went down, Jason brought a knee sharply up into it, simultaneously using one end of the staff to punch him behind an ear with lethal preciseness.

Taking a split second to look around, Jason saw that Nagel had snapped out of it and was bringing his staff clumsily up. Deirdre, on the other hand, used hers to thrust at a bandit who was rushing at her, grinning. His grin disappeared, as did the center of his face, when the end of Deirdre's staff punched into it with a crunch of bone and cartilage.

The sight of a woman fighting back was evidently a shocking surprise. The remaining attackers, who hadn't reached their quarry yet—they were too stupid for a coordinated attack—hung back, mouths agape. The only sound was the squalling of Deirdre's would-be rapist. Jason decided that the sight of cold steel—oh, all right, bronze—would probably suffice to send them running, now that they'd lost their numerical advantage. He dropped his staff and reached for his sword-dagger.

"Enough of this."

The voice was deep and had an odd timbre to it. And it came from above.

At first the sheer, inexplicable wrongness of it held Jason motionless, even though the bandits had gone to their knees and dropped their weapons. A moment passed before he could look up in the direction from which that impossible voice had come.

A platform of some kind was descending with a faint humming sound Jason hadn't noticed before. It was a lovely thing of oddly curving lines and oven odder ornamentation, made of some unidentifiable metal alloy. And it was none too large even for its one passenger. As Jason watched, that passenger stood up and leaned on a low railing, clearly illuminated in the twilight by the running lights.

He was wearing robes not unlike those of the local royalty, but richer than anything they'd seen, with colors that seemed to shimmer and change. He was, Jason estimated, at least seven and a half feet tall. His hair was a shining, wavy mass of gold-shot silver, and his face was pale. That face was long, tapering to a narrow chin. His high cheekbones tilted upward in a way that was mirrored by the long eyebrows over his huge, oblique eyes. His nose was long, thin and sharp, but with flaring nostrils. His mouth was wide, thin-lipped, and set in lines of sublime haughtiness. There was something odd about his ears. . . .

And he was holding an unfamiliar-looking object. It fitted over his hand, and was fashioned to resemble a face. But to Jason, the way he held it screamed *weapon*.

As the three of them gaped upward, he brought the object to bear on Deirdre. It soundlessly flashed ruby light. Deirdre toppled forward to the ground.

As the tube swung toward him, Nagel's shock turned abruptly to terror. He turned and ran toward Jason. He'd almost made it when the weapon flashed again. His face was instantly leached of expression, and he fell as Deirdre had.

Jason recognized the thing for what it was, however curious its design: a neural paralyzer, its energy pulse carried on a laser guide beam which was the source of the flash. He also knew what his only possible option was. He dropped, with his legs bunched up in the direction of the weapon, and tried to roll behind Nagel's motionless form.

He didn't complete the roll before his legs went horribly numb. He gasped, unable to move them, and forced himself not to move anything else. He wanted the weapon's wielder to think he, like his companions, was unable to move a single voluntary muscle—as he would have been if that beam had struck his head or torso.

So he lay perfectly still. Fortuitously, his head was at an angle from which he could, out of the corner of his left eye, watch what now transpired.

The platform settled to the earth. The bandits bowed low, murmuring worshipfully. The tall being surveyed them with cold contempt and spoke in that disturbing voice.

"So I myself must intervene to save you from two men and a woman?"

The bandits groveled. "We are worms," moaned the one who seemed to be the leader. "Worthless worms!"

"Too true. Since you are useless for any other purpose, place the woman in my chariot. The men, and their belongings, you may have despite your bungling."

For the tiniest of instants, rebelliousness flickered in the bandits' expressions. They'd undoubtedly hoped to keep Deirdre themselves, partly for the usual reason but also to vent their feelings concerning their comrade's ruined face. But the instant passed. They meekly did as they were commanded, picking up her stiff form and transferring it to the "chariot," which then departed without another word from its occupant.

Jason continued to feign helplessness as he watched the bandits' leader order one of his followers back to their encampment with the one whom Deirdre had injured. Then the remaining two examined the sacks and whooped with delight when they discovered the windfall of treasure the sacks contained. As they did so, Jason very slowly moved his right hand atop the hilt of his sword-dagger, which he had been careful to cover with his body. He had barely finished doing so when they drew their doubtless-stolen bronze knives and turned their attention to their paralyzed captives.

As Jason had hoped, they decided to have fun with Nagel first.

His legs were starting to experience the painful tingling which presaged the wearing-off of the paralysis. But he still couldn't quite move them. He would have to take two men without the use of his legs. Luckily, they stood over Nagel with their backs to him, only a few feet away. And one end of his staff lay just barely within arm's reach.

With a pouncing leopard's abruptness, his left arm shot out and grasped the staff. With all his strength, he swept it around in an arc to catch the bandit leader behind the knees. With a curse, the man went down, colliding with his companion and knocking him over as well.

Dropping the staff, Jason used his left arm to roll himself over, toward the bandits who were trying to disentangle themselves from the heap in which they had fallen. The leader staggered to his feet just as Jason rolled up to those feet—and thrust upward with his blade, between the chief's legs.

The shriek of agony was still in progress when Jason whipped his sword out and pushed the body away, into the other bandit who had stumbled erect and was rushing in. He fell over Jason, who almost choked on the sour body odor that enveloped him. But, legless though he was, he managed a wrestling hold and pulled the struggling bandit over atop himself. He got his left arm around the man's throat, pulled back on the chin, and with his right arm brought his blade across the hairy throat in a slash that left the head flopping loosely, connected to the body by little save the spinal column itself. He pushed the blood-spurting corpse away and, with another shove of his left arm, rolled himself over to the writhing body of the bandit chief, whose squalling he ended with another throat slash.

After that, he massaged his legs into sensibility, then staggered over to Nagel and worked frantically and a little roughly to bring the historian around. They had to get away, lest the bandits should return, and find a place among the swamp's fringes to make camp. Afterwards, there would be time to confront the incomprehensible nightmare from which they would not be able to awaken for another three months.

CHAPTER SIX

"I think I know what has happened," said Nagel from across the campfire. "At least I have a theory."

They sat under a rocky ledge at the base of one of the hills fringing the swamp. Jason had helped Nagel to its shelter, after which he had barely had time to gather firewood in the gathering dusk. Afterwards, they had consumed in silence the rough bread and rougher wine that Acrisius had given them for their journey. And now, Nagel was the first to broach the subject of the unthinkable. Jason had to respect him for that.

"What theory is that?" There was, of course, no need to ask what Nagel was talking about.

"I listened when Ms. Sadaka-Ramirez—"

" 'Deirdre,' Sidney," Jason broke in wearily. "I think

we can be on first-name terms now. If nothing else, it will save lot of syllables."

"Very well—when Deirdre was describing those old fictional treatments of time travel she had read. All of them had to somehow deal with the Grandfather Paradox. Some of them did so by theorizing that travel into the past isn't really travel into *our* past at all. They postulated an infinity of alternate timelines."

"The 'many-worlds hypothesis,' " Jason nodded. "It's been flatly disproved."

"But it *must* be true!" Nagel leaned forward, and the firelight revealed the terrible urgency in his face. "We've proved it! Time travel really involves travel *sideways* as well as backwards, into a parallel world, superficially similar to ours but where our myths are real. And we're in it now! There's no other explanation. In fact," he pressed on, warming to his subject, "perhaps the peculiar qualities of this world allow occasional, uh, spontaneous transferences into ours, thus accounting for our ideas about mythical beings."

"I've been back as far as the thirteenth century A.D.," Jason reminded him. "While I was in the Middle Ages I never saw any unicorns or dragons or anything like that. Just gritty normalcy."

"Well . . . suppose the differences between the universes grow less marked with the passage of time, due to a gradual fading out of the supernatural in this world. Thus, the two worlds are effectively identical in recent times, and were pretty much so in Medieval times. But now, with this unprecedented expedition, we've gone back into an age when the gods of the ancient pantheons were real—and we've fallen afoul of one!"

Jason laughed softly. "It's an ingenious theory. There are just two problems with it. First, as I mentioned, it's been ruled out in terms of quantum physics. I'm not qualified to explain why; you'll have to ask Rutherford when we get back. And secondly, I happen to know that was no supernatural being we saw today."

"Oh?" Nagel tilted his head back, the better to peer down his nose. He must, Jason decided, be coming out of shock; his personality was unfortunately reasserting itself. "And what, precisely, leads you to believe you know this?"

"The weapon he used on us." Jason briefly explained the nature of the paralyzer. "It didn't look like our designs, of course. In my opinion, ours are a lot more practical. And judging from the time it took for the effect to wear off, it was pretty underpowered. Still, our culture could manufacture one just like it, if we wanted to. Likewise with his 'chariot.' It had the same overdecorated, inefficient look as the stunner, but it was an obvious application of the kind of propulsion our aircars use." He shook his head decisively. "No. I've seen nothing to compel belief in the 'many-worlds hypothesis.' Rutherford rules it out unequivocally, and that's good enough for me. You know how cautious he is."

Nagel lost some of his snippiness, but remained argumentative. "How, then, do you account for what we saw?"

"I can't account for it. He—I assume he was a 'he'—didn't belong to any nonhuman race we've encountered. If fact, we've never met *any* nonhumans even close to our technological level, nor any that looked even remotely similar to us. No, I have no idea who or what that being was, or what he and his advanced technology are doing in our world's past. All I'm certain of is that this *is* our world's past."

Nagel didn't offer the further argument Jason had expected. Indeed, he seemed relieved, as though he had hoped to be persuaded of this very conclusion. "Very well," he said briskly, "I must accept your professional judgment. It follows, then, that our expedition's original objective is as valid now as it ever was."

For a few seconds, Jason could only stare at him. "Did I just hear you correctly? You expect to simply resume your studies, on a business-as-usual basis?"

Nagel looked puzzled at the other's reaction. "But I thought I understood you to say that we are, in fact, in the actual past—the *legitimate* past, as it were. Therefore our findings from archaeology and other disciplines actually reflect this milieu, and our inferences from those findings can be checked against observed reality, since—"

A harsh bark of laughter escaped Jason. "Sidney, forget it! Until further notice, this expedition's original purpose is superseded. Our first and only priority is to rescue Deirdre."

Nagel blinked, as though he hadn't thought of that. "Well, er, yes. Of course I am as appalled as you are at what has happened to Ms. Sadaka-Ramirez . . . to Deirdre, I meant to say. And I would do *anything* to save her. But surely you must realize the futility of such an attempt. First of all, we have no idea where that being took her."

"Yes, we do—or at least *I* do." Jason smiled. "There are certain things we don't normally tell the non-Service members of temporal expeditions. But circumstances force me to take you into my confidence. The fact of the matter is, the TRDs implanted in you and Deirdre also incorporate a microminiaturized tracking device."

Nagel's features went blank, then grew suffused with

outrage. "Do you mean to say that . . . that . . . that a *cybernetic* device was implanted *without my consent* . . . ?" He spluttered to an inarticulate halt.

"Now you understand why we don't exactly emphasize this. No point in upsetting people with things they don't need to know. If the expedition had gone as planned, we would have returned to the linear present, your implant would have been removed, and you would have been left wondering how I'd always seemed to know where you were. You see, the device is completely passive, and hooked into my computer implant. Whenever I call up a map of our surroundings to be projected directly onto my optic nerve, your location and Deirdre's appear on it as red dots. So I know where she's been taken. And that's where we're going."

Nagel's indignation was now gone, driven out by alarm verging on horror. "You can't be serious! It's hopeless. This . . . this exercise in quixotry will accomplish nothing except our own deaths—and the loss of an absolutely unique opportunity to resolve important questions about a crucial period of history. You can't—"

"Actually, I can. Which reminds me . . . Excuse me, please." Jason's eyes lost their focus, and his voice took on an uncharacteristically formal tone. "As a result of hostile action by an unidentified nonhuman entity, a member of the expedition is now in unforeseeable danger. Therefore, in accordance with Title III, Chapter Five, Section 17 of the Revised Temporal Precautionary Act of 2364, I declare that a state of extraordinary emergency exists as of the date and time of this recording." He blinked, and focused again on Nagel, who was staring wide-eyed.

"What I just said has been recorded by my computer implant," he explained. "I remind you of what you already know, or should know, from the Articles of Agreement you signed. Under conditions of extraordinary emergency—which I have the authority to declare at my sole discretion—I have equally extraordinary enforcement powers." Jason paused, and chose his next words with care. "I also remind you that I just killed four armed men—two of them while paralyzed from the waist down. I mean no reflection on you when I say that you could not stop me even if you had the legal right to try."

There was absolute, dead silence. Jason let it continue for a couple of heartbeats, then leaned forward into the firelight and spoke in a very different tone of voice.

"Listen, Sidney, I intend to bring *all* of us back alive. I've never lost a single member of an expedition I've led, and I see no reason to start now. Together, you and I can get Deirdre back. Whoever this bogus god is, and wherever he came from, he's accustomed to pushing around frightened primitives. He doesn't know what he's dealing with. When he finds out, he's going to be one very surprised deity. That will be our advantage."

The pep talk seemed to have an effect on Nagel. He swallowed once, and looked a little less frightened. He still wore a lost look, though. "But . . . where has Deirdre been taken?"

"Not far," Jason assured him. "Only about seven or eight miles, in fact—to Tiryns."

"Tiryns? But why there?"

"Who knows? Maybe the local *wanax* works for this 'god' like those bandits. We'll just have to see what the situation is when we get there—which we'll do tomorrow."

Jason used the point of his blade to draw a simple map in the dirt beside the fire. "Tiryns is to the east, around the head of the Gulf of Argos. We'll go there directly, skirting the gulf. It'll mean going through more swamps, but we can make it by nightfall. How much can you tell me about what we're likely to find there?"

"Not a great deal," Nagel admitted. "What we *won't* find are the massive cyclopean walls for whose ruins Tiryns will be noted in our day. Those date from a period three centuries from now. There will doubtless be some kind of fortification on the summit of the rocky promontory, but it will surely be a wooden stockade like what we saw at Argos. Oh, and Tiryns is practically on the coast now; the sea, which in our century will be a mile away, is believed to have come within a hundred yards of the wall in this era." Nagel paused, then resumed reluctantly. "There is one other thing. Ordinarily, I would not give it much weight, as it is pure legend, without any archaeological verification. But now . . . after some of the things I've seen . . ."

"Yes?" Jason prompted.

"Remember what I said about Acrisius?"

"Yes. You said that the myths include a ruler of Argos by that name, who had a great-grandfather named Danaos."

"Well, according to those same stories, Acrisius had a twin brother named Proetus. The two of them were bitter enemies, and fought a succession war. It was finally resolved by an agreement under which Acrisius kept Argos while Proetus got Tiryns."

"Oho! So now we know why Acrisius was so relieved that we were going to Lerna and not to Nauplia, past

Tiryns and brother dearest. I bet it also explains why he was so reticent about the bandits infesting the swamps. They probably work for Proetus, infiltrating the borders. And since they also work for this 'god,' it means that Proetus is tied in with him . . . so he naturally took Deirdre to Tiryns. Yes, it all fits."

"I caution you that this is all pure legendry, and not necessarily to be relied on." An afterthought seemed to overtake Nagel. "Oh, yes; the stories also mention that Acrisius had no sons, just a daughter named Danaë. Proetus seduced the young Danaë, his own niece—one of the reasons for the bad blood between the two brothers."

Jason nodded sagely. "That would do it."

"Afterwards, however, Danaë—"

"That's enough for tonight, Sidney," Jason yawned. "Let's get as much sleep as we can, and start out at dawn. My implant will wake me." He rolled over, wrapping his cloak around him, and composed himself for sleep. Nagel could only follow suit.

One thing at Tiryns was as per expectations: the entrance ramp that led up the eastern side of the low promontory to the fortress that sat atop the usual straggle of huts, sheds, shacks, stables, artisans' workshops, and all the refuse-strewn clutter that artists' conceptions of archaeological sites in their heyday never seemed to show.

The fortress itself was the expected wooden affair; as they ascended the ramp they were not overshadowed by the massive cyclopean tower and casemated galleries that would later make this one of the most remarkable pieces of military engineering to survive from the Bronze Age world. But the stockade enclosed the same general area as the later stone citadel, Nagel observed, and the rooftops visible above it suggested that the palace occupied the same location.

Jason listened to him with only half an ear, for he was more interested in the group of guards ahead of them, at the top of the ramp outside the gate. In the August twilight—he and Nagel had taken their time, arriving from the marshes to the west and working their way around through the inner town—those guards stood dressed and equipped exactly like those Jason had seen at Argos. They also held the same kind of spears, and their leader also had a short thrusting sword not unlike Jason's. Their hands tightened on those weapons as the two strangers approached.

"Rejoice," Jason greeted them formally. "We seek the hospitality of Proetus' hall." A few conversations in the lower town had established that the local *wanax* indeed bore that name. "I am Jason, a warrior of Aetolia. This is Synon, a cousin of my father, who was a steward to the house of Oeneus."

The captain of the guard showed no reaction at the last name, and Jason mentally sighed with relief. Nagel had recalled Oeneus as a mythical king of Aetolia, and they had been betting that he, like Danaos here in the Argolid, had been real, and that his descendents still ruled.

"Very well, then. You may enter. But things are a little unsettled." The bearded face under the boar's-tusk helmet wore a look utterly foreign to Jason's world, but which he had come to recognize in this one. "The *wanax* was visited by a god last night! Eurymedon himself!"

Jason and Nagel made the appropriate signs. "A high

honor for Proetus," Jason said respectfully, while making surreptitious eye contact with Nagel, who he was sure would later tell him who Eurymedon was, or was supposed to have been. At the moment, his uppermost thought was, *not Hyperion.* Evidently there were at least two of these beings at large on second millennium B.C. Earth, unless one was playing multiple roles.

"I myself saw the god's chariot descend," the guard captain continued as he motioned his men to open the gate. "He bore a woman with him."

"A woman?" Jason wondered how many questions he dare ask. At least he need not ask if she was still here; he knew she was. "Was she a gift for Proetus?"

"How should I know? It's not my place to ask about such things. Just be on your best behavior, that's all."

They passed through the gates and up an inner ramp, covered by its own overhanging stockade, then turned right through another gate into a courtyard opening onto an inner court beyond which was the megaron. Jason was reflecting that it was more impressive than Acrisius' establishment in Argos when he felt a tug on his tunic sleeve. It was Nagel, drawing him a little back to whisper in his ear.

"This is very similar to the palace that Schliemann will excavate in the nineteenth century! They'll build the stone walls around it later, but any rebuilding they do in here will follow the original plan closely. I could almost find my own way through here."

Jason shushed him, unable to share his archaeological enthusiasm but hopeful that he wasn't fooling himself about his knowledge of this fairly labyrinthine place—a knowledge that might prove useful. Then they traversed the porch and entered the throne room itself.

The evening's drinking by Proetus and his warriors had already commenced, presided over by the *wanax* from a throne set against the wall to the right of the central hearth. He was, Jason immediately decided, not really Acrisius' twin. (Come to think of it, there were an awful lot of twin brothers in Greek mythology. Maybe Nagel could explain why that was.) He wasn't quite as tall, and his features were narrower. He was also significantly younger, though still of above average age for an active man—which one got the definite impression that he was—in this era. His beard was still solid dark brown, and worn with the fashionable turned-up mustache that Jason had been trying to cultivate.

The guard captain stepped before him. "Son of Abas, Jason and Synon of Aetolia seek to serve under you." It was the standard formula for introducing strangers who were requesting the hospitality that was almost always granted in the absence of a good reason not to (for one never knew when one was going to need it oneself). But Jason wondered if Proetus might take it literally. Word in the lower town was that he was aggressively recruiting.

The *wanax* raised his right hand in formal greeting and gazed at them with the intense concentration of the partially drunk. "Rejoice. What brings you from the house of Oeneus?"

Jason had been expecting that. "There was a blood-feud, lord. We ourselves were not directly involved in it, but certain of our relatives were. We wished to commit no acts that would require purification—"

"Wise," Proetus nodded.

"—so we thought it best to remove ourselves to the

south for the time being. Naturally we sought out the hall of a ruler known to enjoy the special favor of the gods." That was the closest Jason dared come to inquiring about last night's visit by Eurymedon. He hoped Proetus would take the cue and indulge in some tipsy self-congratulation over his intimacy with the immortals.

Unfortunately, the *wanax* merely gave an indulgent gesture. "Be welcome. Sit down and drink. We will talk further when—" The guard captain approached, and whispered something in Proetus' ear. The latter looked annoyed, and muttered something Jason couldn't quite make out. The captain whispered anew, with more urgency. Proetus sighed, took another pull on his wine, and addressed his new guests.

"You must pardon me. A servitor of mine—a low fellow, but not without his uses—has arrived, with a report he insists will not wait." He nodded to the captain, who turned to the door and gestured peremptorily.

Two guards led in a scruffy-looking type who looked very out of place in this hall. Jason overheard a mutter of disapproval from the aristocratic warriors behind him. Proetus silenced it with a wave and glared at the new arrival.

"Well, you miserable puddle of dog vomit, what is this news that cannot wait for my regular report from Lydos?"

"Lydos is dead, lord," the man mumbled. "All of us are dead, except me and Brasidas—and he has a ruined face. You see, Lydos sent me back to our camp with Brasidas after—"

"Talk sense, clown!" roared Proetus. The man groveled. Jason now recognized him, and he held perfectly still, and hoped Nagel was doing likewise. "Tell me what happened from the beginning."

"Eurymedon appeared to us, lord!" A gasp of indrawn breath filled the hall at the blurted declaration. "He commanded us to take a party of two men and a woman who were traveling south from Argos. They showed fight, though, and killed two of us—but then the god himself came, carrying one of the heads of the Hydra which spout flames and turn men to stone!"

Now the hall was suspended in a silence of primal fear. Jason considered trying to make a break for it, only to reject the idea. Nagel's reactions would be too slow, even if he didn't freeze up altogether.

"Afterwards," the bandit resumed, "the god departed with the woman. That was when Lydos sent me back with Brasidas. Afterwards, I returned . . . didn't want to miss my share of the loot, y'understand. But Lydos and Paralos were dead—and the two men who'd been turned to stone were gone!"

"What?" Proetus rose to his feet in a rage. "You lie, pig! You stole the loot for yourself, and now you want my protection when Lydos and the others come looking for you. Guards, beat the truth out of him!"

"No, lord! By all the gods, I speak the truth!" The bandit looked around wildly at the approaching guards . . . and his eyes bulged as he glimpsed Proetus' two new guests. "*It's them, lord!* The two who were with the woman!"

For an instant, Proetus stared openmouthed and the guards halted in confusion.

"*Get out, Sidney!*" Jason yelled, shattering the hall's stunned silence. Simultaneously, he drew his sword and, with a foot, sent a low bench skidding across the floor into two guards' legs. As they fell in a heap, he ran for the door, grabbing Nagel by the arm.

The tableau was broken, and Proetus' guests rose, bellowing and fumbling for their weapons. Jason propelled Nagel toward the door with a shove and turned on the crowd, cutting the air with a series of whistling sword slashes that made them draw back. One man dived under the sword and tackled Jason's legs. Jason brought the sword's pommel down on his head and felt the grappling arms go limp. He kicked the unconscious form away and brought his sword back up just in time to thrust it into the belly of an onrushing warrior. He withdrew it with a twist, and a string of entrails came out with it. He reversed it and stabbed another man. Then he was free of the press and sprinting for the door . . . and, out of the corner of his eye, saw a guard grasping Nagel from behind while another man punched him repeatedly in the stomach.

Muttering a curse, Jason turned away from the beckoning door and threw his sword-dagger. It wasn't intended as a throwing weapon, but it flew straight. Missing Nagel's head by inches, it pierced the eye of the guard who was holding him. At appreciably the same instant, Jason arrived, kicked the second guard in the crotch. He yanked his blade out of the already-dead guard's head and grabbed Nagel—who was moaning and trying to go into fetal position—and tugged him toward the door.

It was too late. A crush of rancid bodies landed atop the two of them, pinning Jason's sword arm to the floor and pressing his face down so that he never saw the club that descended on his head, sending him into an oblivion of exploding stars followed by darkness.

CHAPTER SEVEN

A kick in the ribs brought Jason sickeningly awake.

He had been lying facedown, dreaming dreams whose general unpleasantness had included a suffocating, inescapable odor which, he now saw, had been altogether too real, for he had been lying on the packed-earth, straw-covered floor of a stable which had seen recent occupancy. He got to his hands and knees, if for no other reason than to get his face out of that in which it had been buried.

"Up, pig!" This time it was a spear butt that jabbed his ribs, toppling him over in a nauseating spasm of pain. Two guards grasped his arms and hauled him upright. Their grip was the only solid thing in a spinning universe. But drilled-in reflexes made him observe his surroundings—especially Nagel, whom a third guard was untying from the post to which he'd been secured. The historian's face was gray, and even as he was prodded forward he remained hunched over, as though an aching midriff made it impossible for him to stand up straight.

The guard captain they had met earlier entered, ran his eyes over the prisoners with none of his former affability, and gave a jerk of his chin. The guards hustled them outside. It was night. They were in a large enclosed area, and glancing to his left Jason saw stronger timber walls topping a higher ridge, with the palace roofs above. They must, he thought, be in the "lower citadel" that would one day have its own cyclopean stone wall. It contained a number of buildings no more prepossessing than the stable. But their destination was the palace, up the ramp they has ascended before. Jason wondered why they'd been imprisoned below. To keep them out of sight, perhaps?

They turned right and entered the outer court. It was heavily guarded and alight with torches. Proetus stood before the columned porch fronting the megaron itself, flanked by his advisors and leading warriors. He looked less like a king holding court than a middle-management underling nervously awaiting the arrival of his boss.

But Jason had no eyes for the *wanax*, or for anything else but the female figure in the filthy tatters of a tunic, sprawled at the foot of a wooden post to which her wrists were lashed. She was unconscious, but seemed to be stirring.

"Deirdre!" Jason started forward, only to go sprawling as a guard cut him across the backs of his knees with a spear shaft.

"Be still, son of a goat," the guard captain rasped in a voice thick with tension. "And stay on your knees."

Another guard pushed Nagel down beside Jason. Then they waited. The fluttering roar as the wind whipped the torch flames was the only sound.

Then, with a faint whining hum that Jason recalled from the road to Lerna, the god came.

It was the same half-gondola, half-throne "chariot" that appeared above the courtyard, running lights ablaze, but the tall figure was seated this time. The vehicle came to a near landing, hovering a couple of feet above the surface in a way that Jason recognized as extravagantly energy-wasteful but useful for making an impression. And this time there were others. Four of the "chariots" drifted down, each holding a "god," two of them female.

Everyone from Proetus on down groveled. The guard captain paused only long enough to shove his two prisoners' faces into the dirt before joining them there.

Even at this moment, Nagel whispered didactically into Jason's ear. "Again, this doesn't quite ring true. The historical Greeks never degraded themselves before the gods—they didn't believe that self-abasement was what the gods wanted. They stood up and prayed aloud—"

"Quiet!" Jason hissed. He was watching as the occupant of the first "chariot" stood up to his full more-than-human height and surveyed the courtyard. Looking at that unhuman face, he could see individual differences from the one he'd glimpsed on the road north of Lerna. This face was heavier-featured, and had a beard which Eurymedon had lacked. It also had a look of mature strength . . . but not an "older" look, for all of these faces had a quality of agelessness.

"Rejoice, Proetus of Tiryns," boomed that indescribable voice. "Have you kept this woman unharmed?"

Proetus raised his head just enough to peek upward. "Yes, Hyperion, Lord of Light. I have done as Eurymedon commanded—even though the woman's two companions sought to inveigle their way into my palace, doubtless thinking to make off with her." He grew bold enough to indulge in a little self-congratulation, rising to a kneeling position and pointing dramatically at the two prisoners. "But my vigilance was too great, and before they could put their scheme into action I—"

The tall being held up a hand, halting Proteus' voice as abruptly as an off switch would have stopped a recording. Then he turned slowly and gave Jason and Nagel an emotionless regard. Jason met those eyes. They were stranger than he had thought: the "whites" were pale blue, and the irises were an opaque azure unlike any human eye color. After a few seconds' inspection, those eyes swung back to Proetus.

"Those ridiculous bandits were commanded to deal with these men."

"One of them is here, lord."

"Kill him. You may also kill these two men. The woman, however . . ." Hyperion stepped from his floating platform, and the general groveling intensified as his feet touched the ground. He walked slowly over to the stake where Deirdre was beginning to return to consciousness. He held an instrument which, to Jason, suggested a sensor of some kind.

Deirdre's eyes fluttered open. She gasped and struggled against the leather thongs.

"Hold her still," Hyperion ordered. Two guards rushed to obey. Then he ran the sensor over her, a few inches from her skin. He halted at the inside of her upper left arm, where a very tiny scar showed. He gave a satisfied nod and turned to Proetus.

"There is a small metal talisman inside her left arm, beneath this." He indicated the scar. "Have someone cut it out of her."

"No!" yelled Jason. He leaped to his feet and lunged . . . only to feel a spear butt impact sickeningly against his already-battered head. Two guards grasped his arms and held him immobile. As his vision cleared, he saw a man who looked like he might very well be Proetus' butcher step forward toward Deirdre, holding a bronze knife.

"Wash the blade first," Hyperion commanded, "as we wish to keep her alive." No one understood the connection, in this era that had never heard of infection, but neither was anyone about to argue. Water was brought and the knife was cleaned, while Deirdre watched with round, unblinking eyes but made no sound.

She continued to hold her jaws clamped shut as the butcher approached, but when the blade neared her arm she burst into a frantic, straining struggle which required three guards to subdue, one grasping her around the knees and one gripping each arm. When the knife stroke laid open her flesh, she finally screamed. She screamed louder as the butcher spread apart the lips of the cut he had made and probed with the knife point.

"I think I see it," he muttered. The knife point began to dig. Deirdre fainted.

"Got it!" said the butcher with satisfaction. He put his thumb and forefinger into the blood-drenched pinkish-gray tissue and pulled. He turned to Hyperion and held out a pea-sized sphere.

"Put it in this." Hyperion held out a flat container—plastic, thought Jason in a small calm corner of his mind. The butcher dropped the blood-dripping object into it, and the "god" snapped it shut. "Now wash and bind her wound," he ordered. "We may have further use for her." Without waiting for an acknowledgment, he turned back toward his "chariot."

It was then that Jason spoke with the recklessness of a man already condemned to death.

"You bastard! Who *are* you?" A hiss of shock suffused the courtyard, and the guards holding him stiffened. He expected another blow, but none came—the guards must have been stunned into immobility by his blasphemy. Hyperion paused, and turned those disturbing eyes toward him.

"Who are you?" Jason repeated. "*What* are you? You don't belong here!"

Without speaking, Hyperion walked over to him and ran the sensor over his left arm—but not, to Jason's relief, over his head, where it would surely have detected the computer implant, whose removal by the butcher did not bear thinking about. The "god" then did the same to Nagel. Then he gazed down from his great height, and for the first time a hint of a smile touched the corners of his wide mouth. "*I* don't belong here?" he echoed ironically, barely above a whisper. Before Jason could try to answer the unanswerable, Hyperion turned back to Proetus and spoke in a loud voice.

"I have changed my mind. Keep the two men alive as well—although you need not keep them comfortable. They also have talismans inside their flesh." Jason could sense the general shudder of distaste. "I will probably want their talismans removed as well, later; but for now the woman's will suffice. It must be studied. Afterwards, we will return and put all three of them to the question."

"All will be done as you command, lord,"

"See that it is. And remember: these men are especially accursed in the eyes of the gods. Keep them closely confined and let no one approach them. The same holds for the woman. Besides, I may have other uses for her." Without another word, Hyperion mounted his "chariot," which drifted upward and swung away over the walls. The other three followed him. Only then did Proetus and his subjects get to their feet.

"Shall we take them to the palace, lord?" The guard captain asked.

"No, idiot! Didn't you hear the god? They're to be kept isolated. Take them back to the stables—but secure them tightly!"

"And the woman, lord?"

Proetus hesitated for the barest instant. "Her too. But confine her separately. Remember what the god said about having 'other uses for her'? Don't let them or any other men have access to her. *Any* other men," Proetus repeated heavily, giving the guard captain a hard look. The latter gulped.

"Yes, lord. You men, bring them!"

Two guards picked up Deirdre's limp form. Two others got Jason and Nagel moving with their spear points. The captain, carrying a torch, led the way from the courtyard and back down the ramp toward the lower citadel. To the right, beyond the main gate, Jason saw a pinkish hint of dawn in the east. He barely noticed, for he was sorting out the implications of what he'd heard.

First of all—and he clung to the thought—Hyperion had made it very clear that Deirdre was not to be harmed by anyone except himself. So presumably she hadn't been molested, save for this night's brutal chopping-out of her TRD. Secondly, that TRD "must be studied" according to the bogus god, who therefore didn't know what it was. In fact, there was no evidence that he knew about time travel at all. That ignorance must be maintained. It was a reason—though not, of course, the most important one—for getting back the implant, without which Deirdre would be a permanent resident of the Bronze Age.

In another compartment of his mind, Jason wondered why he and Nagel hadn't been bound. He suspected it had something to do with the ingrained assumptions of a warrior class that dominated this world through its monopoly of expensive bronze weaponry. Unarmed men didn't need to have their hands tied to be helpless and contemptible. It was an attitude Jason meant to encourage.

All of this ran through the back of Jason's mind as he carefully observed the route they were following. It took them to a sturdily built shed against the base of the ledge topped by the upper citadel and the royal megaron. The two guards carrying Deirdre dumped her on the straw-covered floor, heedless of whether they caused her bleeding to resume, and locked the door with a kind of large wooden bolt. As they did so, Jason made himself slump as though barely able to stay on his feet. A guard contemptuously hauled him upright.

"You two can go on," the guard captain told Deirdre's erstwhile bearers. "We'll take the others to the stables." The dismissed guards departed by the pale dawn-light.

The captain motioned with his torch in the direction of the stables and walked ahead.

They had only gone a few steps when Jason stumbled realistically. "Move!" snapped his guard, prodding his back so sharply that the spear point broke the skin. With a single smooth motion, Jason went to his right knee, shifting to the side, and simultaneously grasped the spear shaft just below the blade. He yanked it forward, then jabbed backwards, ramming the butt into the startled guard's midriff.

Before the captain realized anything was amiss, Jason sprang forward, yanking the spear from the doubled-over guard. His grip on the spear near the top of the shaft was an awkward one. But he stabbed the blade into the base of the captain's neck, severing the spine.

Nagel's guard reacted faster than Jason had thought him capable. With a quick curse and a shove, he sent his own prisoner sprawling, and turned on Jason, thrusting with his spear. Jason, grasping his own spear near center-shaft, batted the thrust aside . . . just in time to be grappled from behind by the guard he'd thought he'd disabled.

Nagel's guard grinned between his helmet's cheekpieces and hefted his spear for a killing thrust. But then his expression went blank and he toppled over, revealing Nagel, staring incredulously at the rock with which he'd just clouted the man from behind, striking the base of his skull just below the helmet.

Jason wasted no time. He raised his spear above his head and brought it down behind him, behind the head of the guard who was grasping him. Then he did a quick forward roll, bringing the man over him to land on his back with a thud. Before he could get his wind back, Jason brought the spear around and plunged it down through the supine man's throat, practically pinning him to the ground.

"Good work, Sidney," he gasped. Nagel did not respond to the compliment—he was still standing in openmouthed amazement at what was doubtless the first act of physical violence in his life. Jason scooped up the fallen guard captain's torch and grabbed Nagel by the arm a little more roughly than was necessary. "Come on! Take one of these spears, and let's go get Deirdre."

Jason didn't know how to work the wooden "lock," so he thrust his spear into the crack between doorframe and door, and pried it open. Holding the torch through the opening, he could see Deirdre was conscious. She was cowering in the far corner.

"It's us, Deirdre!" he exclaimed. With a small cry of relief, she sprang to him and held him tightly with her right arm . . . but only for a moment, until she remembered herself. Then backed away and looked at him levelly.

"They took it out, didn't they?" she asked, indicating her uselessly hanging left arm with its blood-stained bandage.

"Yes." Jason saw no point in lying.

She sucked in a breath, but when she spoke her voice was steady. Too steady, Jason thought. "Then I'm here for good."

"Like hell you are! We're going to get it back. You'll just have to be very careful to not lose it over the next three months," Jason added with an attempt at lightness. "Maybe we can find a local jeweler to make it into an earring or something."

"But how—?"

"I can locate it. Never mind how; I've already explained

to Sidney, but I don't have time to go over it again now. We've got to move." Jason turned to Nagel. "You said you could find your way through this place. How can we get out without going back up the ramp and past the upper citadel?"

Nagel thought for a moment. "In later times, there was an underground cistern just outside the wall at the northwest corner of the lower citadel—the opposite end from where we are now. Not far from that was a kind of sally port. Was . . . or will be." He looked annoyed. "Kyle Rutherford had a point about the need for new tenses, didn't he?"

"Sidney . . . !"

"Oh . . . ahem! Yes. Well, perhaps there are earlier versions here and now."

"Let's find out." They crept from the shed and picked their way among stables, barns and stock pens in the gathering dawn until they reached the stockade. They worked their way around the inside until they reached the cistern, and the small opening in the stockade that gave access to it. Slipping out, they clambered down the low bluff—only an occasional sound of pain escaped Deirdre—and entered the straggling seaside town to the west of the fortress. Few people were about as yet, and they made themselves walk without apparent haste or furtiveness. Then they were clear of the crude structures, and a road stretched ahead of them in a west-northwest direction—a road that didn't look like it had seen much use lately. Jason summoned up his map, and unconsciously nodded.

"Do you know where we're going?" Deirdre asked. She looked even worse than Nagel, who was showing the effects of weariness, hunger, and emotional reaction. Jason didn't imagine he looked all that much better.

"Yes," he nodded. "This is the road to Argos. We'll go back there and claim Acrisius' hospitality. He won't mind that we're in trouble with his brother—he'll probably give us a good-conduct medal. We'll stay there just long enough for me to take a proper look at your wound, and for us to get a little rest. Then we'll resume our original plan and take the road to Lerna. It's more imperative than ever that we get passage on a ship."

"Why?"

"Never mind." He could have told her why, because he knew where her TRD had been taken. But this was no time for lengthy explanations. "Come on, let's move."

They trudged on into the gathering heat of the August morning. They had covered about three miles—almost halfway to the Inachos and the border between the feuding brothers' territories, in fact—when Jason heard the rumbling behind them, growing louder in pursuit. Even as he whirled around, he knew in the pit of his stomach he was going to see chariots.

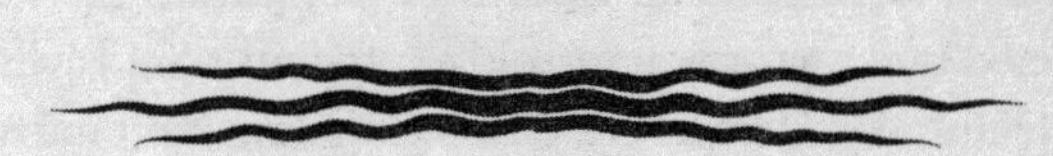

CHAPTER EIGHT

There were three of the chariots, thundering down the road from Tiryns.

Jason knew about them from his forced-draft orientation. They were light, with four-spoked wheels, and axles set well to the rear for mobility. Two-horse teams could draw them at high speed, even though those horses were small—more like ponies to Jason's eyes—and had inefficient chest-strap harnesses. Each carried a lightly clad charioteer and a full-armed warrior.

Earlier in this century, such chariots had overturned the world as thoroughly as stirrup-using shock cavalry would do two thousand years in the future, enabling barbarian invaders to conquer the already-ancient civilizations of the Near East in a series of blitzkriegs. Yet those barbarians had used them as mobile platforms from which opposing infantry formations could be crumpled up with showers of arrows and then finished off with a charge. The Achaean Greeks, if Homer was to be believed, had regarded archery as not quite the thing, and had used the new superweapon as a mere prestige vehicle. It seemed absurd, as though some Industrial Revolution-era army had used tanks to transport soldiers to battlefields where they alighted and proceeded to fire volleys with muzzle-loaders. Nagel had speculated aloud that Homer, a few centuries later when chariots had fallen into disuse, might have misunderstood the old oral epics.

Now it looked as though they were going to find out the truth at first hand.

Jason looked around frantically. They were in fairly flat country; the surrounding terrain was only marginally less suited for wheeled vehicles than this "road." The only possible sources of cover were the occasional olive groves and orchards. There had been a few cultivators visible in the distance, but they were now disappearing as fast as their legs would carry them—a common reaction, Jason imagined, to the sight of war chariots.

All these thoughts took Jason less than a second. "Run!" he yelled at his companions, pointing with his spear at an olive grove, and he suited the action to the word. Deirdre and Nagel needed no further urging.

The chariots veered off the road on a course calculated to intercept them. It was a bumpy ride for them, and as the lead chariot got closer Jason saw that the warrior was holding onto a balance thong attached to the car's rim with his left hand lest he be jolted out despite a highly trained sense of balance. His right hand gripped a spear underhand, which indicated that these people really did wield weapons from their chariots, even if they drew the line at using bow and arrow against human prey. Jason halfway expected Nagel to pause for a lecture on the subject.

And he might just as well, he thought with a sudden onrush of despair. They quite obviously weren't going to make it to the dubious shelter of the grove. Jason alone couldn't even have made it, in his hunger and exhaustion, much less Deirdre with her loss of blood and Nagel with his middle-aged wind.

They were not so much running as staggering when Jason came to a gasping halt, muttered "Shit!" and turned to face the onrushing chariots with spear at high port. "Keep going!" he snapped at the other two. "I'll try to delay them."

To his astonishment, Nagel disobeyed him, pointing his spear and making an attempt at a fighting stance that would have been funny in any other circumstances. Deirdre simply took a deep breath and stood.

"Shit," Jason repeated. The lead chariot was getting close. Jason faced the thundering hooves with upraised spear and waited for death.

Out of the corner of his eye, he glimpsed something flash past him from the direction of the olive grove.

Before Jason's mind had even had time to process that glimpse, a thrown spear transfixed the lead chariot warrior at the base of his throat. Spurting blood, he fell heavily against his charioteer, who lost control of the team. Neighing wildly, the horses slewed around in too tight a turn for even the highly maneuverable chariot to handle. It capsized, crushing its occupants and bringing the horses down in a maddened, screaming tangle, trapped by their harness and traces.

The other two charioteers veered desperately away to either side, barely avoiding a collision. It gave Jason a respite, and he turned to stare in the direction from which the spear had come.

A man was approaching at a run—presumably the man who had thrown the spear, although if so it had been a phenomenal throw. He was hefting a second spear as he ran, his long hair streaming in the wind behind him and his mouth open in a wordless war cry. He was running toward the chariot that had turned off toward Jason's left, and whose charioteer was now bringing it around to resume its charge.

The stranger drew back and hurled his spear, all in one continuous, flowing motion at which Jason, even at this moment, gawked. But this chariot warrior was ready. He raised his shield at an angle, and the spear clanged off it. But the effort caused the warrior to get in the way of his charioteer, and the momentum of the charge was broken. And the stranger had gone directly from that beautiful, Olympic-quality javelin throw into a dead run that brought him up to the chariot even as its charioteer was trying to get the team back under control. He grasped the bridle of the right-hand horse with his left hand, giving a twist which made the animals rear and spill the chariot's occupants.

The fallen charioteer had had enough; he sprang to his feet and set out at a dead run in the direction of Tiryns. But the warrior hefted his shield—round, and small enough to use in a chariot, unlike the great figure-eight shields favored by the local infantry—and advanced on the stranger, flourishing a long, narrow thrusting sword of the kind the archaeologists would, with a certain poetic license, call "rapiers."

The stranger drew from its sling a sword-dagger like the one Jason had been divested of at Tiryns. Simultaneously, he took off a cloak he wore over his tunic and twirled it around his left forearm in lieu of a shield.

A rumbling from behind reminded Jason of the third chariot. It had taken longer to make a hundred-and-eighty-degree turn, but now it was approaching, its warrior raising his spear for a throw at the stranger. But then the charioteer had to swerve to avoid the wreck of the first chariot, spoiling the spearman's throw and partially killing the vehicle's momentum.

Without pausing for thought, Jason plunged forward, hitting the ground and rolling up to the wheels, now turning slowly enough for their four spokes to be individually visible. He thrust his spear between two of those spokes.

He couldn't possibly have done it with a more advanced, many-spoked wheel. But he managed to get the spear shaft through both wheels before it was snatched out of his hand . . . and slammed up against the bottom of the car, an instant brake. The light chariot kicked forward like a catapult, sending its occupants sailing forward over the backs of the loudly protesting horses. The charioteer thudded to the ground at exactly the wrong angle, and lay still with a broken neck. The warrior staggered to his feet and turned on the now-unarmed Jason with one of the long slender swords. Jason got to his feet and into defensive stance . . . just in time to hear a yell off to the left.

It was Nagel, charging in with clumsy enthusiasm. The dismounted chariot warrior turned aside and, in a motion of visibly contemptuous ease, knocked the historian's jabbing spear aside with his shield. He was drawing back his sword for a thrust when Jason sprang forward and crashed into him. The long sword was not designed for close quarters; its wielder could do nothing as Jason got an arm around his neck and, with a quick vicious sideways motion, broke his neck as thoroughly as that of his charioteer.

"Well done, Sidney," Jason sighed as he got to his feet. It hadn't been, really, but he felt no inclination to quibble about technique. Besides, he was watching with interest as the stranger confirmed his own theory of the short sword-dagger's superiority, sending his opponent tumbling to the ground trying to hold in his spilling guts.

Briskly businesslike, the stranger walked over to the overturned first chariot, whose horses still thrashed about in their pain and confusion. He cut their throats. Blood gushed forth to soak into the ground.

Deirdre stared, speechless with horror, and Jason thought Nagel was going to be sick. He wasn't immune to their feelings himself. But he recognized the act as one of mercy—the only realistic mercy for those broken-legged little horses. The other two teams, he noted, were walking around slowly, munching grass and pulling the inconsiderable weight of their unoccupied chariots. They must have been trained not to run off in the absence of their charioteers.

The stranger finally turned to them. "Rejoice," he greeted conventionally, with a smile of guileless friendliness. The face wearing that smile was nearly beardless. Jason hadn't noticed his youth before, probably because of his size—tall even for Jason's native milieu, extremely tall for this one—and the awesome physical competence he had just displayed. But viewed close up he was clearly under twenty and built like a, well, Greek god. His features were regular, with a wide, rather thin-lipped mouth and a narrow, straight-bridged nose. His long thick hair was a richly deep, dark chestnut brown, his eyes bluish-gray, his complexion fairer than the local average but well-tanned and currently somewhat flushed from exertion.

To Jason, there was a vague half-familiarity about that face, which dissolved like the memory of a dream when he tried to put his finger on it.

"Rejoice," Jason responded cautiously. He knew nothing about this formidable kid, including how he stood with respect to Proetus of Tiryns. "We are in your debt."

"Not at all. I was resting in that olive grove—I've had a long journey, you see—when I heard the chariots on the road from Tiryns." The fresh young face came as close to a scowl as it could manage, and Jason began to relax a little. "Did Proetus send them?"

"Yes. We escaped during the night from Tiryns, where Proetus had imprisoned us. Do you know of him?"

"I do indeed. He is my great-uncle." Jason's apprehensions returned in full force, for he wasn't at all sure he relished the prospect of going up against this character, kid or no. But then he noticed that the handsome face had gone expressionless. "Some people believe—wrongly—that he is also my father, for he dishonored my mother, his niece Danaë."

Behind Jason, Nagel gasped. Jason ignored it, for he thought he saw an opening. "Well, then, you will understand why we fell afoul of him. He wished to dishonor this lady, Deianeira." He launched into the stock story of their lives, and added a heavily edited account of their recent adventures, omitting all mention of the gods and attributing their incarceration at Tiryns simply to Proetus' lust. Then another thought occurred to him. "Acrisius of Argos must be your grandfather—and he is the enemy of Proetus. We were on our way there, to seek his hospitality. Would you—?"

"No." The young face took on an incongruously grave look. "Acrisius may not be quite as much of a pig as Proetus. But after my birth, he cast out my mother, his own daughter, for he would not believe her when she told him who my true father was. He put the two of us on a ship and exiled us to the island of Seriphos. Sooner or later," added the youth matter-of-factly, "I will take vengeance on him and Proetus both."

Nagel spoke up. "But that is not why you are in the Argolid now, is it?" He asked the question as though he already knew its answer.

"No. I'm on an errand for King Polydectes of Seriphos, who was guardian to my mother until I came of age. But I must avoid Acrisius—and so should you. He is not to be trusted."

"Hmm. . . ." Jason still wasn't sure how far he could confide in this affable young man. "We have an 'errand' of our own. We must recover a very valuable article belonging to the lady Deianeira. And we need to find a ship. We were hoping to find one at Lerna."

The stranger brightened. "Lerna! There must be fate in this. May I accompany you?"

"By all means." There was, Jason reflected, something to be said for traveling in the company of someone this handy in a fight. "Of course, if we're to avoid Argos, we'll have to leave the road and travel southwestward."

"So much the better. We need to leave the roads in any case; that one charioteer who escaped will tell Proetus. Unfortunately, we won't be able to take the chariots." The stranger turned to the grazing teams. Deirdre sucked in a breath as though she was afraid he was going to do to them what he'd done to the injured ones. But he merely smacked their rumps and sent them on their way. Jason, who had been wondering how he was going to disguise his amateurism at driving the things, was relieved. He was also curious.

"What takes you to Lerna?" he asked the stranger, after the latter had finished a businesslike looting of the chariot warriors' bodies.

"It's my errand. I must bring Polydectes one of the heads of the Hydra. Since Lerna is where the Hydra is supposed to have lived, it seems the natural place to start looking, don't you think?'

"No doubt," Jason managed. He remembered what a "head of the Hydra" really was, for the bandit had used the term in Proetus' hall. Surely this innocent-seeming young man could have no idea that he was talking about a weapon forged by a technology that had no place in his world.

He pulled himself together. "Well, I wish you luck. And we welcome your company. Oh, by the way, you never told us your name."

"Perseus," the young man said politely. "Son of Zeus," he added.

They stopped that night at a goatherd's hut not far from the marshes. Jason could have gone further, and Perseus wasn't even breathing hard, but Deirdre's color was worse and she could barely continue reeling forward, although she'd be damned and in hell before she'd admit it. The goatherd offered them the poor hospitality his means permitted—the custom evidently applied up and down the social scale. He also looked healthily apprehensive at the presence of armed men, although Perseus treated him with the same sunny amiability he seemed to show to anyone he didn't have reason to kill. The hospitality became downright effusive when the goatherd learned he was hosting a Hero.

Apropos of which, Jason needed badly to talk to Nagel.

First, though, he removed Deirdre's bandage and examined her wound closely. It wasn't oozing anything, nor was there any redness around it, to his relief. The broad-spectrum immunizations that everybody routinely got in their world weren't an absolute guarantee against infection, but they helped. In conjunction with the very basic precautions Hyperion had ordained, they evidently had been enough. Jason prevailed upon the goatherd to boil some water in a ceramic pot—metal implements were only for the wealthy in this world. Then he replaced the bandage, tying it as tightly as he dared—and as Deirdre could stand—to hold together the lips of the wound, whose looks he didn't like. If he'd had any sort of needles and thread, he would have done some stitches, using wine as a disinfectant. But he didn't. At a minimum, she was going to have one hell of a scar. At least, he jollied her, it was in an inconspicuous place. Then he poured enough of the goatherd's wine (by courtesy so called) into her to dissolve her resistance to letting exhaustion and pain take her. She was giving out ladylike snores by the time he finally gestured to Nagel to follow him outside, under the sky of an Earth with no electric lighting.

"It's what I was trying to tell you before we reached Tiryns," the historian jittered. "The legends are quite explicit that Perseus' mother was Danaë, daughter of Acrisius . . . and that his father was Zeus."

"Zeus?" Jason echoed. "*The* Zeus?"

Nagel nodded. "Of course, in this era he's not regarded as the king of the gods, as he will be in Homer's time. He's simply the weather god. And I suppose we must assume he's one of the . . . entities we've seen."

"Entities that are obviously nonhuman. I don't care what the Greek myths say; they can't possibly have issue with humans!"

"Of course not!" said Nagel peevishly. "I can't account for that part. But everything else fits, including his 'errand' for Polydectes, king of Seriphos, where he and his mother were exiled. The legend says Polydectes was holding over him the threat of raping his mother, but it's possible that he's too embarrassed to tell us that part."

Jason waved the point aside and thought hard. "Look, Sidney, I don't pretend to your knowledge of this stuff. But wasn't it Perseus' task to bring back the head of the Gorgon Medusa?"

"Yes—the head that turned men to stone if they looked on its face. But Medusa and her sister Gorgons were linked with the Lernean Hydra, whose heads also had magical properties, such as shooting out fire—a laser guide beam, as we know."

"What was the linkage?"

"They were both descended from the sea deity, Phorcys. The Gorgons were daughters of his; the Hydra was a child of his daughter Echidne—the prototypical mermaid, being half beautiful woman and half sea serpent—by the monster Typhon. Confusion on the part of the later myth compilers was understandable."

"But they got the genealogies so exactly!"

"Royal genealogies were orally transmitted with great care. This was a necessity. But with monsters, it was permissible to let the fancy have free rein." Nagel permitted himself a dry chuckle. "To take just one example, in the legends as they have come down to us, the Hydra is killed by Herakles, a descendant of Perseus. But here we have its heads already believed to be available as portable weapons in Perseus' lifetime!"

"I suppose you're right. And at any rate, I don't suppose it matters. As you say, we know what this 'head' really is, no matter who it's supposed to have belonged to or who is supposed to have cut it off. Let's go back inside—no, wait a minute!" Jason summoned up his neurally projected map, and scrolled it northwestward by mental command. "Sidney, this 'Echidne' who was the mother of the Hydra: is she connected with the Echinades Islands, up on the far side of the Gulf of Corinth?"

"Why, yes. They were supposedly her home, and were named after her. Why do you ask?"

Jason looked at the flashing red dot for a moment, before dismissing the map and turning to Nagel. "Because, Sidney, that's where Deirdre's TRD has been taken."

CHAPTER NINE

Thanks to Perseus, they made better time than Jason had dared hope. It wasn't that he helped with Deirdre, although he was always ready with polite—and, to her, infuriatingly patronizing—offers to do so. Rather, she kept up on her own out of grim determination to avoid accepting those very offers. It also helped that in August the Inachos was fairly easy to ford even near its mouth. They reached Lerna late in the afternoon, following the coast around the northern end of the Gulf of Argos.

Lerna pretty much lived down to expectations, although Nagel was happy as a clam at high tide as he compared what he was seeing to the conventional wisdom about this much-excavated site. There was even a barely visible remnant of the wall of mud brick, built atop a foundation of limestone blocks, that had guarded the settlement the barbaric Proto-Greeks had burned four centuries earlier. Before Nagel could wander off in search of the "House of Tiles" as the archaeologists had dubbed it, Jason firmly hustled him on toward the docks. They were here to find a ship.

There were a surprising number of ships in port. Some of them were from the various islands. Nagel, listening to the unintelligible conversation of their crews, could barely contain his glee at the confirmation of yet another of his theories. Those sailors' language, he declared breathlessly, belonged to the Hittite-Luwian branch of Indo-European. Jason, who couldn't have cared less if they had been speaking Swahili, made noises of polite interest and devoted most of his attention to the ships themselves.

They were wide-bodied merchantmen, the largest only about sixty feet long. Jason's expert eye recognized plank construction using mortise-and-tenon joining. These were single-masted square-riggers with a single square sail, and their ability to beat upwind was consequently very limited. Nevertheless, that sail was the primary propulsion, with a few oars (typically eight) used for maneuvering in and out of harbor with the aid of crude rudders. This held the crew requirement down to only a dozen or so, hence minimizing the amount of cargo space that had to be devoted to their stores.

All in all, the ships were exactly what Jason had expected in this time and place. He didn't have to worry about adjusting to any surprises. What he did have to worry about was getting passage.

If they'd still had their high-value trade goods, he would have simply chartered a ship. But their wealth now languished in the storerooms of Proetus of Tiryns, which

Jason found objectionable on principle as well as damned inconvenient. They would have to offer to work for their passage on a ship that was going to stop at the Echinades anyway. He was optimistic about finding one. As Rutherford had pointed out, they were well within the March-through-October sailing season.

Perseus was skeptical, in his invincibly cheerful way, when he learned that they wanted to go to the west of the Peloponnesus, which was as specific as Jason was willing to be about their destination. "I don't know, Jason. Most of the ships' captains around here trade in the Cyclades, or south to Crete. To get from here to where you want to go, you have to round the Cape of Malea, at the southern end of the Peloponnesus. You know how treacherous that is."

Jason didn't, really. "Even at this time of year?"

"There's no good time of year down there. Remember, the summer winds are almost always from the north or northwest. You'd be going against them the whole way." Perseus shook his head ruefully, with the sunny smile he wore even when he was throwing the proverbial wet blanket. "Also, traders have no incentive to go to Messenia and Elis. Nobody there but warring robber-chieftains." This, Jason knew from his orientation, was an accurate description of the western Peloponnesus before the foundation of the Homeric kingdom of Nestor of Pylos, almost four centuries in the future of here-and-now. "And before you even get there, you have to round Cape Taenarum, which means passing too close for comfort to the gates of Hades."

He would *say something like that just when he was starting to make sense*, Jason groaned inwardly. "But won't anybody be going to Corcyra?" he asked, using the current name for Corfu. Homer and the archaeologists agreed that there would be a rich kingdom there in later times, at least.

Perseus gave him an odd look. "That's an awfully long way, Jason." He had been, and continued to be, too well-bred to question them directly about their itinerary. "Besides, to get there you'd have to pass the Echinades . . . and of *course* nobody wants to go there!"

Jason, naturally, had to find out for himself. He left Perseus and Nagel to find accommodations and set out with Deirdre to make the rounds of the ships. His choice of a companion was a calculated one, based on the theory that shipmasters, after one look, might find the idea of having her as a passenger appealing. Needless to say, he did not discuss this strategy with her. And at any rate, it did no good. Nobody was going west. And on the rare occasions when he got as far as mentioning the Echinades, his listeners' reaction immediately went from disinterest to downright alarm, as though they were confronted with a dangerous lunatic.

They were growing both tired and disgusted when Perseus tracked them down. The Hero was, of course, above indulging in I-told-you-sos. "Come with me," he urged. "I found the house of Sotades, a merchant from Seriphos who is loyal to my mother. He's taken us in."

Sotades was out and about on business when they arrived at the house—Jason would have called it a hut, and he imagined his fellow time travelers' terms for it would have ranged downward from "hovel"—but the servants provided them with wine and very basic food. Thus fortified, Jason turned to Perseus and spoke in a voice he carefully kept from seeming too eager.

"Perseus, you say Sotades is beholden to your mother Danaë?"

"Yes, ever since Poseidon washed her ashore on Seriphos, carrying me. Diktys, the brother of King Polydectes, took us in. Sotades was a young sailor on one of Diktys' ships then, and it was he who fished her out of the water, where she had been clinging to a piece of wreckage while keeping me above water. Afterwards, he knew his fate was linked with ours." The word he actually used for "fate" was a recognizable ancestor of the Classical Greek *moira*, which implied a great deal more.

"Well, then, do you suppose you could persuade him to take us to our destination?"

"Probably—if I were going. In fact, I'm sure he'd be willing to take me anywhere. But . . ." If Perseus didn't feel genuine regret, he was a better actor than Jason took him for. "I'm truly sorry, Jason, but my task for Polydectes must come first. As much as I'd like to accompany you, I have to stay here in Lerna until I've found a head of the Lernean Hydra."

Jason considered for a moment, then threw caution to the winds. "Perseus, I haven't been altogether candid with you about our destination—"

"I know," nodded Perseus, with no visible resentment, as though he understood Jason's reservations about his relatives.

"Well, the time has come when I must tell you. We are going to the Echinades."

Perseus' eyes grew round. "The Echinades? But Jason, you must know there's nothing in those islands but the pirates who infest them. The scum of the earth! Squatting there just north of the entrance to the Gulf of Corinth, they've practically brought commerce to a standstill."

"Why hasn't someone mounted an expedition to root them out?" Nagel asked, curious.

Perseus gave him an odd look. "Why, they are protected. Everyone knows that. They are under the special patronage of certain of the Old Gods."

The Old Gods. It was, Jason thought, the first time he'd heard that particular turn of phrase. He started to open his mouth to ask for an elucidation, then immediately closed it. He and Nagel had already exhibited quite enough curiosity about matters of common knowledge.

"Nevertheless," he said firmly, "we must go there. Remember I told you of a precious article belonging to the lady Deianeira? Well, it has been taken to the Echinades. Never mind how I know this; the knowledge has been granted to me in ways of which I may not speak. By the same means, I also know that at least one of the heads of the Hydra is there as well. We ourselves encountered it, and were lucky to escape with our lives. If you come with us, we'll help you gain that head—if you help us with our errand as well, starting by getting all of us passage on Sotades' ship."

Perseus leaned forward, his eyes alight with youthful enthusiasm. "Yes! We can help each other. I'm with you, Jason."

Jason's conscience stirred. He wasn't quite sure why. He knew that recovering Deirdre's TRD should have been his only consideration. But there was something about this kid . . . "Perseus, there's one other thing I haven't mentioned to you before. The Hydra's head of which I'm speaking was in the hands of one of the, uh, Old Gods.

They seem to be in alliance with Proetus, and they regard us as their enemies. I feel obliged to tell you this, since they may regard you the same way if you aid us."

"So much the better! Am I not the son of a god? What a chance for glory! What a—ah, here comes Sotades. I'm sure he'll feel as excited as I do!"

Sotades, of course, felt nothing of the sort. He would have been instantly recognizable as a hard-bitten old salt in any time or place—some stereotypes transcend centuries and cultures—and Jason fully expected him to reject the whole idea with a snort of surprised contempt. And in fact his reaction was dour and pessimistic. But he yielded in the end. Clearly, he could refuse the son of Danaë nothing—and not just because he was also the son of Zeus. Perhaps there was, in this culture at least, something to Perseus' assumption that saving someone's life created an obligation that worked both ways.

So they departed a few days later, as soon as Sotades had finished rounding out his crew. It was a problem at first, once word of their destination got out. But Jason promised to fill one billet himself. He also suggested the discreet release of rumors of fabulous treasures in the Echinades, coupled with assurances that all hands would share in the loot. It worked, just as it would work all down through history.

So they sailed south, along the eastern coast of the Peloponnesus. Jason forced himself to enjoy the scenery and not yield to impatience as he recalled the swiftness with which Rutherford's aircar had whisked them along this same route. At least the winds were with them for this part of the journey. Then they turned west, and in defiance of Sotades' pessimism they rounded the Cape of Malea without incident. The skipper's habitual scowl actually relaxed a trifle, but then resumed its accustomed intensity as they turned west and beat against the winds between the mainland of the Peloponnesus and the island of Cythera. Then Cape Taenarum appeared ahead and to starboard, with the crags of the Taygetus Mountains looming beyond the sheer cliffs . . . and the sailors started to make surreptitious signs against evil.

Jason drew Nagel aside. "What's this 'gates of Hades' stuff? Perseus said something about it."

"The Classical Greeks had various ideas about entrances to the underworld of the dead. In a country this mountainous, there was naturally no lack of caverns. One well-known one was at Eleusis, near Athens, where Persephone was supposed to have reemerged after her abduction by the god Hades. In Roman times, they built a temple, the Ploutonion, over that cave entrance. But here—" Nagel pointed at the cliffs that were beginning to recede astern, to the visible relief of the sailors "—was generally believed to be the entrance guarded by the giant three-headed dog Cerberus, where Herakles entered to capture Cerberus and liberate Theseus. Clearly, that tradition had its origins in this era."

But then they were past Cape Taenarum, and shifted course to the north-northwest. The winds became even more unfavorable. At least they didn't become severe, for which Jason was thankful; Nagel suffered a couple of attacks of seasickness, and Deirdre lost color a few times, and he hated to think how they'd react to seriously heavy seas. But beating against even these winds became a three-steps-forward, two-steps-back affair that tried the patience of people for whom the age of sail lay half a millennium in the past.

Sotades, of course, took it in stride. As they worked their way up the western coast of the Peloponnesus—the region known as Messenia—he stopped each night in some more-or-less sheltered cove, as was standard practice. Given the inhospitable reputation of the locals, they generally went ashore only briefly to replenish the water (which there was currently no way to preserve fresh for more than a few days) and then spent the night on board, stretched out on deck under the stars. There were no quarters on a ship like this, even for the captain, and Deirdre had plenty of opportunities to demonstrate her indifference to traditional notions of physical modesty in coed settings.

Jason, with his experience in low-tech sailing, made himself useful enough to earn Sotades' occasional grudging grunt of approval. After a time he was even able to draw the captain into conversation.

"Tell me about the Echinades, Sotades," he urged one day, as they were taking advantage of a lull in the work.

"Haven't been there in donkey's years," the captain growled. He was in his late forties; he looked at least ten years older, but preserved in brine. His hair and beard were iron-gray, and the former had receded to reveal a scalp that sun and wind had turned as leathery as the rest of his hide. Most of that hide was revealed by the loincloth that he, like the least of his sailors, habitually wore on his stocky form. "I was young then, and a fool like all young men. Poseidon alone knows how I managed to escape with my life."

"But you don't mind going back now?" Jason queried.

"Mind?" Sotades gave him an odd look, and then shrugged as though the question was meaningless . . . or, at least, had an answer so obvious it was difficult to put into words. "Perseus asked me," he finally said, with the air of someone stating the obvious.

"Yes, he told us of your ties to him and his mother. And, of course, he's a Hero, born of the gods." Cautiously, Jason probed for more information. "At the same time, isn't everyone, if you go back far enough?"

Sotades gave him another slantwise look. "Maybe. I don't know about such things. But only the Heroes were actually begotten by gods on mortal women. Yes, I suppose quite a few people, and all kings—all *real* kings, anyway—are descended from them."

"Like Acrisius of Argos and Proetus of Tiryns," Jason prompted.

Sotades spat feelingly over the rail. "Right. You can see how the blood of the gods gets diluted! But Perseus, now . . ." Sotades glowed with pride. "It's been renewed in him. Because the New God Zeus sired him on a mother descended from the Hero Danaos, so he has some divine blood on both sides."

Jason was careful to agree emphatically. Later, he reported the conversation to Deirdre and Nagel. "It's the same thing I noted shortly after we arrived here," the historian declared. "The matter-of-fact acceptance of divine ancestry in the immediate past. I still don't know what to make of it."

None of them did.

CHAPTER TEN

They made a final watering stop at the mouth of the Alpheios River, then let an unseasonably favorable wind take them northwest, between the westernmost point of Elis and the island of Zante—modern words to which Sotades' names bore a ghostlike resemblance. Then it was a few degrees to starboard, and presently the large island of Cephallenia loomed up off the port bow. In the distance, and partly concealed by Cephallenia's bulk, the hilltops of Ithaca could be dimly glimpsed. Jason sternly reminded himself that at least another four hundred years were to pass before Odysseus—assuming that he ever lived at all—would leave Penelope pining on that island. He had other things to think about . . . specifically, the body of water that lay dead ahead, defined by Ithaca to the west, Levkas to the north and the mainland to the east. The wind had died down and those enclosed waters were like a smooth silver setting for dozens of islets—the Echinades.

There was something uncanny about that seascape, studded with islands, most of them rugged and barren, almost desertlike, some of them pine-covered, and some showing evidence of habitation. It was a scene of stern and austere beauty, had Jason been in a mood to appreciate it. But he kept calling up the map spliced into his optic nerve, and the red dot of Deirdre's TRD showed on the largest of these islands: Taphos, just a narrow channel away from Levkas. The second red dot of Nagel's TRD, moving at the rate of the ship—slowly on this scale—showed their own location.

Jason shifted scale and zeroed in on Taphos. The dot shone on the western coast, inside an inlet that sheltered behind a headland. He dismissed the map and turned to Sotades.

"What we are looking for," he explained to the captain, "is on Taphos. Here is where we need for you to take us." With his swordpoint, he lightly scratched an outline map in the rough deck timbers.

Sotades' eyes and mouth grew round, then clenched into an expression of bulldog immovability. "I used to think you were mad. Now I know you are. Man, that's the hideout of the pirates that infest these waters—the cavern where their fleet shelters. That we've come this far without encountering any of their ships is a gift of the gods. And now you expect me to sail like a fool right into their very harbor!" He crossed his arms. "No! Not even for Perseus and his mother!"

"Well," argued Jason, "maybe you could let us off somewhere on the coast." He had no plan anyway; he'd known all along that this was going to have to be sheer improvisation.

Sotades' scowl was unabated. "That island's coast is all cliffs, except for a few inlets—and there are villages overlooking all of those. You couldn't possibly get ashore unobserved."

"There *must* be a way!" Jason summoned up the map of Taphos again, knowing that his eyes must be taking on an unfocused look that was unlikely to improve Sotades' opinion of his sanity. The red dot glowed tantalizingly . . .

And, as Jason looked, it turned the color of clotted blood and flickered out.

Malfunction in the display, came the automatic thought. He enlarged the scale to take in the entire archipelago, and their ship.

The dot that marked Nagel's whereabouts still glowed steady and scarlet.

Sheer, howling panic seized Jason's mind. He felt strong hands grasping his upper arms. He deactivated the display, blinked, and looked into Sotades' gruffly solicitous face. He saw Deirdre peering over Sotades' shoulder, with Perseus and Nagel in the background.

"What's the matter? What happened?" Deirdre's voice was charged with concern.

"Nothing," he said, as firmly as he could manage. "Everything's all right." He met her eyes—the eyes of the woman who trusted in his ability to get her home.

Hell, no, everything's not all right! he wanted to scream.

The TRD was supposed to be effectively indestructible. Its molecular-level circuitry was solidly embedded in a sphere of super-dense metal. To the denizens of lower technological levels—even the twenty-first century, the most recent attainable era—the thing would seem nothing more than a small ball bearing, hardly bigger than a BB, a little heavier than it ought to be. Smashing it with a sledgehammer, or throwing it into a fire, would do nothing. Reducing it to plasma would serve . . . but anything that could do that would leave the individual in whom it was implanted too dead to care. And anyway, such things were beyond the capabilities of earlier eras.

But, thought Jason, face to face with nightmare, *we never knew what truth was lurking behind some of those earlier eras' myths, did we?*

He pulled himself together. It didn't necessarily follow that Deirdre's TRD had been destroyed. Maybe the "gods" had the capability to do that, but it was also possible that they had something that could block the transponder, and that they had now moved the TRD inside that something. He had to proceed on that assumption, because the alternative was hopelessness.

He shook Sotades off. "Really, I'm fine," he assured his companions. He gave Deirdre a smile, but said nothing. A mocking inner voice reminded him of what he had once told Nagel about worrying people with things they didn't need to know. He turned back to the shipmaster.

"Listen, Sotades, we've got to get to that cavern!" *The TRD's last known location.* "Maybe . . . Perseus, are you a strong swimmer?"

"Of course." There was no boastfulness in the Hero's voice, just a mild surprise that the question was even being asked.

"Good. Sotades, after dark I want you to bring us in as close to that inlet as you dare. Perseus and I will swim the rest of the way."

"I'm coming too!" flared Deirdre, drawing an astonished look from Perseus.

"So will I." Nagel's voice held a sense of obligation rather than enthusiasm.

Jason considered. He could use Deirdre's imperfectly healed wound as an excuse to exclude her. But she was entitled, given what was at stake for her. As for Nagel, Jason's first impulse was to tell him to remain on the ship. But if he, Jason, didn't get back, he doubted the historian would survive long in this world. He might as well let Nagel tag along.

"Very well," he told Deirdre. "You're in, if you think your left arm is up to it." Perseus' astonishment grew comical, and Sotades clearly shared it. Jason turned to Nagel. "You'll also have to keep up."

"I can swim," the historian pouted. This, Jason knew, was true. It was one of the abilities would-be time travelers had to demonstrate to the Authority's satisfaction before being allowed to venture into the past.

"All right. Now let's get as much rest as we can. It's going to be a long night."

The night was very clear, and there were more stars out than anyone had seen from Earth's surface since electric lighting had become ubiquitous in the late twentieth century. This despite a three-quarter moon that lay a silver trail across the waters.

That moon was fortunate, for it enabled them to see where they were going. The bulk of Levkas' three-thousand-foot mountains occluded the star fields to the west. Southwestward, the outline of Ithaca was visible, as were other islands in other directions. But as they slipped into the dark water their attention was focused on the cape that loomed up ahead.

They were all stripped to the minimum. The men wore loincloths through which they had secured their weapons: Jason's and Perseus' sword-daggers and the knife with which Nagel might conceivably do some good. Deirdre also had a knife, thrust through the sash of the light tunic she wore. She could actually have gotten away with less than that in this culture, where above-the-waist female nudity was standard for ritual purposes and acceptable elsewhere. But twenty-fourth-century human civilization had reverted to clothing standards whose conservatism would have surprised the people of three centuries earlier.

They struck out for the headland. Jason used the kind of survival breaststroke that sacrificed speed for endurance—a trained swimmer could sustain it for about as long as he could have walked. Perseus' technique was one to which Jason couldn't even put a name; all he could say was that it was powerful. He also got the impression that the Hero could have kept it up all night. Perseus was obviously holding back in deference to Jason—all the more so inasmuch as Jason himself was letting Deirdre and Nagel set the pace.

They rounded the headland and entered the cliff-walled inlet that lurked behind it. In a line of four, heads bobbing darkly above the moon-glistening waters, they swam along the western cliff. Jason watched the sheer rock face for the opening he knew must be there. Finally it appeared, barely visible in the moonlight—a cavern vast beyond Jason's imaginings, its opening at least sixty feet high and almost that wide. They swam up the central channel, into a subterranean world whose darkness was relieved by flickering fires up ahead and whose silence was broken by the soft nighttime fluttering of the gulls and swallows that nested above among the stalactites.

From Sotades' description, the water here was almost as deep as the ceiling was high, and the chill of it began to seep into their bones despite their exertions. But further along it grew more shallow until it finally formed a gravel beach where the pirate galleys were drawn up. Normally, the pirates—a dark, beak-nosed breed of obscure origin, though including in their ranks renegades of all stripes—lived in villages perched like eagles' nests atop the cliffs. Only a few would be down here with the ships in their deep-water shelter at any given time—especially at night. Those few had built the fires that gave Jason and his companions light to swim toward.

Jason briefly activated his map display to confirm his recollection. There was no possible doubt: this was the last confirmed location of Deirdre's TRD. But what could have happened to it here in this primordial marine cavern, among these primitives whose muttering voices echoed among the cathedrallike spaces?

He raised an arm above the water and gestured toward the right. The others followed as he swam to the narrow strip of gravel that lined the cavern wall. It was so narrow, in fact, that they could only move along it in single file. They began to edge along it toward the moored ships and the fires and the clusters of men around them.

Jason told himself to look on the bright side. There were no sentries out. Why should there be? Who would be crazy enough to voluntarily come into the innermost lair of the Echinadian pirates? *Who, indeed?* gibed Jason's inner critic.

The figures of the pirates showed in silhouette against the firelight as they sidled closer. Something else was visible in that flickering light: a crudely carved statue, seemingly of a very stylized man, standing against the cavern wall. The pirates—who, come to think of it, seemed oddly quiet and subdued—cast occasional uneasy glances toward it. *Odd,* Jason reflected. *You don't usually think of pirates as being all that religious. . . .*

He dismissed the thought as one of the silhouetted figures detached itself from the group and walked along the narrow gravel shingle in their direction. But they hadn't been spotted; the man, oblivious to the four motionless figures in the darkness, put one of the ships between him and the group, faced the water, and hitched up the front of his kilt.

Jason smiled; evidently some standards of modesty prevailed even among this lot. And it gave him his opportunity. He stepped silently out of the shadows and, as the sound of tinkling water stopped, grasped the pirate around the neck in a choke hold. Jason dragged the struggling figure back into the darkness, where Perseus placed his swordpoint against the pirate's belly just under the rib cage, putting an end to his thrashing. Jason relaxed his hold just enough to let him breathe.

"Tell us the truth and you won't get hurt," Jason whispered into his ear. "At least one god came here, bringing a little box of a strange material, right?"

The pirate, his eyes bulging, nodded.

"Very well. I'm going to let you speak. Tell us what happened to that box, and where it was taken. If you raise the alarm, it will be the last sound you ever make. Understand?"

The pirate nodded again.

"Good. Perseus, back off a little." Jason eased up on the pirate's throat.

The pirate drew a deep breath, let it out, and . . . *"Help! Summon the gods!"*

Sheer, startled surprise at that scream held Perseus motionless for a heartbeat. Then he rammed his sword in and upward.

It was too late. The other pirates leaped to their feet and came running.

Jason cast the dead pirate aside. *Now what did he want to do* that *for?* he wondered in a calm corner of his mind as he drew his sword and stood to face the onrushing gang. Behind them he saw one man face the idol and say something in an unknown language—another display of unexpected piratical piety. Perseus had already turned on them, waving his bloody sword and bellowing a war cry.

They halted, screamed, and drew back in obvious terror.

Perseus, looking boyishly pleased with himself, turned to Jason with a smile . . . which instantly turned to a look of blank horror. Nagel and Deirdre, Jason saw, were staring in the same direction with the same expression. He turned and looked behind him, and saw the being that was emerging from the water.

It was a biped, somewhat larger than a man—although its exact height was difficult to judge, for it stood with a forward-leaning posture balanced by a long thick tail that ended in flukes. What it stood on were webbed feet, and the two arms ended in hands that weren't really hands but rather clusters of four long claws connected by thick webbing. The body was bulky but lithe, with what looked like gills to the side. The incongruously slender neck supported a long, narrow head tapering from a large braincase behind to a snout or muzzle which held small nostrils and a lipless mouth. The eyes were large and dark, and nictitating membranes periodically blinked back and forth across them like antique camera shutters. The ears were mere holes, protected by bony ridges. The skin was lightly scaled, and as far as could be told in this dim light it was gray-green, shading to light gray on the belly. The being was nude save for a kind of harness bearing unfamiliar devices.

It wasn't until later that Jason took in all these details. In that first instant, he could absorb the overall impression . . . and feel a tantalizing sense of familiarity, as though he ought to recognize the being. He was thinking about it when the mouth opened and the alien spoke in a strange Achaean: indescribably accented as a result of being produced by nonhuman vocal apparatus, but with the fluency of long, long practice.

"Come with me." One of the strange hands pointed at the water.

Jason could only stare.

Then he heard a commotion among the pirates. Beyond them, beside the idol, there was a wavering in the air, not at all like that caused by rising heat, but rather a disturbance of something more fundamental, of reality itself.

"Quickly!" said the alien. "Follow me if you wish to live!" Without another word, the being turned with a sinuous twist of its entire body that would have been impossible for the human skeleton, and dived smoothly into the water.

At that instant, Jason remembered the source of that half familiarity.

At the same instant, the region of disturbance beside the idol seemed to solidify into a circle within which something other than the cave wall behind it was visible. The tall form of a "god" appeared in that circle, silhouetted against whatever it was that lay beyond.

Jason came to quick decision. "Follow him!" he yelled at the others.

They stood, held in the grip of shock.

"I said move!" He grabbed Perseus and shoved him toward the water. "Dive in and follow him!" He turned to Deirdre and Nagel, who at least knew of aliens and didn't consider them supernatural.

"What . . . what . . . ?" stammered Nagel.

"Never mind! Jump in and swim underwater, both of you." A sudden afterthought struck him. "And . . . whatever happens, don't tell that alien that we have interstellar travel."

They both stared at him in bewilderment.

"I said *move!*" He turned toward the water. Perseus was still paralyzed.

"What are you, too cowardly to follow me?" Jason yelled. Perseus jolted as though an electric shock had gone through him.

Jason could only hope it was enough to get the Hero moving. He took a deep breath, dived into the cold, deep water and struggled downward. Below, a light glowed.

He took time for a look backward over his shoulder. Three other forms had entered the water. Without taking time to feel relief, he continued downward toward the light.

That light was the oval interior of a vessel with sleekly submersible lines. The bubble which normally covered it was raised and the alien was there, motioning to them.

As soon as they were inside, the bubble clamshelled shut and the water began to flow out of the compartment to the sound of pumps. They were all feeling the agony of suffocation clamp around their chests by the time the water level dropped below their heads and they were able to gasp for air.

The alien was paying them no heed. He was too busy at the controls. (Jason found himself thinking of the being as "he" despite the absence of any recognizable sexual organs.) The humans sat down in what appeared to be recliners designed for their host's species—they had openings to accommodate the tail, which made them awkward seating for the human form. They did so none too soon; the vessel was already moving, and when the last of the water drained from the compartment the alien manipulated additional controls, and the vessel surged with what Jason recognized as the amazing acceleration of a supercavitating submarine using reactionless propulsion. In the dim glow of the outside lights, they saw the underwater walls of the cavern flash past and then vanish. They were in open water.

Still gasping, Jason turned to Perseus. "I beg your pardon for what I said," he began . . . but the Hero wasn't hearing him. And his eyes weren't blinking. And his mouth wasn't closing, even though a trickle of saliva oozed down from one corner of it. He was staring fixedly at the gleaming high-tech interior with its artificial lights, and the being in front who was piloting it, and his mind had simply shut down under an unacceptable overload of the incomprehensible. At least it would be a while before he was in any shape to take up the little matter of what Jason had called him.

Jason examined his other two companions. Nagel was having more difficulty breathing than anyone, but he seemed in no danger. Deirdre seemed to be in the best shape of any of them, with neither Perseus' paralysis nor Nagel's apnea. "Are you all right?" he asked her.

She nodded jerkily. "Yes, I think so. And I won't even bother asking you what the hell is going on here. But . . . what did you mean about not telling—?"

He shushed her with a gesture. "I'll explain later. For now, let's just say that I recognize his race." He indicated their still-preoccupied pilot.

"You do? I've met some nonhumans, but never any like him."

"Of course you haven't," Jason said, lowering his voice. "In our era they don't exist anymore."

CHAPTER ELEVEN

After a while, with the marine cavern well behind them, the alien turned off the outside lights, reduced the bubble's inboard illumination to a dim red glow, and allowed the little craft to drift. In the semidarkness, their weariness began to creep up on them, and Jason felt he could easily have dozed off.

But then their rescuer-*cum*-pilot stood up and approached them, and Jason came instantly wide awake.

The alien examined Perseus with eyes whose nictitating membranes left them fully exposed in this light, then spoke in his indescribable but intelligible Achaean. "Your companion appears to be in shock. I will give him a sedative that is appropriate for your species." They watched in silence as the being applied what appeared to be a hypospray injector to the Hero's arm and extended the recliner to full horizontal position. No covers were needed; the passenger compartment's air temperature would have been uncomfortably high had their garments been less scanty and less wet.

"Thank you," said Jason as Perseus began to snore. "I think he was somewhat . . . overwhelmed."

"Understandable." The alien turned his strange eyes—there was no visible distinction between iris and pupil—on the humans. His expression, if any, was unreadable. "He is obviously native to this time."

Jason did not dare let himself make eye contact with the other two humans. He could only give the alien a look of innocent incomprehension—not that the alien would necessarily recognize it as such—and hope the others were doing the same. "What do you mean?"

"Our time is limited," said the alien. "So let us not waste it with denials. You clearly belong to this planet's dominant species. Yet you are evidently familiar with advanced technology, for you failed to react to it as did your companion here. This merely confirms what I and the Teloi already know."

"The . . . ?"

"Those whom this planet's inhabitants call 'gods,' " the alien explained. "Eighty-two of this planet's years ago they detected an energy surge of unknown nature—certainly nothing that the local cultures could produce. When your probe appeared and subsequently disappeared, they drew the obvious conclusion—as did we." For all the impossibility of reading emotions in an alien face and body, Jason would have sworn that this being somehow wore a look of bemused wonder. "We had always believed time travel to be a fundamental impossibility. But it was the only hypothesis that accounted for the facts."

Nagel had been sitting silently, passive almost to the point of listlessness. Now, with startling abruptness, he came out of his stupor and spoke in a rush. "Wait a minute. Wait a minute! What is *happening*? Who are these 'Teloi'? What are they doing here, in our world's past? What are *you* doing here? And who *are* you?"

"Yes!" Deirdre leaned forward fiercely. "Who are you? What's your *name*, for God's sake?"

Jason sighed. There was obviously no further point in trying to deny that they were time travelers. "It *would* be nice to have a name to address you by," he said reasonably.

The alien's posture seemed to relax a bit. Indeed, Jason thought he could detect a distinct sense of relief. "You may call me Oannes. And as for the rest . . . you really *don't* know, do you?" He cast a glance at the instrumentation. "There is no real danger of detection, and the submarine's automatic pilot is holding position. And I see some explanation is in order.

"The Teloi, as you have doubtless inferred, are of extraterrestrial origin. Their superficial physical resemblance to this planet's primates is sheer coincidence—a rare case of convergent evolution. About a hundred thousand of your years ago, a group of Teloi landed on this planet—or, more accurately, were left stranded on it."

"What?" Jason struggled to understand, fending off the soft blubbery arms of physical exhaustion. "You mean they were exiles?"

"Not really. Their 'exile' was entirely self-imposed." Oannes seemed to gather his thoughts. "This may not be easy for you to understand. The Teloi are a very old race, whose development halted long, long ago. They are the end product of ages of . . . breeding for selected traits." Jason recognized this as the closest one could get to "genetic engineering" in the Achaean Greek that was their common language. "Their ancestors sought to turn their race into gods. On their own terms, they succeeded. For one thing, they became immortal."

"That's preposterous!" snapped Nagel. "Nothing in the universe lasts forever—not even the universe itself."

"Oh, not literally immortal, in the sense of living for eternity. But they do not age during the entire course of their lifespans, until the very end. And those lifespans are, if not eternal, close enough to it as makes little difference on your time scale . . . or even on mine, and my race lives many times as long as yours. So neither of us can really conceive of what it must be like. It must be hellish beyond our capacity to imagine."

"People have always thought of immortality as the ultimate gift," Deirdre said quietly.

"That is because they have never had the opportunity to actually experience it," Oannes said bluntly. "A limited lifespan is all we know, or can know; so we take for granted the significance our lives derive from their brevity. An endless existence is also a meaningless one."

"How can *you* possibly know this?" challenged Nagel. "You said before that you aren't immortal, even though you live longer than we."

Oannes was unruffled. "We know it from observation. We have been in contact with the Teloi for a long time . . . and have been at war with them for almost that long."

Jason put awe into his voice. "So you have the ability to travel among the stars?" He risked a quick, quelling glance at his companions. Deirdre evidently remembered his earlier admonition, for she maintained an expressionless silence. Nagel seemed about to blurt out his bewilderment, but clamped his mouth shut at the last instant.

"Yes." Oannes showed no sign of having noticed the byplay, to Jason's relief. "Long ago we discovered how to get around the fundamental structure of the universe and evade the limiting velocity of light. So it seems each of our societies has achieved something the other regarded as impossible. But at any rate, we have known of the Teloi for some time. We know of their lives. They attempt to fill the emptiness with pleasure-seeking and elaborate intrigue and—for the minority so inclined—scholarship and art that for ages have merely excavated deeper and deeper strata of pedantry and abstraction. Creativity is no longer even a memory for them. The selective breeding that produced them has left their minds so structured as to be incapable of escaping into outright madness, although one may doubt how truly sane any of them are by now. Their war with us must have come as a welcome relief; it gave them something real to do. But interstellar warfare, by its nature, can occupy only a relatively small cadre of specialists. The rest were thrown back on diversions that were ever more decadent and bizarre. And even before that, their capacity for flights of whimsy had been incomprehensible to other minds. In particular, they sought more and more to isolate themselves. Over eons, I imagine, the presence of one's fellows grows ever more irritating.

"Thus it was, a thousand of your centuries ago, that certain Teloi arranged to have themselves permanently marooned on this world. It was well off their usual spacelanes, but an exploratory probe had revealed a habitable planet with a presentient lifeform which resembled the Teloi's own evolutionary forbears enough to be thought of not simply as animals but as a kind of sub-Teloi."

"*Homo erectus*," Jason breathed. Perforce, he used his own language.

"Whatever. A certain group among the Teloi—Clan? Club? Who can say?—arranged to make this world their private preserve. Here, cut off from their own society, they would be the gods their race had always aspired to be. And here they would remain.

"Now if one is going to be a god, the first requirement is worshipers. And, as a practical matter, sentient slaves were necessary. So, using the most promising indigenous species—*Homo erectus*, did you say?—as raw material, the Teloi created them."

Deirdre looked like she was struggling to awake from nightmare, only to find that it was real. "Wait a minute! Are you saying that these Teloi, by, uh, breeding for certain traits, created . . ." She couldn't go on.

"Yes," said Oannes with a gentleness that transcended races and worlds. "They created your species. They strove, if only unconsciously, toward an aesthetic ideal represented by themselves. So the physical appearance of the result represented a compromise between *Homo erectus* and the Teloi."

Apes and angels, Jason found himself thinking in some calm mental storm-center. *Only . . . the Teloi aren't exactly angels.*

"But," Nagel demanded, "what about *Homo neanderthalensis*?" Seeing incomprehension, he elaborated. "Another species of the same genus as ours, in this part of the planet during the last . . . time of extended cold." Achaean didn't lend itself to "glacial epoch" either.

"Oh, them. They were an irrelevancy from the Teloi standpoint—a product of independent evolution. *Homo erectus* evolved into them in the natural course of events, in response to ice age conditions in Europe and western Asia."

"We think of them as an evolutionary dead end," said Deirdre softly.

"Your ancestors saw to that," remarked Oannes with unmistakable dryness. "They might have turned out to be so in any case. Or they might have evolved further. The question is moot now. They were doomed the moment your race began moving north from its cradlelands."

"Moving north?" Jason struggled to understand. "But I thought you said the Teloi bred *Homo sapiens*—that's us—as slaves."

"That was the intention. Your ancestors lived at first in the region of northeast Africa and southwest Asia—not as effectually separated at that time as they have subsequently become—in societies of the Teloi's own definition. But the Teloi had miscalculated. They had no real conception of the species they had created—the individual variability of its members, and the difficulty of controlling them. Almost immediately, the more independent and adventurous ones began to escape from Teloi control and spread out over the planet, gradually differentiating into the linguistic and physical varieties that exist now."

"But what about *you*?" Nagel persisted. "Where do you come from?"

"Another star, of course. Its location would mean nothing to you. As I mentioned, my race—the

Nagommo—have been at war with the Teloi for a long time. Or, to be precise, I should say that we *had* been at war with them for a long time a little over two thousand of your years ago, at which time we learned of their ancient expedition to this world. Your planetary system is as out of the way for us as it is for them, but one of our survey ships, operating more or less independently as such ships customarily did in the absence of any kind of practical communication with their bases, went to investigate. I was a member of that ship's crew." He seemed to notice his listeners' expressions, and added parenthetically, "As I mentioned, a Nagom lives a long time. At any rate, when we approached this planet we were attacked by the robotic weapons the Teloi had emplaced in orbit to safeguard their privacy. We destroyed them, but in the process we suffered critical damage. Many of us were killed. Those who survived were lucky to manage an emergency landing—a controlled crash, really—in a body of water to the southeast of here, into which the two rivers of a major river-valley system flow from the north." *The Persian Gulf*, thought Jason. "So, like the Teloi, we were castaways on this world. The difference is that we were involuntary ones."

"How did you survive?" Deirdre wondered aloud.

"This planet is habitable for us, even though the air is less dense and less damp than we like, and the average temperature lower. But fortunately we had crashed in fairly low latitudes. And, as you have probably gathered, we are amphibians, so escaping from our sunken ship was no particular problem. Nor was nutrition; a fair number of the local food products are compatible, and we had instruments for determining which those were. At first we entertained hopes of a rescue. But as time passed and no ship arrived, we relinquished our illusions. This world is out of the way, as I mentioned, and no one had known we were coming here. No, we were on our own."

"Did you have children?" asked Deirdre.

"That was out of the question."

"You mean all of your group were of one gender?" Nagel ventured.

"Not in the sense you mean." Oannes looked uncomfortable. "We are fully functional hermaphrodites. But our reproduction involves . . . Well, our home planet's rotational cycle is very different from this one's. Its day is exactly two thirds of its year, which in turn equals only a little more than a hundred of your days. Our reproduction is closely tied to this. On your planet, it simply didn't work."

Jason nodded unconsciously. Such a "resonance lock" was the normal fate of a planet in an eccentric orbit within its primary star's tidelock zone, like Sol's Mercury. In the case of the smaller, dimmer stars—the M and late K classes—this could coincide with the liquid-water zone where life-bearing worlds could exist. It was a fairly uncommon state of affairs, but he had seen an example . . . and it was one more confirmation of what he already knew but could not (or would not) admit that he knew.

"That's terrible!" Deirdre was saying.

Oannes gave a gesture so similar to a human's fatalistic shrug that Jason assumed he had picked it up locally. "There were compensations. At least we were able to continue pursuing our basic mission."

"Your 'basic mission'?" Deirdre queried.

Oannes gave her an odd look. "Why, yes. There were Teloi here for us to combat."

They stared at him. Jason finally broke the silence. "Uh, Oannes, wasn't the war kind of over for you and your shipmates?"

Oannes stared in his turn. "But," he said carefully, as though feeling he must have been misunderstood before, "there were Teloi here, and we knew it. Wherever we find them, we *must* thwart them if it is within our power to do so. They are . . ." The alien's voice trailed off, silenced by something too obvious to be put into words, and his body clenched with some strong emotion.

It would seem, Jason reflected, *that to know the Teloi is not to love them.*

"But," Deirdre protested, "how could it have been 'within your power' to hinder them? You were a handful of castaways!"

"We were not altogether without resources. Though our ship was wrecked beyond any hope of repair and had sunk to the bottom, it wasn't too deep for us to salvage a good deal of equipment from it, including many devices designed for survey operations on primitive planets. This vessel, for example."

Nagel's old self resurfaced. "It looks in remarkably good repair after two millennia!"

Oannes took no apparent offense at the sarcasm. "Not so remarkable, when one considers that the Teloi's equipment is still functioning after a *hundred* millennia. In point of fact, we and they both use metals that can . . . restore themselves."

Nagel shut up, and Jason and Deirdre nodded. All three of them understood what Oannes was trying to convey in Achaean. Not that it was common in their world, where the social trauma of the Transhuman movement had largely relegated nanotechnology to a manufacturing technique in orbital factories. But it was possible, though expensive, to leave the construction nanobots permanently active in a manufactured item, to regenerate any damage or deterioration. It couldn't last forever of course; if nothing else, the cumulative effect of cosmic radiation would either kill or "mutate" the molecular-sized robots. But until then, such a device would show no rust, corrosion or other signs of aging, and any major damage to it would self-repair within certain limits.

None of the humans even bothered asking about power sources. It would have been impossible for Oannes to explain in Achaean, and at any rate they already had a pretty good idea. Total conversion of matter directly into energy was a theoretical possibility for their own civilization. Such a power unit could be made very small, and used such minute quantities of matter—any matter—as to be effectively inexhaustible. When the bugs were worked out, it would put an end to an energy problem that hadn't been all that urgent anyway since the development of safe, controlled fusion. Clearly, the Teloi and the Nagommo had, in fact, worked out those bugs.

"So," Oannes continued, "marooned though we were, our technology made us seem like gods to the humans we encountered, on the lower reaches of the two rivers flowing into the waters where we had arrived. We taught them the arts of civilization, at the limited rate at which they were able to absorb the teaching. We started with an elementary form of writing, and moved on from there. We helped them to rebel against the Teloi. They tore down the slave society in which the Teloi had imprisoned them, and built their own civilization out of its ruins."

"The Sumerians!" blurted Nagel. "I *knew* I had heard the name 'Oannes.' Not that Mesopotamia is my field, you understand. But the Sumerians had a legend of a kind of, uh, fish-man from the sea who brought the arts of civilization."

"Yes," said Oannes ruefully. "Our efforts to prevent primitive humans from regarding us as supernatural have always proven unavailing in the long run. At any rate, we subsequently worked against the Teloi elsewhere, in the various river valleys where they had erected their slave societies. It wasn't easy, as we had to act covertly. And as the centuries went by, more and more of us died off, either by violence or old age. I am nearly the last," he added, with an offhandedness that a human could not have matched, "and I am getting along in years. But the Teloi gradually lost ground, despite their attempt to reestablish their dominance through the creation of Heroes."

That brought Jason up short. Oannes had used the Achaean word, with its implicit capital "H." "Uh, you mean like . . . ?" He indicated Perseus' sleeping form.

"Yes. The Teloi decided to create a superstock, physically and mentally superior to the general run of humans, to serve them as proxy rulers over the human masses. They used selected human females as surrogate mothers of artificially produced embryos. The public story was that these women had been impregnated by gods, so the offspring were half-divine.

"But once again they miscalculated. The Heroes proved no more amenable to control than ordinary humans—if anything, rather less so. And they were interfertile with other humans—they took spouses among them, and this had the inevitable effect on their primary loyalties, by processes that lie beyond my race's understanding. In short, the Heroes broke loose from Teloi control, and led their fellow humans into rebellion. A certain Gilgamesh was among the first.

"However, the Teloi are not noted for flexibility and adaptability. By now they have largely withdrawn from the affairs of the more anciently civilized areas, leaving only legends, and are most active in fringe areas like this where the humans are less sophisticated and—" a modest gesture "—there is less interference from us Nagommo. They travel back and forth between here and northern India and northwest Europe and other lands, where they are known by different names—"

"So now we know where the Indo-European pantheon came from," Nagel muttered to himself. "And why rulers in those same lands always claimed to be descended from demigods."

"—but they find it very difficult to change their technique. They have persisted in creating Heroes, even though the results have continued to be mixed at best."

Understanding came to Jason. "Like Danaos of Argos?"

"Among others. In recent generations the Teloi, incapable of abandoning the approach but seeking to refine it, have taken to using women of part-Heroic ancestry, in an effort to reinforce the traits of the . . . breed." Achaean wasn't up to "subspecies."

"His mother," Deirdre said, very softly, looking at Perseus.

Jason nodded. It explained a lot of things about their friend. It also explained something else. If the Teloi, like Oannes, knew Deirdre was a time traveler, they might well have looked at a woman from a future age, with who knew how much further evolution programmed into her genes, and seen fresh breeding stock.

I may have other uses for her, Hyperion had said in the torch-lit courtyard at Tiryns.

Jason saw no useful purpose to be served by mentioning it to Deirdre.

"I trust I have answered your questions," said the Nagom. "And now I hope you will have the courtesy to answer some of mine."

"Well," said Jason, "we certainly owe you that much, at least. But first of all, I must ask you one more question—although I think I know the answer already. The, uh, phenomenon we observed in the cavern, beside that idol . . . ?"

"Ah, yes. The Teloi who had themselves marooned on this planet were not *entirely* insane. They were careful to provide themselves with a sanctuary—a refuge from any imaginable dangers. It is a device for creating . . . that is, shaping—"

"Never mind," Jason cut in. "I'm certain I know what you're trying to express." Deirdre and Nagel weren't so sure, judging from their expressions. But then, they weren't *au courant* with cutting-edge dimensional physics. Jason wouldn't have been either, except that the field impinged on temporal physics—a connection Oannes' people evidently hadn't discovered. Humans had, and perhaps it was the resulting diversion into time travel that had prevented twenty-fourth century researchers from discovering a practical way of creating a "pocket universe" isolated from all physical phenomena of the familiar continuum, even though they knew it was a theoretical possibility.

"I know what you mean," he reassured Oannes again. "And I know how difficult it is to describe. Just tell me how this . . . gateway can be. . . ." *How do you say "interfaced with" in Achaean?* he wondered desperately.

But Oannes' alien body language somehow exuded good-natured relief. "I see that you know what it means. And the answer to the question you are trying to ask is that it can only be opened from the outside—from our world. But the device that does so can be timed in advance to open at a predetermined moment. Or it can be activated by voice." Jason spared a fraction of his consciousness to marvel at how clear Oannes was making these concepts in their common language. The Nagom's expression shaded over into the first inarguable amusement Jason had observed. "The designers of your probe were not the only ones to think of the idea of concealing a piece of advanced instrumentation in what appeared to be a primitive idol. The Teloi long ago used the same kind of . . . housing for the controls concerning which you inquire. The location of that idol determines the location of the gateway. The pirates' leaders had been given verbal formulas to recite in case of emergency. I became aware that the device was being activated—there is an instrument aboard this craft that can detect the peculiar energy surge involved—and intervened at that point."

"Yes, I saw the gateway opening," said Jason absently. Here, he thought, was the solution to the mystery of what had happened to Deirdre's TRD. The Teloi had taken it into their private extradimensional mini-universe for further study, pulling familiar space-time in around themselves so the transponder could no longer make contact with Jason's computer implant.

"So," he heard Oannes saying, "now that I have satisfied your curiosity on that point, perhaps you will explain your own presence here, and what you were trying to accomplish in that cavern."

Jason had always regarded telepathy as a singularly unbeautiful dream. Now, for the first time, he wished it was real, so that he could communicate silently to his two companions a simple message: *Keep your mouths shut and let me do the talking!*

"I will not attempt to deny that we come from this world's distant future," he began. "The device that enables us to travel through time is implanted in our flesh." He released a silent sigh of relief when Deirdre and Nagel remained silent for this half- (or quarter- or eighth-) truth. He then proceeded with a reasonably factual account of their adventures. "Oannes," he concluded, "you have been aiding our race for two thousand years, and we thank you for it. Now I ask you to aid us once again. Help us recover the device that was cut out of Deirdre's arm. Without it, she will be forever unable to return to her proper time."

The large, strange eyes held inarguable compassion. "I believe you are telling the truth—or as much of the truth as you are permitted to tell. And I will give you all the cooperation I can. But I must tell you that this will be very little."

"Why?" asked Deirdre, almost too quietly to be heard.

"As I previously explained, my overriding duty is to advance my race's struggle with the Teloi. This must take precedence over all other considerations—including my very real sympathy for your plight, and my inclination to help you."

Jason leaned forward and held those alien eyes.

"Oannes, there is no conflict between your 'inclination' and your duty. Consider: if the Teloi are given the opportunity to study this device at their leisure, they may be able to duplicate it. They would then have the secret of time travel. And they know when and where you and your shipmates arrived here. They could be there at the time, prepared to blast your ship into atoms before it even hits the water!"

Silence fell, and Oannes' nictitating membranes fluttered back and forth in what Jason hoped reflected an agony of panic-stricken indecision. He continued to hold those eyes, thankful that neither of the other humans had said anything to reveal the outrageous mendacity of what he was saying. But then, he reflected, maybe that mendacity wasn't as obvious to them as it was to him.

"And consider this also," he resumed, lying *con brio*. "If the Teloi on this world travel back far enough in time, perhaps they could lay the foundations and develop the industrial capacity to return to space by this era, and reestablish contact with the rest of their race. Then they could go back even further—to the origin of your civilization—and abort its future!"

Jason was growing more and more confident of his ability to read the Nagom's expressions. And he was certain he saw a twinkle—or, more accurately, a glint—of shrewdness as Oannes replied. "I have some small experience of observing your race. And I perceive that you are not being altogether candid with me. Furthermore, your very presence in this era suggests that the course of history is not as easy to change as you are suggesting. If it were, time travel would be a philosophical as well as a practical impossibility."

Jason forced himself to remain expressionless. *"Some small experience" indeed,* he thought belatedly. *Like two thousand years of it! And he's gone straight to the heart of the matter of history's malleability, or lack thereof. I couldn't trick him for a second. I was a fool to try.*

"However," Oannes continued after letting Jason hang in suspense for an instant, "in light of my total ignorance of time travel, I cannot ignore the possibility of catastrophic consequences if this 'device' is not retrieved from the Teloi. This obligates me to aid you." He became brisk. "Our first step is to proceed to a locality where we can obtain advanced equipment. My people have, over the centuries, taken pains to leave caches of such equipment in areas where the Teloi were active. I will set our course at once." He started to turn toward the control panel, but then paused and turned back to Jason. He spoke with restrained eagerness. "Tell me one thing first. You are from this world's future. Do I understand that you have never . . . ?"

"Yes," said Jason, and he had never been gladder in his life to be able to tell the complete truth. "In our era, on this planet, the Teloi are forgotten. The 'gods' they pretend to be are only tales to amuse children."

At once, he was sorry he had spoken, for something seemed to go out of Oannes. He stepped forward in alarm, extending his hand to offer support before the old Nagom could collapse. But Oannes stood up straight, and Jason understood that he'd been overcome by a surfeit of gladness. "No, I am all right. It is only . . . We *succeeded.* Or would it be more accurate to say that your race will succeed, with whatever help we were able to provide? It doesn't matter. The point is, the Teloi will fail. Thank you for the gift of that knowledge." He stood for a moment, clearly in the grip of an emotion to which Jason doubted he could have put a name. As for Jason himself, he did not trust himself to speak, for if he had he might have blurted out that which he knew. But then the moment was past. Oannes' briskness returned, and he went to the controls.

Deirdre gave Jason a curious look, unable to read his expression. She leaned close. "What did you mean earlier, when you said you knew of his race?"

"Out beyond my home system of Psi 5 Aurigae," he whispered hastily, "there's a dim orange star—a class K9v—with a liquid-water, life-bearing planet resonance-locked to it. An expedition from Hesperia discovered it a few years ago. Normally, nobody goes there except archaeologists. But I stopped there once—we were pursuing some smugglers—and saw what they've found: the remains of an ancient civilization, with horribly degenerated, gene-twisted monstrosities skulking among the ruins. The archaeologists concluded that the race had destroyed itself by unwise tinkering with its own genotype—what we humans narrowly escaped with the Transhuman movement. Only . . . there were indications that they might have escaped it too, if their civilization hadn't already been weakened by a great war. In fact, that war might have been what caused them to yield to the temptation to try to genetically engineer themselves into specialized castes, including supersoldiers. And there were plenty of artistic representations to show what the race had looked like in its natural state."

Horror awoke in her eyes. "You mean . . . ?" Her gaze flickered to Oannes.

"Now you know why I don't want him to know we have interstellar travel. He'd naturally wonder if we have any news of his civilization. And I don't want to lie to him any more than necessary."

Nagel, who had been listening, took the next step into the regions of horror. "If this is true, and if the war was the one Oannes says they were fighting with the Teloi, then . . . it could be argued that their species unknowingly died defending ours. Or, I should say, that it *will* so die."

"You had it right the first time," said Jason grimly. "Radiocarbon dating showed that the collapse had occurred about forty-five hundred years before our time. Which means that as of now it has already occurred."

They all stared at Oannes—one of the last of his race, not just on Earth but in the universe.

CHAPTER TWELVE

Oannes rejoined them. He took no apparent notice of the embarrassed and abrupt halt to their whispered conversation.

"I have set in our course. Ah, we are moving now." They felt a slight surge.

"Should we get seated again?" asked Jason.

"No. We are proceeding at a leisurely rate. This craft's full speed would bring us to our destination in little more than an hour. But the energy expenditure involved would make us easier for the Teloi to detect, besides imposing an uncomfortable acceleration." Jason didn't doubt this in the least; he knew what submersibles with supercavitating hulls could do.

"What about the ship that brought us?" asked Deirdre.

"It is moving on a southerly course. Evidently the

captain decided to depart when you failed to return. His action is understandable, given these waters' grim reputation."

"Will he escape?"

"Probably. I have detected no indication that the Teloi have connected that ship with you, or that they are taking any action against it."

"Good," Jason said, and meant it. He liked Sotades.

There was a stirring from the direction of Perseus' recliner. "Your companion is awakening," Oannes observed. "Perhaps you should—"

"Let me," said Deirdre quickly. "Maybe I can, well, ease him into things if I'm there for him when he comes to."

"Maybe you're right," said Jason. "And now, Oannes," he continued as Deirdre went to Perseus' side, "tell us about this 'destination' of ours."

"It is one of the equipment caches I mentioned. We Nagommo established it several centuries ago, when the Teloi were first beginning to take an interest in this region."

"Will others of your race be there?"

"No. I am the last in this sea. As I indicated, we are spread very thin these days. The others—even older than I—have gone to the islands off northwestern Europe, where the Teloi have become more active in the identities they long ago assumed among the Celtic peoples. They will do what they can there."

"The Silkies," Deirdre breathed, as she knelt beside Perseus. Jason wondered what she meant.

"The cache in this region," Oannes continued, "was positioned to be close to the Teloi activities on the island of Crete." He used the current word for Crete: *Keftiu*. "There, the Teloi were in the process of establishing the kind of society they always try to create: the closest approximation they can manage to the glorified slave pens into which they originally crammed their human subjects. We have been able to ameliorate it, although it will probably take a conquest by the mainland Greek-speakers—the kind of conquest that has been going on for the past two generations in the Middle East—to completely sweep it away."

A totalitarian theocracy, thought Jason. He made eye contact with Nagel, and for once they shared a moment of wordless empathy. *So much for Arthur Evans' innocent, carefree, peaceful, egalitarian, et cetera Minoans. They're just as imaginary as Margaret Mead's Polynesians.*

The difference is that Evans was merely too opintonated—and his opinions were mistaken. He, at least, wasn't falsifying evidence to advance the twentieth-century Western intelligentsia's ideology of self-loathing.

"Unfortunately," Oannes was saying, "we put it a little too close to Crete. The island on which it is located has become a major center of Teloi-inspired activity, and will therefore be hazardous to approach. It is only about seventy miles north of Crete, you see, and—"

"A circular volcanic island?" Deirdre said, rising to her feet and speaking like a robot.

"Why, yes. The island of Kalliste."

"We know of it," Jason heard himself say. "In our time it's called Santorini."

The little vessel wasn't comfortable for humans, but at least the voyage was short.

Deirdre turned out to be right about her ability to help Perseus adjust. She explained everything to him in terms of Oannes as a benevolent sea deity and the submarine as his "chariot." It all proved surprisingly easy for him to accept. He had grown up with a matter-of-fact attitude toward the supernatural, given his background.

And that reminded Jason of something . . .

He took it up with Oannes as soon as they had an opportunity to talk privately. There were more such opportunities than he might have expected, since Perseus was spending a lot of time with Deirdre. At the time, Jason noted it with nothing more than gratitude.

"Oannes," he said, "earlier Perseus spoke of 'the Old Gods.' Naturally we couldn't admit that we didn't know what he was talking about. We merely warned him that we might run afoul of some of them. Do *you* know what he meant?"

"Ah, yes. As I explained, the Teloi live an incredibly long time, but not forever. Thus the . . . breeding that produced them allows them to have children, but only very infrequently. Childbirths are exceedingly rare events for them—but not occasions for great rejoicing. The Teloi," Oannes added in an unmistakable tone of studied understatement, "are not noted for deep filial feelings. Nevertheless, a second generation appeared on this world. There have been no subsequent births, however. We Nagommo do not know why. Presumably there is something in this world's environment which in the long run—the *very* long run—interferes with their already very problematic fertility.

"The younger generation worked with their elders about as well as the Teloi generally do—which is not well at all by the standards of either of our races. They can act in concert whenever their self-interest requires it, of course, but they have no deep wellsprings of mutual loyalty. Absent the pressure of an outside threat, they compulsively intrigue against each other—sometimes for motives which, at best, are obscure to us and, I would imagine, to you."

"Yes, you indicated as much," Jason ruminated. The reasoning of the ages-dead genetic engineers was clear: the near immortality of the Teloi had *had* to be accompanied by drastically reduced fertility, lest every environment available to them be smothered in a mass of Teloi flesh. And since the parenting urge could no longer be fulfilled, it had been edited out of the genetic code. Only . . . how widely, and in what unforeseeable directions, had that void spread through the psyche? It was just the kind of unintended consequence that the Transhuman movement, in its hubris, had ignored.

"Perseus told us his 'father' is Zeus," he said cautiously. "Is that—?"

"Yes," Oannes nodded—another of the human mannerisms he'd had centuries to pick up. "He is one of the second-generation Teloi. That is his name in the local human belief system, where he has carved out a niche as the weather god. There are others, with names like Hera, Poseidon, Ares—"

The Olympians, thought Jason with an unconscious nod of his own.

"—and the rest. As part of their ongoing low-level rivalry with their elders, they seek to create Heroes of their own. Zeus made use of a female descendant of Danaos for this purpose."

Jason nodded again. Most of his questions had been answered. He only wished he knew what to do with those answers.

* * *

They proceeded beneath the waters off the western shores of Elis and Messenia, then turned east to round the Peloponnesus. Jason occupied his time by observing Oannes at the controls and trying to memorize as much as possible, just in case.

Mountainous Cape Taenarum was off the port bow in Oannes' light-gathering periscope, when the attack came.

Jason got his first intimation of it when Oannes tensed, and bent over his instrument panel with a concentration he'd never displayed before. At first Jason thought nothing of it. But then came a soft beeping and a blinking of lights.

"What is it?" Jason asked quietly, maneuvering himself between the controls and the other humans' suddenly curious eyes.

"A pattern of seeking missiles has been dropped into the water in our vicinity. These missiles have a submersible function. They are now homing on us." Oannes spoke as quietly as Jason had, as though recognizing the need to keep this from the latter's companions—especially Perseus. He indicated a screen. The symbology meant nothing to Jason. But he saw the semicircle of tiny glowing dots beginning to converge on the larger dot at the center of the screen. He also felt the surge of acceleration as Oannes manipulated the controls. Deirdre and Nagel felt it too, for they looked up in alarm. But the little predatory dots in the screen must have accelerated in response, for there was no sign of escape from their encirclement.

"Uh, Oannes, what can be done?" Jason kept his voice level.

"It is already being done." The Nagom manipulated

more controls. "The missiles, of course, use the same kind of motive power as this craft—"

"Of course." Reactionless drives converted the angular momentum of their cores' atomic particles directly to energy and angular momentum. Jason knew better than to expect an explanation in Achaean.

"—and there is a device that can nullify this power within a certain radius. We carry such a device, and I will now activate it."

"Well, then . . ." Jason felt his tension dissolve in relief. Such an interference field was a theoretical possibility in his own world, although no one had actually built one—or at least the public wasn't allowed to know if anyone had.

"There is, however, one complication," Oannes remarked as he manipulated his controls.

"What's that?" The question was barely out of Jason's mouth when the acceleration halted with an abruptness that forced him to grab onto the edge of the control panel to steady himself.

"The device affects *all* such propulsion within its radius of effect, including our own."

"*What?*" Jason yelped. There was no longer any point in keeping his voice down, for the other humans had felt the sudden cessation of acceleration and looked almost as alarmed as they should have. He looked at the scope. The missiles were drifting aimlessly. The blip of their own craft was lent a spurious steadiness by the fact that it was, by definition, the center point of the display.

"There was no other alternative," Oannes said quietly. "However, now that we can no longer maneuver, I am releasing the water from the ballast tanks. Our momentum and the current are taking us toward Cape Taenarum, and we should not be too far from shore when we surface."

"But, Oannes, why surface at all? Why not wait it out down here? Their missiles can't maneuver either."

"Now that we have been detected, they will find another way to attack us—and we will be unable to evade it. It is going to become necessary to abandon ship. And for that, we must surface, because . . ."

Because we nonamphibious humans are along, Jason finished for him mentally, thinking what the alien shrank from voicing. Their eyes met in a moment of shared understanding and mutual embarrassment. The other humans looked on, bewildered.

But then the little submarine broke the surface under the sunset sky, with the peaks of the Taygetus Mountains black against the darkening east. It rose from the water like a released cork, and hung for a bare instant before flopping back down and hitting the surface. The impact sent them all staggering, but Oannes swept one alien hand across the controls while holding on with the other. The transparent canopy clamshelled away, leaving them exposed to the first stars that were beginning to appear.

"Abandon ship and swim for shore!" the Nagom shouted, and in a movement of otterlike fluidity he was over the side and into the water.

The humans scrambled to obey. They were clambering over the side when Jason glimpsed the lights sweeping in on them—the running lights of the Teloi "chariots."

"Jump!" he yelled. It wasn't fully out of his mouth when a coherent lightning bolt stabbed out with a crash like thunder.

Some kind of charged particle beam weapon they've attached to external hardpoints on their aircars, thought Jason, with a calmness that surprised him, as he dived. He hit the water just as the artificial lightning struck, staggering the little submarine and disabling all its electronics in a shower of sparks.

He raised his head above the water and looked back. Nagel was jumping clumsily from the rapidly listing craft . . . and Deirdre was falling from it, apparently unconscious. She sank, and did not come up.

Jason started to swim frantically toward her.

"I'll get her!" shouted Perseus between powerful strokes. He was swimming toward the spot where she had sunk, and he was closer to it than Jason.

In the sky behind him, Jason saw another of the "chariots" swing around, lining up for a shot.

Trained survival reflexes thought for Jason. He pulled his knees up under him and plunged underwater.

The water above him exploded into steam, scalding him and sending him into an uncontrollable spin. He somehow managed to continue holding his breath, and reestablished the rhythm and direction of his strokes.

His lungs were knots of unendurable agony when he finally broke the surface, took a gasping breath, and looked around. There was no sign of Perseus or Deirdre. There was also no sign of the glowing predators in the sky.

He couldn't let himself think about it—at least not yet. He located the shore and started swimming for it.

The sun had finished setting by the time Jason crawled ashore, lacerating his hands and knees on the shale of the narrow beach beneath sheer cliffs.

He took stock. His sandals were gone, and his tunic was the worse for wear, but he still had his sword-dagger. He looked around in the twilight. A short distance down the beach, a cavern gaped at the base of the cliff. In the opposite direction, a prone figure was vomiting weakly. It was Nagel. Jason forced himself to his feet and staggered to the historian's side. He grasped Nagel by the shoulders and shook him into awareness.

"Have you seen Deirdre?" he demanded.

"No . . . no," Nagel said vaguely, and collapsed as soon as Jason released him.

"Nor have I," came an unmistakable alien voice.

Oannes was still wearing his utility harness with its array of devices. One was an incongruously ordinary-looking flashlight. Its wavering light approached them through the gloom. "I came ashore well before you," he said. "I have seen no sign of your female companion, or of the local male Perseus."

"He was trying to rescue her." Jason felt leaden in a way that transcended mere physical exhaustion. "They must have both drowned." *Or been cooked by that particle beam, or boiled alive* . . . He veered hurriedly away from that line of thought.

"Perhaps," Oannes acknowledged. "But there is another possibility, suggested by your account of the interest the Teloi—specifically the one called Hyperion—took in her. They may have retrieved her from the water and conveyed her to their . . . sanctuary. You will note that they ceased to attack us just after the female vanished."

Jason forced his battered mind to think. He checked his implant display. There was still no sign of Deirdre's implant, so it must still be inside the Teloi's private pocket universe. "So you think the Teloi brought the . . . idol here from the Echinades?"

"Actually, I know they did. As you may recall, my submersible had a device which could detect the . . . opening when it activated. This occurred just before the attack. I had time to note the location." Oannes pointed down the beach toward the cave mouth. "It is in there. In my judgment, that is where the female has been taken"

"No!"

They all whirled around at the sound of that despairing scream. Perseus stood statue-still in the shallows, with small waves lapping his knees. Even half seen in the gloom, his expression was chilling. No one of Jason's world would have worn it—or *could* have worn it, for it held a primal terror that not even those remaining religious believers who self-consciously rejected the rationalistic world-view could any longer feel.

"So Deianeira is dead," he said in a hollow voice, staring down the beach at the mouth of the Underworld.

"She may be, Perseus," said Oannes, "but I do not believe she is. Unless I am mistaken, she still lives, but the Old Gods have taken her into Hades for purposes of their own."

Without warning, Perseus threw back his head and howled—a long, quavering howl that prickled Jason's skin and raised the hairs at the base of his neck. As its last echoes died away, Perseus fell to his knees in the water. Then, with just as little warning as that eerie scream, he spoke in a voice that was thick with emotion but rock-steady.

"They have taken the living into Hades! This is a wrongness in the heart of the world. By this, the Old Gods have forfeited all that I have ever felt for them except fear. And fear is no longer enough." He got slowly to his feet. "I failed to protect Deianeira. This is a disgrace I must wipe out. I must go into Hades and bring her out."

For a moment that stretched into eternity, they all stared at him.

Nagel was the first to speak. "You would dare to violate the wall between the realms of the living and of the dead?"

"The Old Gods have already broken that wall. I am the son of one of the New Gods. He will help me, even though I have nothing here to sacrifice to him." Perseus turned to Oannes. He did not kneel or otherwise abase himself. That, Jason recalled, had not been the way of the historical Greeks, who had stood like men before gods who did not view men as worthless.

Could it be that we're seeing the start of that right here and now on this beach? Jason wondered.

"Oannes," said Perseus, "you are a deity, and I know you are no friend of the Old Gods. Will you help me?"

Oannes' eyes met Jason's, across a few feet of space and an abysm of biology and culture and inability to speak openly in Perseus' hearing. The Nagom had lost his submarine and all his technological wonders except those he carried on his person. He owed nothing to Deirdre or Perseus or any other human. But . . . the Teloi were in that cave, and the struggle with those bioengineered abominations was what he was for.

"We may not succeed, Perseus," he said. "Indeed, we probably will not. But if you are resolved to try, I will do what I can to aid you."

"We all will," Jason added. He looked through the

gathering darkness at the deeper blackness of the cavern. Then, for what he knew was probably the last time, he looked around at the sea and the stars and the world, and smelled the salt air and listened to the wind.

It was, he decided, a good night to harrow Hell.

CHAPTER THIRTEEN

Oannes' lamp, set cautiously low, lit their way as they entered the gaping cave mouth and scrambled down a treacherous slope.

"There is a more direct route, through another cavern at the end of an inlet a short way along the coast," the Nagom explained. "But its very directness means that it will be watched. They feel no need to guard this one; the fears of the local populace are enough."

"I can believe it," muttered Jason. He had seen the look of arcane terror return to Perseus' face as they had passed the threshold of what was, to him, the realm of the dead. But the Hero hadn't even paused. Jason knew he could never fully appreciate the kind of courage that lack of hesitation implied.

"We have almost reached—" Even as Oannes said it,

Jason momentarily lost his footing . . . and gasped in shock as his feet landed in ice-cold water.

"Perhaps we need more light," Oannes conceded. He adjusted the power output.

Jason gasped again, but this time not from cold.

"The River Styx," Perseus breathed.

They were on the bank of an underground river whose beginning and end were lost to sight in the distant gloom. Its waters were pellucidly clear, and in the light of Oannes' high-tech torch the bottom glowed emerald-green. Overhead was an inverted forest of gleaming, multicolored stalactites. The banks were narrow and gravelly, lined by what looked like abstract sculpture in eons-shaped semiprecious stones.

It was like being inside a jewel.

"We have no boat," said Oannes matter-of-factly. "So we must proceed along the bank. Fortunately, we are on the correct side. *Very* fortunately, inasmuch as the water is extremely cold."

"So I noticed." Jason couldn't help thinking Oannes could have given him some warning. It reminded him that he might need to talk to the Nagom in private. "We're obviously going to have to go in single file. Perseus, scout ahead."

For a moment, the young Hero didn't move. Jason had never imagined anything that could faze Perseus' resolve. But this was too close to his innermost horrors.

"Perseus," Oannes said slowly, "you are going to find that some of the things you have been taught are . . . not untrue, just not precisely as you have interpreted them. In particular, the actual realm of the dead is on a lower level of Hades. What you are going to see at first is reserved for the *living* dead: the prisoners the pirates of the Echinades bring here and work to death with the consent—and, indeed, at the orders—of the Old Gods."

The fear vanished from Perseus' face, replaced by the anger of disillusioned faith. "So . . . another betrayal by them. My father Zeus doesn't treat mortals so." He hefted his weapon and went ahead on point, sidling along the narrow bank. The others followed. The crudely statuelike formations were more fragile than they looked. Whenever Jason brushed against them, fragments of topaz or amethyst broke off. It seemed like a desecration.

The underground waterway seemed to go on forever. But presently Perseus signaled back to them, pointing at a small side tunnel through which a narrow tributary trickled. They had to stoop to enter it, and the bank became so narrow that they had to step into the shallow but icy water. Oannes adjusted their light to the minimum they could see by, which made the tunnel seem even more confining. It was, Jason thought, fortunate that full-blown claustrophobia was one of the things that automatically disqualified would-be time travelers. Still, sweat gleamed on Nagel's face in the dim light.

They went about a hundred yards, although it seemed longer. Then a faint glow appeared up ahead. Oannes turned his lamp off altogether, and motioned them to proceed with caution. They crawled forward in the chill shallows, seeking the light.

They emerged into a scene that took away whatever breath Jason had left after his partial immersion in the freezing water.

They were looking out over a large, roughly circular cave, illuminated by many torches inserted in sconces chipped out of the rocky walls. The stream they had been following trickled down a slope and over a steep pile of fallen rocks into a pool that reflected, mirrorlike, the inverted forest of stalactites fifteen yards or so above the corresponding stalagmites that fringed the motionless dark water. Around the perimeter of the cavern, dark corridors branched off.

But Jason barely noticed these natural features. He was staring at the activity that filled the central cave and the portions of the branching passages that could be seen.

Everywhere, moving through the flickering torchlight like resident demons, were armed, leather-armored men, mostly of the swarthy eagle-nosed Echinades breed. Many of them carried whips. Jason saw none of those whips used. The barely human creatures—grime-encrusted, shaggy-headed, cadaverously thin, practically naked despite the subterranean chill—who labored in the cavern had evidently been brutalized into a level of submissiveness where that was no longer required. They cringed and whimpered at the mere approach of one of the guards, then returned hastily to their tasks—most of which seemed to involve one phase or other of pottery-making.

"It is a sideline of the pirates," Oannes answered Jason's unspoken question, and pointed toward one end of the central cavern. There was a pit where clay was being tempered. Beyond that was a huge, crude kiln. Smoke from the latter was rising straight up; nature had obligingly provided an efficient chimney. It must, Jason thought, also be drawing up the smell from another pit, where, as he watched, the guards tossed the limp form of a slave whom death had liberated. It landed on top of a heap of corpses in varying stages of decomposition, all the way down to skeletons at the bottom. The vent above could not remove the stench altogether, but no one seemed to mind it. Jason suspected that the guards were very little further above the subhuman level than their charges.

Jason glanced at his companions. Nagel looked like he was going to be sick. Perseus was staring with horrified fixation.

As well he might, thought Jason. *If this isn't really Hell, it's close enough.*

Still, alarm bells began to sound in Jason's mind. There was something disturbing about the Hero's expression, something Jason knew was beyond his own understanding because it belonged to a mental universe his own world had left behind. Perseus' features were firm—it was hard to imagine them any other way—but the firmness had something brittle about it. Something, in short, that suggested his behavior was unpredictable. In a situation like this, unpredictability was the last thing Jason needed.

Oannes pointed again, indicating the largest of the openings. "That leads to the surface, through a cave mouth at the beach . . . and it is guarded. The others extend further into the depths, in all directions. They are lined with niches where the prisoners sleep. And then there is that one. . . ." He pointed at an exceptionally large opening about fifty yards around the cavern's perimeter, to their right. "If the readings I obtained are to be trusted, the . . . gateway is in there."

"We've got to get to it," said Jason.

"It will be difficult to do so, unnoticed. But there may be a chance, if we stay very close to the wall of the cavern, where it is ill-lit. Unfortunately, the poor lighting also works against us. Be careful to avoid the crevice there."

Jason bit off a sarcastic retort. At least the Nagom had warned him this time. "Lead the way."

Crouching, Oannes led the way down a slippery slope toward their right. The humans followed, trying their best to emulate the sinuous movements that made him seem merely a part of the flickering shadows. Presently, Jason felt the edge of a precipice with his foot, which dislodged some gravel. He waited to hear it striking the bottom. He never did. He continued on, even more cautiously than before.

They edged their way to the great tunnel mouth and crept into it, still keeping behind the deep fissure. They gazed into a vast, vaulted cavern arching upward to a height of almost a hundred feet but hung with translucent arrays of stalactites. The floor looked like it had been laboriously flattened out. At the far end, flanked by torches was the crude-looking idol Jason had seen before in another cave, in the Echinades. It was guarded by a number of armed pirates, but no one else was in evidence.

It was all like some profane cathedral.

"Oannes," Jason whispered, "you told me before that the gateway can only be opened from . . . this side." Which, he reflected, made sense. No energy expenditure inside the Teloi's pocket-universe "sanctuary" could affect anything outside it, unless the gateway was already opened.

"That is correct. As I explained, it can be . . . ordered to do so at a certain point in time. This is done as a routine precaution when the Teloi enter it and close it behind them. But it can also be opened by a spoken signal by anyone on the outside."

"I don't suppose you know this 'signal'?"

"No. It is a secret the Teloi only share with their most trusted human servitors."

Nagel had been listening. He indicated the men in the cavern. "Maybe we could capture one of them and force him to tell us."

"No," said the Nagom. "These are mere guards. Only the priests are allowed to know—and not even all of them. They always make a great production of opening it, to enhance their own prestige. The Teloi humor them in this, even letting them do their mummery when the Teloi themselves are present and there is no need for it."

"Naturally," Nagel nodded. "The priests must inspire awe in the ignorant, if they are to be useful."

Jason wasn't listening. With part of his mind, he was worrying that Perseus might be overhearing this. But a glance reassured him that the Hero was paying no attention, just staring fixedly ahead with who knew what going through his Bronze Age mind. So Jason concentrated on worrying about what to do next.

Oannes says they always set it to open on its own after a certain period of time, just in case. But we have no way of knowing how long we have to wait for that to happen, with nothing to eat and the constant chance that someone will blunder onto us—

Jason's thoughts were interrupted by a commotion from the central cavern behind them. Looking over his shoulder, he saw pirates scurrying frantically toward the cave of the gateway. And behind them was a glow that held a quality of artificial light that had no business in this world.

"Down!" he hissed at his companions. They flattened in the narrow darkness between the cave wall and the crevice, while the pirates—some of them wearing regalia of long robes and high-crowned headdresses that must mark the priesthood, ran unseeingly past them and arranged themselves in ceremonial order behind the "idol."

They were none too soon. The glow intensified, and with the faint, eerie hum Jason remembered, a graceful flying platform, ablaze with running lights, swept into the cavern. A chant arose from the priests, and the guards groveled.

Jason was getting better about recognizing individual Teloi. So he recognized this one even before the chant reached his ears: "Hyperion! Hyperion!" *It's him, all right,* he thought, forcing cold calmness on himself. *The one who might have had "further use" for Deirdre.*

The "chariot" hovered a few feet above the floor while the priests made their obeisances. Finally, under Hyperion's patiently condescending eye, the priest with the most elaborate headgear stepped before the idol.

There's more to it than Sidney thought, Jason reflected. *Having flunkies do things for you that you could do yourself is a universal status symbol.* He strained to hear what the priest was saying, but couldn't make it out. *Of course not,* he told himself. *Did you really expect him to blurt out the secret in the hearing of all the guards and low-echelon priests? He's probably murmuring just loud enough to activate the pickup.*

Then, as he watched, a circular area about three yards in diameter began to define itself, in midair off to the side of the idol. A worshipful moan went up from the guards and acolytes as reality began to waver in the same indescribable, disturbing way Jason had seen once before. Then, as before, the disturbance was gone, leaving a hole in the universe.

The high priest and his underlings bowed deeply as

Hyperion's platform floated through that immaterial ring. The "god" was gone . . . but the gateway remained open.

"Energy conservation," Oannes whispered, answering Jason's unspoken question. "Another Teloi must be coming—or perhaps one is about to leave the sanctuary."

"Is that the gateway to the true realm of the dead?" Perseus rasped harshly.

"In a manner of speaking," said Jason absently. He would have given more thought to his reply, but he was looking hungrily at that opening. Suddenly, on a hunch, he thought a command to his brain implant. The visual display appeared, on the minutest scale of which it was capable.

The red dot marking Nagel's TRD showed steadily, on a detailed map of this area of Cape Taenarum, showing where the historian crouched a few feet from him. And off to the side was the other dot, flickering and wavering as though the implant couldn't decide just exactly where it was, or even if it was really there at all.

So, Jason thought, *as long as that gateway is open, it admits signals, and I can pick up the transponder, even though the TRD is nowhere on this map—or even, strictly speaking, in this universe.*

"The device of which I spoke is definitely in there," he whispered to Oannes.

Perseus overheard him. His eyes grew round. "Does that mean Deianeira herself is beyond the gateway?"

"Almost certainly," Jason told him. "All the more so because Hyperion just arrived. I believe he wants . . ." *How do you explain genetic engineering and artificial insemination to this kid?* "I believe he wants Deianeira," Jason finally settled for saying.

Perseus' eyes grew even huger. All at once, Jason realized it had been the wrong thing to say. He opened his mouth to utter a qualifier.

He never got to say anything. With the suddenness of an explosion, Perseus cried out—the same ululating, blood-freezing howl they had heard on the beach. And without any more warning than that, he whipped out his sword and bounded across the chasm that separated them from the main body of the cave.

Jason had absolutely no chance to urge him to stop—nor would there have been any point, with the guards and priests already looking up in startlement at the sound of that cry. So he yelled, "Follow him!" Without waiting to see what Oannes and Nagel were doing, he leaped the chasm—it was deep but not wide—and ran in Perseus' wake.

It was a wake of spurting blood, flying severed limbs, and screams of agony, littered with dead and dying bodies.

Jason had seen Perseus in action before, on the road from Tiryns, and he knew he had no business being amazed at the human killing machine that was the Hero. But it was impossible not to feel horror-stricken awe as Perseus sliced his way through the press of pirates like some elemental principle of death, barely slowing down as he ran unerringly toward that incomprehensible opening. Jason had little to do but fend off the occasional guards who converged from the sides as they came out of their stunned surprise. He battered one such guard's spear aside with his sword, then whipped it around across the man's throat. Simultaneously, he took a split second for a glance backward; Oannes and Nagel were with him. Then he looked ahead again. Perseus was almost at the gateway cutting down the last guard who could interpose himself. The high priest alone stood before him, immobilized with shock, doing nothing.

Of course, came Jason's flashing thought. *The Teloi naturally wouldn't tell their human servitors how to* close *the gateway from the outside. They may be crazy, but they're not stupid.*

The high priest screamed something. The scream changed in quality as Perseus thrust his sword into the priest's belly and withdrew it with a disemboweling twist, trailing a rope of entrails. Then, without breaking stride, the Hero was through the portal.

Even at that moment, Jason found himself wondering what kind of courage that took for someone native to Perseus' mental universe.

But he had no time to appreciate it as he dived through the hoop of energy himself.

He landed on a smooth floor whose material he couldn't identify. He heard Oannes and Nagel coming through behind him. No one else followed, and the pandemonium on the other side of the portal suddenly died in a collective gasp of horror over what the strange men and the sea god had just done.

Jason looked around frantically, unable to mentally process all his eyes were seeing. But he saw a kind of instrument panel to the right, and he saw Perseus grappling with an unfamiliar Teloi male, getting an arm under the being's jaw and pulling upward to expose the throat to his blade.

Even at that moment, the Teloi croaked out a command—a meaningless series of syllables in his own language.

The portal vanished.

CHAPTER FOURTEEN

For a long moment, the tableau held in silence.

Perseus finally broke it, standing up and letting the dead Teloi slide to the floor. He stared at his hands and forearms, red with blood—but a paler red than the blood of humans. He continued to stare in silence.

As well he might, thought Jason. *By his own lights, he has just killed a god.*

Jason also got to his feet. He thought he felt a little lighter. The temperature was comfortable—perhaps a couple of degrees warmer than humans would have set it. He turned to Nagel and Oannes and addressed the latter. "I thought you said—"

"I said the gateway could only be *opened* from the outside," Oannes stated with pedantic exactitude. "No such limitation applies to *closing* it."

"Right," Jason said sourly. He looked around. Gradually, strangeness faded enough for their surroundings to begin to register.

They were at the center of a large circular chamber with a lofty domed ceiling. Everything was constructed of the same unidentifiable material as the floor, in muted colors and crafted into decorative motifs on which Jason's mind could not get a grip. The central area was sunken, surrounded by several broad concentric steps rising to a higher level. Spaced equidistantly around the circumference of that level were five archways, sized to Teloi proportions. Between them were softly glowing wall panels that provided the light he was seeing by. Through the archways, Jason could see corridors receding. It was almost like an artificial reflection of what nature had crafted in the central cavern through which they had recently passed, beneath Cape Taenarum . . . wherever that was relative to where they were now, Jason thought. But of course, the question was meaningless. Cape Taenarum was in another universe.

The thought reminded Jason to activate his display, at the largest possible scale. No map appeared, of course; the computer in his skull had no referents to attach its inertial positioning system to. But it could and did show the two red dots, floating in isolation before his eyes.

"Oannes," he asked, "how big is this . . . place?"

"How should I know? I have never exactly been invited here, nor have any of the Nagommo. Such a . . . construct can be of practically any desired size, and once it is established, maintaining it requires no . . . work." This, Jason recognized, was the closest Achaean could come to "energy expenditure."

"But," Jason persisted, gazing down corridors that seemed to recede into infinity, "why do they need, or even want, for it to be *this* big?"

"Certain fundamental laws require that it be at least a certain minimum volume, which is far from small. And it is created around a structure—a practical necessity, because otherwise the occupants would have to look on the naked face of . . . something with which finite minds cannot cope."

Jason nodded. The mind quailed at the thought of the nearby event horizon that must lie beyond these walls. And unrestricted nanotechnological construction techniques allowed for the creation of *very* large structures. None of which was particularly helpful with his immediate problem.

"Sidney," he told Nagel, "run as fast as you can over there." He pointed at one of the archways.

"Why?"

"Just do it!" Jason reined in his temper and explained. "I need to establish an orientation for the return I'm getting for Deirdre's TRD. Right now, it's just floating in limbo."

The historian didn't look like he really understood, but he got to his feet, took a deep breath, and made his best effort at a sprint in the indicated direction. It was a clumsy run, lurching forward as though the leg muscles were applying too much power. It confirmed Jason's impression that the gravity here was a little less than one Earth G. Presumably the Teloi came from a lower-gravity planet—which made sense, given their height and build—and had set their artificial gravity generators accordingly. *It must, he thought, be a great comfort to them to be able to come here and luxuriate in their accustomed weight.* But these thoughts occupied only a small corner of his mind. Mostly, he concentrated on the display that seemed to float before his eyes.

Even on the scale to which Jason had set the display, Nagel's dash across the domed chamber covered only an insignificant distance. But to Jason's tightly focused eye, the red dot of his TRD seemed to jerk almost infinitesimally sideways, at about a sixty-degree angle to the imaginary line from it to the other red dot. He immediately deactivated the display, applied that angle to the direction in which Nagel had run . . . and found himself looking at one of the archways.

It was a poor basis for a plan of action. But it was all he had. And he owed it to the others to project more confidence than he felt.

"Deianeira is down that corridor!" he declared, loudly enough for Perseus to hear even through his shock. He pointed theatrically. "Let's go, Perseus! We can still snatch her from the realm of the dead before . . . before . . ." He cast about through his recollections of Greek mythology. "Before she's eaten the food of the dead."

Something seemed to crystallize in Perseus. He stood up straighter, and his features and his voice held nothing but steadiness. "Yes. After that it will be too late for her. Jason, I do not understand by what power you know where she can be found. But I do know there is a power in you. I will follow where you lead."

Jason examined the Teloi Perseus had killed. No paralysis beamer or any other weapon, of course; that would have been too easy. "Let's move, then." He strode off in the direction of the archway, and through it. Oannes quickened his steps and drew abreast of him, and spoke too low for Perseus to hear.

"I believe I know what this 'power' of yours is, although this language lacks the vocabulary to describe it. The time-travel device has a . . . quality which you can perceive at a distance. Although, come to think of it, this quality probably did not function when the device was . . . here, and you were not."

Jason sighed. There was, he knew by now, no point in trying to conceal things from this old member of an old race. He maintained a silence which Oannes recognized as the acknowledgment it was.

"But," the Nagom continued, "how do you know that the female is in the same location as the device, which was removed from her?"

"I don't know, of course," Jason whispered harshly. "But it's all I've got to go on. Do you have any better suggestions?"

"No," the alien admitted. "And it is not unreasonable that they would be keeping her in the same general area where the device is being studied, inasmuch as she is, herself, an object of study. Lead on."

Jason did so, through endless empty corridors, navigating by means of his display. As he did so, he noticed that the implanted computer, using the data it received through his eyes, was building up a new map—or, more accurately, floor plan. Order was emerging from chaos, although Deirdre's TRD still lay in the murky realms beyond the pattern of corridors that grew like a living organism in the display as fast as Jason saw them. Through that pattern, the other red dot moved at the rate of Sidney's walk. At least the implant now had a firm basis for distances, and the rate at which the two dots grew closer together enabled Jason to estimate how much further they had to go, relative to how far they'd come. And he became more and more nervous.

"Oannes," he whispered, "why are we being allowed to walk further and further into this . . . structure? Why aren't the Teloi swarming all over us?"

"They may not be aware of our presence."

"But surely they've detected us!" Jason looked around nervously for anything that looked like cameras or sensors.

"Remember, they have never required security measures within this . . . realm. And even if they had, vigilance tends to wear down over the course of a hundred thousand years. Furthermore, our lack of any advanced tools other than the small ones I am carrying on my person has a good side: we are not conspicuous at a distance."

No high-energy emissions, Jason thought with an unconscious nod. "But what about the one Perseus killed?"

"For the same reasons, they probably were not in continuous contact with the one on duty at the portal. Perhaps he reports in at regular intervals. But until he fails to do so, they have no cause for alarm."

Jason breathed a little easier. It seemed to hold up.

"At the same time," Oannes continued serenely, "it is also possible that they have been observing us all along, and are merely allowing us to penetrate deeper into their stronghold so that we can be more easily captured."

It was, Jason thought, a remark that could just as easily have been left unsaid.

"You know, Oannes, it's too bad you'll never be able to return with us to our time. There's a man named Rutherford I'd like to introduce you to. You and he have a lot in common."

"I am gratified to learn of the evolutionary heights your race will attain in the future."

"That's how Rutherford himself would see it," Jason sighed.

Nagel was not amused. "So we could be walking into a trap!"

"Perhaps." Oannes' serenity was unruffled. "But if so, the trap is not of a highly advanced nature. I have . . . means of perceiving such things."

Jason looked at him sharply. Was he referring to one of the "tools" hanging from his harness? Or—a possibility that had never occurred to him before—did the alien have a brain implant similar to his own, but equipped with sensors that could detect any automatic energy weapons or gravitic capture fields or any such high-tech security systems? He wondered how tactful it would be to ask.

He was still wondering when an open space appeared up ahead.

They emerged onto a terrace encircling a vast open well whose top and bottom were lost in shadows. Jason began to appreciate the concept of a "minimum volume" as applied to artificially created pocket universes.

Perseus halted, and looked around openmouthed. But then he stepped forward onto the terrace. Jason could not imagine what was keeping the Hero going, in an environment even more disorientingly alien to him than it was to his companions. But, he reflected, Perseus had had a lot of practice at adjusting to the unimaginable lately.

Jason checked his display. Deirdre's TRD still lay dead ahead. He looked across the chasm and saw an entryway of hangarlike proportions. Nothing could be made out in the obscurity beyond.

"We'll have to circle around," he told the others. He led the way through the archway and began to move along the rail that encircled the edge of the seemingly bottomless shaft. An updraft blew against his face. The breeze was welcome after their tension-filled trek through this warm place.

In fact, it was so refreshing that it slowed his responses just a trifle. Or maybe it was the fact that the faint whine behind them was a little higher-pitched than he had heard in his previous encounters with Teloi flying platforms. Those had been moving with self-consciously godlike stateliness. The Teloi who now zoomed out of the corridor from whence they'd come and whipped around the corner was in a hurry.

In fact, he was clearly as surprised by them as they were by him. He instinctively swerved to avoid them, while applying a braking thrust that raised the whining to a jagged scream. The platform skidded against the railing, sending them scattering in all directions. Jason hit the floor and rolled out of the craft's way just before it came to a halt. Then he sprang to his feet, drawing his sword-dagger, ready to spring at the Teloi—male, somewhat more heavily built than the norm, bearded like Hyperion but in some indefinable way younger-seeming that the others Jason had seen—who stood in the "chariot" and regarded them with the expression of pitiless *gravitas* that seemed habitual with his race. Jason gathered himself for a leap.

The Teloi touched something on the platform's little control panel . . . and Jason could not move.

Capture field, he thought in his despair.

It was a common tool of twenty-fourth-century police

forces. Utilizing the control of subatomic forces that made artificial gravity possible, it held the major muscles of the limbs in an unbreakable grip, while leaving functions like breathing and speech unimpaired. But those twenty-fourth-century police weapons involved a directional beam, or a two-dimensional field across an entrance. Apparently the Teloi, in the course of their immemorial history, had learned how to generate a *spherical* capture field. Jason could still turn his head, and he saw Nagel and Perseus pinned in the field's immaterial but irresistible embrace. No doubt the field had an inner boundary within which the platform's occupant was unaffected.

A handy security system for a vehicle, he grudgingly approved. *And since this Teloi didn't activate it until now, Oannes didn't detect it.*

Speaking of which . . . He looked around again. *Just where* is *Oannes?*

The Teloi alighted from his slightly-the-worse-for-wear "chariot" and gave them a look whose curiosity spoiled its imperiousness. "Who are you?" he demanded. "And how did you gain entry into regions which are forbidden to mortals?"

Jason tried to formulate a response, balancing the need to withhold information against his desire to say something defiant or even smart-ass. But Perseus saved him the trouble. The Hero's voice rang out like a clarion.

"I am Perseus, descendant of the divine-born Hero Danaos! And I claim as much right to be here as those gods who have brought the lady Deianeira here, ignoring the proper boundary between the living and the dead!"

"What?" It was the first time Jason had ever seen a

Teloi taken aback. The unhuman face went slack with amazement. "You are *Perseus*?"

"Yes!" The Hero pressed what he perceived as his advantage. "And besides being descended from the god-born Danaos, I am of divine birth myself. Yes, my mother Danaë was looked on with favor by a god. I claim the hospitality of the immortals, for I am the son of Zeus!"

The Teloi recovered his self-possession. But he did not resume his race's usual look of cold remoteness. Instead, his wide mouth quirked upward and a smile gleamed through his beard.

"This is all very interesting," he said in a voice beneath which amusement bubbled. "Especially inasmuch as I am myself Zeus."

CHAPTER FIFTEEN

In the silence, Zeus—Jason decided to think of him as that, since it was the name he went by in this culture—reached back into his "chariot" and withdrew an overelaborate but basically tube-shaped object Jason had seen before.

"A head of the Hydra!" Perseus gasped.

"Yes. You know what it can do. So I release you from that which I laid upon you before." Zeus touched another of the controls, and deactivated the capture field. Jason's large muscles were free again. But as an aftereffect he knew was characteristic of the field, they initially collapsed in a series of mild spasms. All three of them fell, willy-nilly, to their knees before the "god."

"So, Perseus," said Zeus in a tone Jason found hard to interpret, "who are your companions?"

The genetically enhanced Hero rose unsteadily to his feet before Jason could even consider trying. "These are Jason and Synon, from Aetolia." Jason silently prayed that Perseus would leave it at that. As so often happens, his prayers went unanswered. "They, like me, come in search of the lady Deianeira. Certain of the Old Gods brought her down here into the realm of the dead before her proper time."

"Ah, yes!" Zeus' strange eyes turned and met Jason's in a moment of shared understanding.

Yeah, he knows, Jason thought. *He doesn't even need to scan Sidney and me for TRDs to know we're time travelers like Deirdre. Hyperion knew that much at Tiryns.*

But the Teloi didn't pursue the matter. Instead, he manipulated another of his vehicle's controls. "I have summoned my fellows," he explained. Then he turned back to Perseus. "So, my son, you have explained why the others are here. But you have not explained why *you* are here. You may have attached yourself to these men's quest, but I cannot believe you did not start out on a quest of your own. I know your kind—the kind we have begotten on mortal women—too well."

Perseus' head drooped. "I was sent by Polydectes, king of Seriphos. He holds my mother's life in his hands—my mother Danaë, whom you once loved!"

Whom you once drugged unconscious and put into a lab! Jason thought searingly. And yet . . . was it his imagination, or did the Teloi's features waver, just for a moment, into an expression he had never seen on their kind? But then the moment was past, and that unhuman face smoothed itself out.

"What does Polydectes want of you in exchange for Danaë's safety?" Zeus asked.

"He commands me to bring him a head of the Hydra," Perseus mumbled, seemingly reduced to unaccustomed humility by the magnitude of what he was saying.

"A head of the Hydra!" Zeus let a tiny smile escape him for a split second, then remembered himself. "Polydectes presumes too much. It is a common failing of mortals. Or perhaps he merely wishes to send you to your death by compelling *you* to presume too much. We will deal with him in due course."

Perseus looked the Teloi full in the face. "Let *me* deal with him, Father!"

"I am sure you would, Perseus. But I still feel that you have not fully answered my question. I sense there is something more to your presence here in the company of these men, whose only motive is to recover Deianeira . . . and, I suspect, an article that belongs to her. Something even stronger than your desire to protect your mother from Polydectes' lust."

Perseus' eyes fell anew. "You see through to my innermost heart, Father. Yes, I have a reason of my own for seeking Deianeira, and you know it well. I love her—and I know she loves me!"

Jason's jaw fell.

Once again, Zeus demonstrated that a Teloi could smile, if only slightly.

"Help me, Father," Perseus pleaded, quivering with the intensity it took to force himself to beg.

"I cannot, Perseus." Jason wondered if what he saw in the unhuman face was really sorrow.

"But, Father, I have nowhere else to turn! Not even the sea god Oannes could help me."

No! Jason groaned inwardly. But it was too late.

The disturbing alien eyes flashed with sudden alertness. "What did you say?"

"He led us here," Perseus explained in his innocence. He looked around, puzzled. "But now he has vanished. I wonder where he could have gone?"

"I think I know," said Zeus grimly. He seemed about to say something else, but then there was a distant whining hum as though from several of the "chariots," and a glow of approaching lights appeared in one of the archways. Zeus went expressionless. "It is out of my hands, Perseus. I cannot help you. No one can. Not now."

Before anyone could say anything else, several Teloi swept into view. Their leader exchanged a few words with Zeus in an unknown language, finishing on a peremptory note. Zeus turned back to the humans. His face wore . . . what? Was it reluctance? Jason was still trying to decide when the "head of the Hydra" came up, and paralysis took him.

They were fitted with a kind of handcuffs and transferred with unfeeling efficiency to three of the flying platforms, which swept away through the hangarlike opening on the far side of the terrace. Lying on the vehicle's floor by the feet of the Teloi driver, unable to move a single voluntary muscle, Jason could only catch occasional glimpses of the inconceivable expanses through which he was being whisked.

Finally, the "chariot" settled to a landing. Jason was unceremoniously offloaded. By chance, he was left at an angle from which he could see that he lay on the floor of a roofless, nearly cubical chamber. He heard rather than saw Nagel and Perseus being dumped beside him. Then the Teloi departed with a whine and a flash of running lights, and it became apparent that their prison cell wasn't roofless after all. The roof rumbled shut above them, leaving them in dim lighting from the ubiquitous wall panels, awaiting the painful tingling of renewed sensation.

Perseus was despondent, believing himself "turned to stone" permanently. He therefore reacted with surprise when he was the first to be able to stand up. It didn't surprise Jason at all. He wondered if the resentment he felt might have something to do with what the Hero had said about Deirdre. At least he had the satisfaction of recovering before Nagel.

Barely had the historian struggled to his feet when the roof above their heads slid away with a grinding roar. A flying platform descended. It held Hyperion and a smaller figure—human, wearing a lost look.

"Deirdre!" Jason yelped, forgetting Perseus' presence.

It didn't matter. The Hero didn't hear the name. He stumbled forward, his eyes eloquent.

Deirdre blinked a few times and looked around, as though awakening to her surroundings. She gave Jason a smile. But then her eyes met Perseus'—and her expression changed to something Jason had to sternly remind himself he had no right to resent.

Hyperion clearly recognized that look for what it was, for he gave a satisfied nod. He touched his control panel, causing Perseus' handcuffs to fall away, and motioned *come*. Before Jason, in the midst of his whirling emotions—and his struggle to understand those emotions—realized what was happening, the Hero stepped onto the platform and took Deirdre's hands . . . and the platform rose upward from the pitlike chamber.

Jason's paralysis broke. "Stop!" he shouted, and rushed forward. But the "chariot" swooped away and was gone. Then a second vehicle appeared above them and began to descend.

This one was very different from the "chariots:" large and bulky, with a minimum of the usual baroque decorative motifs. It carried two Teloi, neither of whom Jason recognized. It also bore a machine that Jason was fairly sure he recognized, despite its alien origin. Form, after all, follows function . . . and this included a recliner with a helmetlike object overhanging one end.

The platform settled to the floor, almost filling the cell. One of the Teloi held a paralysis beamer on the humans, while the other beckoned.

"I'll go first," Jason sighed. Before Nagel could argue, he stepped onto the platform, settled onto the Teloi-sized recliner, and allowed the helmet to be fitted onto his head. His captors strapped him in and began fiddling with the controls.

"Wait a minute—" Jason began, suddenly alarmed.

But the Teloi, unlike the Temporal Regulatory Authority's technicians, were clearly unconcerned with the effect of imposing new language patterns by direct neural induction on a brain that was not cushioned by drugs . . . at least not when that brain was merely a human one. They ignored him and activated the machine.

Jason managed not to scream too much before he fainted.

He awoke lying on a pallet in a room that was small on the Teloi scale. Nagel was on another pallet beside him, still unconscious and very obviously still suffering from the indescribable dreams that had held Jason in thrall. At first he felt relief at having escaped from them. But after assessing his condition—nausea, splitting headache, black depression—he decided the dreams hadn't been so bad after all.

But there was no going back to sleep. He concentrated on exploring the new language that had been brutally and unnaturally forced on his brain.

It was worse than any such adjustment he had ever had to make before. There were, he decided, two reasons. The other languages he had acquired this way had been human and, for that matter, Indo-European. The tongue that now resided uncomfortably in his mind was altogether alien, with a structure and a body of assumptions that had begun to diverge the moment the first proto-Teloi and the first proto-human had begun to utter something more meaningful than grunts. And in the second place, those human languages had belonged to societies less advanced than his, and therefore had contained no concepts beyond his horizons. The Teloi language, on the other hand, was peppered with words that were mere noises to him, for he had no referents. It was unsettling.

Nagel finally awoke, even more wretched than Jason. They were given food—nothing startling, just the local human fare—but not allowed the rest or the antidepressants they would have gotten in Australia. They were forced to their feet and conducted through one oddly proportioned hall after another, finally emerging into a large octagonal chamber with walls and floor of a shiny, silver-veined black. A round table rose from the center of that floor like a natural outcropping, with Teloi-sized chairs arranged around its gleaming top. Only half of those chairs were occupied: a semicircle of about a dozen Teloi of both sexes. Hyperion sat at the center. Jason also recognized Eurymedon . . . and Zeus.

"Now we can talk," said Hyperion in the language Jason now more or less understood.

"May we sit down?" asked Jason. He hadn't had an opportunity to practice with the language, accustoming his vocal apparatus to it. He was sure his pronunciation must be nearly incomprehensible, so he spoke with great care.

Hyperion evidently understood him. Just as evidently, he was taken aback by something other than automatic, cringing subservience. And, it occurred to Jason, this was the first time the Teloi had dealt with humans inside their private universe.

"If you wish," Hyperion said indifferently. Jason settled uncomfortably onto one of the outsized chairs, directly across the table from Hyperion. Nagel followed suit.

"So," said Jason after as long a pause as he calculated he could get away with, "what do you want to talk about?"

"This should be obvious, even to you. We have given you our language, using the same technology we have used to give ourselves the languages your species has evolved in its various cultures, so that we can converse without the limitations of the primitive local language you already know. So let us proceed. I trust you will not waste our time by denying you are time travelers from this world's remote future."

Jason considered doing just that, if only to annoy the Teloi. He reluctantly concluded that the emotional satisfaction involved was outweighed by the chance of obtaining information by playing along. Besides which, he had to admit, if only to himself, that it was a great relief to be able to communicate in a civilized language—even though he had to concentrate to understand Hyperion, despite the effort the Teloi was making to speak slowly and distinctly.

"There's no point in denying it," he said carefully, "inasmuch as you've already obtained one of the devices that enables us to travel in time, by chopping it out of our companion Deirdre." He risked a quick side-glance at Nagel, with a glare he hoped the historian would correctly interpret as *Shut up and let me do the talking.* Fortunately, Nagel still seemed too listless to blurt anything out.

"Yes," Hyperion nodded. Jason wondered if the Teloi did that naturally, or if they had picked it up from humans. "She has admitted to being a time traveler. We only need for you to verify certain elements of her story."

Classic interrogation technique, thought Jason, with his law enforcement background. "Where is she, by the way?" he temporized.

"With the genetically modified specimen known as Perseus. He, like most of his kind, has proven unsatisfactory in various ways." Hyperion gave Zeus a supercilious glance, which the latter stonily ignored. "We had already intended to use her as breeding stock. Being from several thousand years in the future, she is presumably a more evolved specimen than is currently available. Now, since she and Perseus have evidently formed a sexual attraction, we have decided to let them breed without any genetic manipulation, thus producing a 'control.' Later, there will be plenty of time to use the two of them in a program of artificial insemination and germ-line genetic engineering in our ongoing efforts to produce a useful, worthwhile variety of your species—a variety worthy of the honor of being our worshipers and servitors, the role we created you for."

Don't do us any favors, Jason thought. It was a mental defense mechanism, enabling him to maintain his self-control and not give way to the various emotions he was feeling—one of which was a suicidal urge to spring across the table and lock his hands around Hyperion's throat.

Nagel abruptly came out of his torpor. He leaned forward and spoke in a reckless rush, his tongue stumbling over the unpracticed phonemes. "This is insanity! What do you hope to accomplish? Doesn't the fact that we've come from the far future of this world—a future that our race rules, a future in which you're nothing but dimly remembered mythological figures from religions thousands of years dead—tell you that you're going to fail?"

"Not necessarily. You come from one possible future. Now that we know of it, we can forestall it. So you see, you blundered badly in coming back to this era. We are going to change destiny itself, and wipe out the perverted future that spawned you! And the final irony is that your world of feral humans will have served a purpose, by providing us with something we have lacked. We have the female's time-travel device; we will have yours, as soon as we extract them from you. Eventually, we will learn their secret, and then we will be able to roam at will through the eons!"

Nagel's mouth hung open. "But . . . but . . . that's not the way it . . ."

Jason suddenly knew what he had to do.

"You sniveling little prick!" he yelled at Nagel, who

stared in shock. "You were always in love with Deirdre! And when she wouldn't have you, you conspired with Perseus!" He flung himself sideways, wrestling Nagel to the floor and locking an arm around his throat. The historian gasped for air.

"Eos! Helios! Separate them!" he heard Hyperion command.

"Sidney!" he whispered harshly into the historian's ear. "Don't tell them the truth about time travel! Deirdre must have been misleading them. Their ignorance is the only weapon we've got."

He felt Nagel's chin bob up and down as he nodded, just before two Teloi pulled them apart.

"Enough of this nonsense," Hyperion said coldly. "Such behavior is only to be expected of feral humans. If you cannot control yourselves, we will continue this on our arrival at Crete."

"Crete?" Even at this moment, Nagel looked transfigured.

"Yes. Most of our fellows—including the most senior among us—are already on the island of Kalliste, where the chief temple of our worshipers is located. But we will go to Crete first—the political center. Certain formalities must be observed. So that is where the pirates are even now transporting the dimensional anchor for this habitat."

Jason thought about it. It was, to say the least, an interesting mode of transportation: a ship carrying the gateway which defined your universe's location relative to the larger universe. Only . . . "What if the ship sinks?" he couldn't resist asking.

Hyperion looked disgusted. "Naturally we have an

aircar aloft in case of emergencies. But why am I wasting time talking to such as you?" He made an impatient gesture. "Take them back to the holding area."

"I'll take them," Zeus said quickly.

Hyperion gave a wave of indifference. Zeus gestured with his paralyzer and they preceded him through the door.

"Why don't you transport the portal device to Crete in one of your aircars?" Jason asked Zeus, breaking the silence as the Teloi conducted them through the labyrinthine corridors. "Why wait for the pirates to row a galley there?"

Zeus looked puzzled by the question. It occurred to Jason that a race with lifespan measured in millennia might well be in less of a rush. Zeus' words seemed to confirm it, for he didn't even address the question of travel time. "We let the priests deliver it to the Minos on Crete because performing such a function enhances their prestige, and hence their usefulness to us."

"But," Nagel wondered, "is the Minos willing to accept anything from outlaws?"

"Why, of course." Again the Teloi seemed surprised at having to explain anything so obvious. "The Echinadian pirates accept his ultimate religious authority. And they have many ways of making themselves useful to him—for example, keeping the coastal communities in a proper state of fear."

Jason found himself nodding. He didn't pretend to Nagel's knowledge of this era, but he had a good grounding in various later periods of history—like the late twentieth century, when terrorists had been the shock troops of totalitarianism, a relationship which many in the West had been strangely unable or unwilling to recognize.

They passed through a final door, and were in what Hyperion had called the "holding area"—a term of which Jason had taken note. The ceiling was in place above their heads, which gave Jason an excuse for looking up. What he was really looking for was some evidence of surveillance equipment. He completed his quick survey, satisfied that there were no cameras or audio pickups in the chamber.

Zeus stood by the door as a robotic servitor floated almost silently in with food and water. "Here you will remain," explained the Teloi. "I am in charge of you, and I will see you are not made unnecessarily uncomfortable, as long as you cause no trouble."

"Thank you," said Jason. "Will we be allowed to see our companion Deirdre? And your . . . son Perseus?"

Zeus went expressionless. "That is out of the question. Their fate is now distinct from yours. Accept this." He seemed about to say more, but then turned abruptly and was gone. The door slid shut behind him.

Nagel slumped to the floor.

Jason sat beside him. "Sorry about what I had to do, back there," he said in a low voice. "But I couldn't let you reveal the truth."

A flicker of puzzled interest awoke in Nagel. "But why are you talking about it now? Aren't you afraid—?"

"No. I'm reasonably sure there are no surveillance devices in here. It makes sense. Remember Hyperion called it a 'holding area,' not a 'prison' or a 'detention area' or anything like that. We're the first intruders to ever get into this pocket universe. They've never needed a prison before. I don't know what they normally use this chamber for, but it's just a makeshift cell. Also, from every thing I've seen and heard about the Teloi, I doubt if they'd be willing to trust any of their number with the authority to emplace bugs here in their private universe. So as long as we don't yell, we can talk with some freedom. That, by the way, was why I was willing to try goading Zeus the way I did."

"But . . . why goad him at all?"

"Because I think he's the weak link in the Teloi chain. Some of the things I've seen . . . things about his relationship to Hyperion and the rest of the Old Gods. But most of all, there's what he didn't give away to them."

Nagel was clearly lost. "Give away to them?"

"Remember how Perseus blabbed to him about Oannes? But Hyperion never asked us about that. Zeus must not have told him. Otherwise, he surely would have been concerned about one of their old enemies being on the loose in here."

"No doubt," came a third voice.

They swung in the direction from which the sound had come, just in time to see a wavering in the air resolve itself into Oannes, looking somewhat the worse for wear.

"You are correct about the lack of viewing and listening devices here," he said into the stunned silence. "I have verified it with instruments. And now . . . may I trouble you for some of your food? I have not eaten in a while."

CHAPTER SIXTEEN

"So," said Jason after the famished Nagom had taken the edge off his hunger, "I suppose you're going to tell us you have some invisibility device that lets you vanish from sight."

"Actually, I do." Oannes pointed to one of the devices hanging from his harness. "It bends light around." This could be said in Achaean, and it made neither more nor less sense than it did in any other human language. Only in Jason's era had generating a field such as the one the Nagom was describing become a theoretical possibility. But in fact, they were using the Teloi language. Ironically, Jason and Nagel now knew it better than Oannes. But the Nagom could get by in it.

"So how can you see while using it?" asked Jason, interested.

"The device compensates. Imperfectly, to be sure. But one can view the outside world in blurred shades of gray." Oannes paused to take another bite. At this rate, Jason reflected sourly, Oannes would leave Nagel and himself on short rations. But, he had to admit, Oannes had been without food quite a lot longer than they, if he'd been skulking around in the corners since they had lost sight of him.

"I gather you also have something in that handy tool kit that shields you from a capture field."

"Unfortunately, I don't. But as soon as I detected that platform approaching, I knew what was going to happen. I immediately activated the invisibility field and stepped away. You didn't notice my disappearance, as you were . . . otherwise occupied."

"That's one way to put it," said Jason drily.

Nagel was less inclined to take matters philosophically. "You might have included us in your invisibility field!"

"As you may note, this is a very small model. It only works for a single individual. That individual's living flesh is the basis for the field, which conforms to the shape of the body. An area-effect field generator such as you are visualizing cannot be miniaturized to this level."

Nagel refused to be mollified. "You could at least have told us what you were going to do."

"There was no time. I had to act instantly, or I would have been captured. This way, at least one of us is at liberty—for now, at any rate."

"You don't sound too optimistic," Jason observed. "Do the Teloi have sensors that can detect an operating invisibility field?"

"They do. But such sensors are short-range, and

directional in nature. Still, I was listening when Perseus blurted out the fact that I was present—and that I had vanished, a feat whose explanation the Teloi know quite well. I'm only surprised that I was able to slip into this chamber so easily while the two of you were gone. I'm sure an organized search for me is afoot, even though I have seen no signs of it."

"In fact, it almost certainly isn't." Jason briefly described their interview with Hyperion and his fellows. "They never asked us about you," he concluded. "Zeus must have kept his knowledge to himself."

Oannes went absolutely silent and motionless for several heartbeats. Human ones, anyway. "This is . . . curious," he finally said. "I must think on it."

"While you're thinking on it, let me tell you what Hyperion *did* say. Their tame pirates are transporting the dimensional interface-*cum*-idol to Crete." The Teloi, of course, had used the current name *Keftiu* for the island, but mentally translating it had become automatic for Jason. "He also mentioned that most of the other Teloi are already on Kalliste, but that the pirates are going to observe the proprieties and take us to Crete first."

"So," said Oannes softly, "a major gathering of the Teloi on Kalliste . . ." He seemed to withdraw into deep thought, ignoring the humans.

"Uh . . . this might make it a little more complicated to get to your cache of Nagom tech on Kalliste, mightn't it?" Jason offered, in an attempt to bring Oannes out of his trance.

"Also," Nagel chimed in, "Hyperion said something about the 'most senior' of the Teloi being there. What did he mean by that?"

"What?" Oannes' nictitating membranes shuttered back and forth a few times, and he seemed to remember where he was. "Oh, yes. These Teloi have no rigidly structured organization, you understand. Such things do not come naturally to their race, and least of all to individuals like these who took up residence on this planet. And their interrelationships are in a constant state of flux due to their incessant intriguing among themselves, barely restrained by their consciousness of a common interest. But certain of their number possess more prestige than others. One in particular: the one known in this culture as Cronus."

"Zeus' father," Nagel breathed.

"Why, yes. How did you know?"

"The relationship is remembered in mythology even in our time."

"Well, he is the most powerful of the lot—the first among equals. The one to whom all the others defer." *The big enchilada*, Jason thought, summoning up a very old expression. "But they are going to be in the personal territory of Rhea, who has made Crete and the nearby islands her particular field of operations. Kalliste is something of a neutral meeting ground for them, but socially they are her guests when they are there."

"Our legends remember her as the wife of Cronus," said Nagel.

"There they are wrong. I daresay the later mythmakers will superimpose the family patterns they know onto their gods. But in fact the Teloi have no institution comparable to marriage. They are the ultimate atomic individuals, held together only by self-interest. And they practice absolute gender equality. It is only because childbirths are so very rare among them that the father is known with certainty."

Deirdre should approve, Jason reflected wryly. He was opening his mouth to ask a question when one of the small devices hanging from Oannes' harness began to beep in time with a flashing light. The Nagom hastily switched it off.

"You are about to receive visitors," he explained to Jason. Without another word, he touched another device, and faded into invisibility.

Jason barely had enough time to raise his lower jaw back into position when the door slid open to admit a Teloi—Jason thought he recognized the one called Helios—and one of the quietly floating servo-robots. Jason wondered if the robot's energy output was what Oannes' sensor had detected. It gathered up the dishes under Helios' watchful eye . . . and the hungry eyes of the humans, who couldn't admit that they hadn't been the ones to consume the food. After it had floated away, the Teloi turned to them.

"The portal device has arrived in Crete. Zeus will come for you soon. Prepare yourselves for departure."

All at once Jason's hunger was forgotten. He stared at Helios, waiting for something further that would cause what the Teloi had just said to make sense. But Helios only turned to go.

"Wait!" Jason called out. "Even if the pirates loaded that 'idol' onto a ship and started out the instant we were captured—"

Helios cut him off in a tone of puzzled contempt. "Of course they didn't. A ship had to be provisioned. And there are lengthy ritual observances that must be performed whenever the object is moved."

"But . . ." Desperately, Jason wondered if the brute-force imposition of the Teloi language on his brain's speech centers had left him with an even more imperfect understanding than he'd thought. "But . . . we *can't* be in Crete already!"

Helios gave him a look of uncomprehending irritation, and was gone. Jason was left staring at the closed door. Presently Oannes shimmered back into visibility.

"Did you hear?" Jason demanded.

"Yes. The field has no effect on atmospheric vibrations. There is another device which does in fact interfere with sound waves, by a process of—"

Jason wasn't in the mood. "Then what was all that nonsense about us already being in Crete?"

Oannes looked at him oddly. "You really *don't* understand, do you? Well, within an artificially created pocket dimension like this one, the time rate relative to the larger universe is entirely arbitrary. The Teloi prefer to arrange matters so that less time passes here than on the outside. Remember I mentioned that they are not really immortal. Of late, they have begun to suffer from intimations of mortality . . . especially their first generation. This is one way they can prolong the time in which they seem unchanged in the eyes of their human worshipers."

But Jason had stopped listening before the last two sentences.

As though from a great distance, he heard Nagel's voice. The historian had grasped one point at least. "Oannes, this is very important: *How much time has passed in the outside world while we've been here?*"

"I cannot possibly answer that question. As I have explained, it depends entirely on the time rate the Teloi have set—which I have no way of knowing."

"Well," Nagel spluttered, "how much time *can* have passed?"

"An interesting question. I do not know if there is a theoretical upper limit on the time-rate differential. However, there is no reason why such an upper limit would be approached in this case. At most, the pirates and their priests were probably allowed a relatively leisurely schedule to prepare for a visit to their overlords in Crete. I would be very surprised if the elapsed time has been more than a matter of weeks, or perhaps months."

"Months! But that means it may be autumn by now! So it's possible that already the—"

Realization of what Nagel was about to say brought Jason struggling up out of shock.

"Well, we'll find out soon, won't we?" he interrupted, forcing heartiness into his voice and clapping Nagel on the shoulder. That brought the historian's eyes around to stare at him. He met those eyes with a look that not even Nagel could misinterpret. Then he turned back to Oannes. "Tell us what's waiting for us in Crete."

"The pirate ship will have landed at Amnisos, the port of Knossos. There, you will be turned over to the Minos and conveyed to the palace."

"We've heard that title before," Nagel said eagerly. "Zeus used it. In our culture's myths, 'Minos' is the name of a king of Crete around whom many legends clustered—several generations' worth of them, in fact. For that reason, it has been widely supposed that 'Minos' was a title, like 'Pharoah' in Egypt."

"That is essentially correct. He is the priest-king. The priesthood in Crete is largely female, due to Rhea's primacy there. But the supreme head is required to be a warrior as well as a priest. That tradition has survived even though all of Crete has long since been so totally subservient to the rule of Knossos and its 'gods' that fortifications are unnecessary."

Another blow to the chops for poor old Sir Arthur Evans, Jason reflected.

Nagel's mouth was half open with another question when Oannes spoke hastily. "They are coming, doubtless to lead you to the portal. While this chamber is open, I will slip away. Remember: you must not reveal my existence to any of them except Zeus, who already knows."

"But what will you be doing?" Nagel asked.

"What I can." And Oannes was gone from sight, just as the door slid open to admit Zeus.

Jason expected to be whisked back to what he thought of as the "reception area" on one of the open aircars. But, as was often the case, Teloi behavior did not follow what seemed wholly logical patterns. They were marched through the endless corridors with Zeus in the lead. A couple of the hovering robots—no waiters these, fitted with paralysis weapons rather than dishes—followed watchfully behind.

"I've had time to think things through," Nagel whispered, emboldened by Zeus' seeming indifference to their presence. "Santorini—or 'Kalliste' as I suppose we should call it, since it's still one large island, not yet reduced to the islets of the Santorini group—must not have exploded yet, even if it is now autumn. After all, if the Teloi are aware that we've arrived in Crete, they must also be aware of conditions there. They could hardly have missed such a cataclysm!" He sounded positively chipper.

"That makes sense," Jason whispered back. "Only . . ."

He hesitated, and once again he heard that mocking echo of his own voice: *"No point in upsetting people with things they don't need to know. . . ."*

To hell with that! he thought savagely. *Sidney has a* right *to know. I told him we're all in this together. Did I mean that, or was I just farting at the wrong end?*

" 'Only' . . . ?" Nagel queried.

"There's something you haven't thought of, Sidney," Jason whispered harshly. "Remember what I told you about the TRDs? They activate automatically, at a preset time. And the timer uses an internal atomic clock. It's been ticking away while we've been in this mini universe—ticking at the same rate at which time moves here."

Nagel still looked blank. Jason drew a deep breath and reminded himself to continue speaking in a whisper.

"It hasn't ticked *enough* while we've been here, Sidney! As far as it's concerned, we've only spent a couple of days while the outside universe—the universe that includes the displacer stage in twenty-fourth century Australia—has spent weeks or months, according to Oannes. It's going to keep on ticking, until it reaches its preset number of ticks—which it won't do until weeks or months after it's supposed to, as far as the linear present is concerned."

Horrified understanding began to dawn in Nagel's face.

"So," Jason continued inexorably, "we won't appear on the stage at the moment we're scheduled to—an event unprecedented in the history of the Temporal Regulatory Authority. Instead, we'll appear at some point in time weeks or months later. Rutherford will have no way of knowing when that will be."

"And therefore won't know when to make sure the stage is clear for us," Nagel said tonelessly.

"You've grasped it," Jason sighed.

Then they could talk no longer, for they emerged into the "reception area"—the tiered, domed chamber from whose circumference the five main corridors receded like the spokes of a wheel. A live Teloi now sat at the small control panel where Perseus had left a dead one, and other tall alien figures stood about, waiting.

But Jason had no eyes for any of it. Another Teloi emerged from another of the five archways, leading another two humans.

"Deirdre!" he called out.

She looked around wildly, and grasped Perseus' arm more tightly. "Jason!" she shouted, spotting him.

But now there was something that had been absent when Jason had been here before, cut off by the dying hand of a Teloi. An immaterial three-yard hoop glowed in midair, and the eye flinched away from what was within it. Then, without any transition the eye and the mind could perceive, the hoop was gone and there was a hole in reality through which the light of the Mediterranean sun could be glimpsed.

Was it just Jason's imagination, or did that sunlight have a quality of autumn about it?

CHAPTER SEVENTEEN

The four humans were herded together and prodded forward. Their accustomed weight returned as they stepped across the intangible boundary and Earth's gravity reasserted control. Then they were through the portal, and the natural world was all around them, marred only by the circle through which the Teloi's extradimensional construct could be glimpsed like a smudge of something that should never have been.

Jason would never be religious. But as he stood in the sunlight and looked around at the sea and the land and the sky as they were intended to be, he thought he understood what it was that religious people felt.

The port of Amnisos was at the mouth of what passed for a river in Crete, a break in the yellow cliffs that made the island's coast so forbidding. The idol was still on the ship, but the portal had opened near the base of a mole which extended out into the water from a rough seawall, behind which brightly painted houses—some of them three or four stories—stood in ranks on the terraced shore. The paint—predominantly blue and white and red—could not compete in gaudiness with the crowd that now sank in one vast genuflection to the ground that Zeus' feet had touched. The peacock feathers on the men's turbanlike headdresses drooped and brushed the ground as they groveled, as did the less showy plumage on the women's small hats. From Jason's standpoint, those hats were the least exotic item of local feminine apparel—and the least interesting. They wore ankle-length, multilayered skirts, and tight, embroidered bodices that left the breasts exposed save for a wisp of translucent fabric. By contrast, the men wore little more than a combination of girdle and shorts. Both sexes wore an astonishing amount of makeup and jewelry.

Zeus spoke in a voice of rolling thunder. Jason decided the artificial amplification probably came from a tiny device stuck with adhesive to the divine throat. His words were addressed to a man kneeling before a thronelike chair on a platform resting on the backs of eight crouching slaves, and were spoken in the language of the islands, which Jason couldn't understand. But the Teloi must have granted permission to stand, for the man rose to his feet amid a general indrawing of breath at the stupendous honor being done him.

Perseus gasped. "The Minos himself! Here! He almost never leaves the palace."

Jason looked at the priest-king more closely. He wore a long, elaborate, deep-blue robe and an even more elaborate golden dress helmet shaped to suggest a bull's head, complete with horns. Even through the makeup that made his age impossible to estimate, his expression was unmistakable: bred-in arrogance currently overlaid with terror. The look was reflected in his voice as he spoke a response.

"Can you understand what they're saying, Perseus?" Jason whispered.

"Partly. On Seriphos, where I grew up, the common people speak a tongue much like that of Keftiu. Zeus has commanded the Minos to take us to the palace at Knossos and present us to the goddess Rhea. He is also to take the idol—it is to be in his care for a time. He also says . . . I couldn't really understand this part, Jason. He said you and Synon and Deianeira have affronted Cronus himself. What does he mean by that?"

Jason remained silent. Behind him, he heard Nagel mutter, "Cronus—the god of time."

"There's something else, Jason," Perseus continued in a troubled voice. "But surely I must have misunderstood it. I thought he said something about the sailing season being over, which was one of the reasons the idol is being left in the Minos' keeping for now. But how can that be, Jason? That's not until the autumn gales blow. And yet . . . the wind *does* seem to be blowing strongly from the west, doesn't it? And it seems cooler than it ought to be. What does it mean, Jason? What has happened?"

"I don't know," said Jason. *What else am I supposed to say?* he asked himself. Himself gave no answer.

The formalities came to an end. Zeus' "chariot" floated through the portal by itself, to a collective sound of rapturous awe from the crowd. *Remote control,* Jason thought, *must seem supernatural here.* Zeus boarded the aircar and flew away to the south. And, at what must have been a preset moment, the portal vanished.

It reminded Jason of something he had neglected for a while. He summoned up the map spliced into his optic nerve, and confirmed his near certainty. Only Nagel's TRD showed. Deirdre's must still be in the Teloi's pocket universe—a hole into which the dirt had just been pulled.

Then he remembered something else. He looked to the north, out to sea, at the horizon beyond which lay Kalliste, whose fragments would later be named Santorini.

Rising from that horizon was a faint tendril of smoke.

He and Nagel made eye contact. No words were needed.

The crowd dispersed, most of the dignitaries going to the slave-borne litters that Jason now noticed in the background. Other slaves, under the pompous supervision of priests, put the idol on a stretcherlike framework that seemed inadequate to carry it. Four of them lifted the framework up and conveyed the idol to a solid-wheeled cart drawn by garlanded oxen. It trundled off between the houses and onto the Knossos road, followed by the Minos on his super-litter (which was what he'd been standing on, atop the slaves' backs). That potentate was now seated but—Jason thought with a certain grim satisfaction—forced to breathe the oxen's dust as the idol preceded him. The prisoners were taken in hand by a squad of soldiers, equipped much like their mainland counterparts Jason had seen at Tiryns, complete with figure-eight shields covered with oxhide, but with more of an air of disciplined military polish. They fell in at the rear of the procession, and trudged along a road that wasn't the same as the one they'd taken from Herakleion in the twenty-fourth century, but which led through a landscape that was strangely similar despite being more forested . . . although the slave gangs toiling in the olive groves and orchards were a jarring touch.

After a time, the road joined the one with which Jason was familiar—or at least its ancestor. So he knew what to expect when they neared the foothills of the distant mountain range. Or at least he thought he did. But then they passed beyond the screen of cypresses.

Jason had seen Sir Arthur Evans' reconstructions, and he had seen numerous artists' conceptions. Neither had prepared him for the sheer impact of tiered and terraced colonnades, crowning the ridge and covering its slopes with loggia after stepped-back loggia, rank after rank of downward-tapering red pillars, the roofline crowned with stylized bulls' horns that arrogantly gored the sky.

His intellect reminded him of the pyramids and the Great Wall of China, and insisted that, like those, Knossos embodied nothing that couldn't be accomplished with enough slaves and enough time. The rest of him knew he was seeing something that did not belong in this era.

He felt the collective motion of the column halting, and looked back over his shoulder. Perseus had stopped dead as though from a blow to the gut. He had never seen, or imagined, such a place as this. *What must he be feeling?* Jason wondered. *The Teloi pocket universe was a thing of the gods, so it was* supposed *to be incomprehensible. But he knows what man-made things are like, and he knows this cannot be one of them.*

Nagel had also halted, but his face wore another expression. It was not an expression Jason could put a name to.

But he knew that if they all died in the next hour, Nagel would count it worthwhile.

"Move, dog dirt!" growled a guard in heavily accented Achaean. He prodded Perseus in the back with his spear butt.

The numbed expression vanished from the Hero's face, replaced by something else. Jason knew what that something was, and he braced himself for the explosion of superhumanly swift violence that would leave half the guards dead or dying and the other half looking down on four corpses. . . .

But then Deirdre touched Perseus' arm and whispered something inaudible in his ear. The moment passed. They all stumbled forward.

The procession followed the road past villas that would have been impressive in any other setting, with an outdoor amphitheater in the distance to the left. Here the oxcart turned left and moved away toward the northern end of the palace. The rest of them continued on before turning, and approached the palace from the west across a kind of open plaza. They entered through a propylon with a great red lintel-column rising from its gleaming floor. "The West Porch," Nagel said, not seeming to care who heard him . . . and Jason knew where he was, in terms of what he had seen in the twenty-fourth century. He also knew that something was missing.

"Sidney," he whispered, as they were waiting for the Minos to descend, stepping on the back of a slave who crouched to serve as his step stool. "Where are the frescoes?"

"What?" Nagel shook himself out of the trance he'd fallen into as he avidly sought to memorize everything his eyes took in. "Oh, yes. They haven't been painted yet.

That has been recognized for a long time . . . that is, it *will* have been recognized for a long time in our era . . . oh, you know what I mean! Anyway, the frescoes we associate with Knossos date from the period of the New Palace—slightly later than this, although much is unclear about just exactly when and how the transition took place. Equally unclear is the reason for the artistic efflorescence that will take place then. But it appears that the basic structure of the palace has reached its final form by now, as has long been suspected."

Then further conversation became impossible as the procession got moving again. They entered through a doorway to the left, and proceeded along a long corridor whose floor of cemented stone slabs had a central causeway of gypsum. ("The Corridor of the Procession," Nagel murmured.) Eventually the passageway took a right turn, and a terrace with a loggia could be glimpsed through openings to the right, giving light. More light came from an open area to the left, which they passed through and entered an elaborate entryway. ("The South Propylaeum," Nagel's monologue continued.) Beyond was a wide staircase, open to the sky, atop which was a vestibule giving entry to a vast colonnaded hall into which light filtered from an open corridor to the left and glinted on the spearpoints of the ranked guards. They turned again, crossing the cement-paved corridor under the sky, and entered the vastest hall yet, its roof supported by two massive central columns. Here, the Minos settled onto a gypsum throne set against the far wall, and the courtiers took their ceremonial places. The guards prodded the four prisoners forward to stand before the throne, at a considerable distance.

It was undeniably an impressive display of architecture, especially considering that all this mass was on the second story. (Jason recalled, with the help of his implant, that it rested on great masonry piers on ground level, where the storerooms for the Minos' treasure were located.) But it all had a hieratic oppressiveness that not even the ubiquitous light wells could alleviate. These walls were painted, but only in uninspired geometric patterns. Nowhere was there any trace of the dazzling frescoes—the naturalistic, life-affirming art that later ages would link admiringly with the Minoans. The insistent background chanting and the pervasive smell of incense didn't help.

Then the crowd parted as a line of women entered from a door to the right. They were dressed in the usual way, except that their breasts lacked even the largely symbolic covering provided by the usual translucent chemises, and their long dresses had even more layers and flounces, dyed in every color of the rainbow. The one in the lead seemed middle-aged—although it was hard to tell, through the makeup that practically disguised her membership in the human family. She wore a tall, gilded headdress shaped like a tapering cylinder, its surface fashioned into a pair of circling snakes. She and the Minos—who appeared to be doing an admirable job of controlling his joy at seeing her—spoke what seemed to be a series of responsive formulas. Then the ceremony ended. The priestesses, as Jason assumed them to be, led the way out, and the prisoners were hustled along in their wake.

"What was that all about, Perseus?" Jason dared to whisper as they crossed the open corridor.

"I'm not sure. They were using an old-fashioned form of the Keftiu tongue, different from what the people speak nowadays. But I think the priestesses are taking us before the goddess Rhea for purification. The Minos has to allow it, before he can do whatever it is he plans for us."

Jason nodded. He didn't pretend to Nagel's knowledge of this milieu, but he had spent time in the Middle Ages, and he recalled the delicate balance between "the Church Militant" and "the Secular Arm."

They returned the way they had come, down the broad staircase and through the vestibule to the processional corridor, but this time they turned in the opposite direction, then turned left. Jason began to understand the legend of the Labyrinth.

They finally emerged into the great central court. This, at least, resembled the artists' conceptions, surrounded by three levels of colonnaded terraces, broken by various staircases and monumental entryways. Then they were across the courtyard and into a stairwell illuminated by clerestories. ("The Grand Staircase," Nagel breathed.) They ascended a flight of steps, threaded more passageways, and then turned into a great multipillared area with three light wells. ("The Hall of the Double Axe," Nagel whispered.) Jason saw the ornamental axes that were to give the hall its archaeological name, mounted on pillars. In the center of the floor was a sunken water-filled basin. But he hardly noticed any of this, for at the far end loomed a statue that was like the image of the chief priestess, only twice her height and incomparably more resplendent—or, some might have said, gaudy—with skin of ivory, hair of bronze, and lacquer dress glittering with precious stones in the dim clerestory light. The arms were outstretched, and around them coiled golden serpents. Also of gold were the nipples and other areas that were covered with makeup on the living version. Imagination failed at the cost of the thing.

The chief priestess abased herself before the statue, and a great deal of responsive chanting went on between her and her subordinates in the archaic cult language. Perseus was clearly straining to understand it, and the longer it went on the more agitated he looked.

The priestess turned her dark, heavily mascaraed eyes on the prisoners, and deigned to speak in accented Achaean. "You are to be purified," she intoned, indicating the lustral basin. "Afterwards, you will be dedicated to the Goddess Rhea. You, Perseus of Seriphos, are to be housed with the woman Deianeira, for the gods have plans for the two of you. The men Jason and Synon are to be gelded, thus rendering them more acceptable to the goddess."

For the first time, Jason noticed a stone table off to the right. It held a set of bronze knives. An older-than average priestess stood beside it, flanked by brawny male assistants. Was it just his imagination, or did he detect a glint of eagerness in her eyes?

He forced his heart rate down as he looked behind him at the ranked guards. *Maybe if I spring forward before the guards have time to react I can grab the chief priestess and use her for a hostage. . . .* No. If all else failed, a Teloi would come and simply paralyze all concerned. And afterwards, the priestesses would really make it last.

So let's see, he thought as sweat began to pop out. *What can I say—what appeals, or warnings, or anything else—that will cut any ice here?*

He was still wondering when Perseus—who, he would have thought, had less cause for alarm than any of them—suddenly stepped forward and cried out in a voice that dispelled the funereal solemnity like a strong wind blowing away dust and cobwebs.

"No! I am Perseus, son of Zeus, and I do not belong to the goddess Rhea, or to any of the Old Gods. I am my father's, for him alone to judge."

Only one guard was able to break free of the general speechless horror. "Silence, barbarian!" he hissed, stepping forward. His tall figure-eight shield was at his side, not covering his bare torso. With his usual hair-trigger swiftness, Perseus rammed an elbow backwards into the unprotected solar plexus. The guard doubled over in a clatter of dropped spear and shield. The Hero took another step forward, and only the basin separated him from the chief priestess, who stood as immobile as the statue behind her.

Perseus met her unblinking eyes, and his voice rang. "I call on my father!"

"Do you?" came a new voice.

Behind the statue, a glow of light appeared. *There must be a doorway back there,* Jason told himself. The sound that went up as the crowd sank to its hands and knees was one of terror held tightly in check lest it provoke something even worse than its object of fear.

The light intensified into an instant's eye-hurting glare, and at that moment one of the Teloi "chariots" drifted out, holding a female Teloi. Even in his present frame of mind, he couldn't help admiring the sheer theatricalism of the entrance. Something else he couldn't help admiring, since the "goddess" was dressed in a version of the priestesses' costume—or, more likely, the original of that costume—was the incontrovertible proof that the Teloi species was mammalian.

The herd sound in the hall sank to a low moan, above which rose occasional wails of "Rhea!"

Even Perseus took a step back. Jason was glad he wasn't on the receiving end of the look Rhea gave the Hero.

"Your kind has always been a disappointment to us, Perseus. Even more of a disappointment than the ordinary human stock, from whom nothing better can be expected." She ran her gaze over the crowd, which cringed with new intensity, as though trying to burrow into the floor and escape those terrible eyes. She turned away from them with disgusted contempt and addressed Perseus alone. "Yes . . . we gods had high hopes for your kind. But instead of guiding the lesser humans into a proper reverence for their creators, you have proven more apt to lead them into even more blatant acts of disobedience and presumptuousness! So it has been ever since the time of Gilgamesh, a thousand years ago. But now you have invented a whole new form of insolence, by seeking the aid of one immortal against another! All the more so because the god you invoke is one of the younger generation, whose filial duty to us of the—"

"I no longer acknowledge the Old Gods!" Perseus' words seemed to hang suspended in the incense-heavy air, and Jason expected a new exhalation of horror at his act of interrupting the goddess. But there was nothing. The blasphemy the Hero had uttered was beyond the threshold of outrage. Even Rhea was speechless.

"The Old Gods broke the link between themselves and mortals when they violated the law that separates the living from the dead," Perseus continued into the silence he had created. "They loosed the bonds that hold together all the certainties that have always existed in the world . . . including their own right to our worship. So now—"

"Be silent!" Rhea shouted, abruptly emerging from her shock into something approaching hysteria. "Do you dare to claim that there are laws governing the world which bind the gods themselves? And that mortals can hold the gods answerable for failure to abide by these laws? This is madness! We owe you nothing, and you owe us everything. You need us!"

"We need gods . . . but perhaps not all the gods. I call again upon my father Zeus!"

"He will not answer. He knows his place."

But then Jason became aware of a second glow of light, this time from behind him. He turned and stared as Zeus glided in, the guards scattering before him and falling to the floor.

Rhea stared, speechless, and her alien face wore an expression Jason could not interpret. But then the spell broke, and she spoke in a peremptory rush.

The crowd wore a look of uncomprehending awe, for this was not the ceremonial tongue of Crete, nor even related to it, or to any language ever fashioned for human throats. In fact, their expressions told Jason they had never heard this language before. He had, for he remembered these sounds, from another dimension. But he couldn't understand that angry staccato outburst. An academically correct form of the Teloi language had been brutally forced upon his brain. It had enabled him to converse with Hyperion and Zeus. But he didn't have a prayer of following this spate of idiomatic invective.

Zeus responded in the same tongue, not with Rhea's asperity but in a low rumble of deep passion—and, from Jason's perspective, just as incomprehensibly rapid-fire. He gestured toward Perseus as he spoke. Rhea replied with rising anger.

The priestesses and the guards were now prostrate, not even daring to moan, and the air of the hall was thick with the bewildered terror of small children first witnessing a violent quarrel between their parents.

Finally, Rhea overrode Zeus with a series of harsh syllables. Zeus fell silent, and sullenly backed away toward the rear of the hall from whence he had come. Rhea drew a deep breath and addressed the chief priestess in the ritual tongue. The chief priestess gave a series of stunned nods and got to her feet. Two of her juniors hurried forward to restore her lofty diadem, which had fallen off. Having it back on seemed to fortify her. She turned back to the prisoners with a glare of indescribable loathing.

"The goddess declares that thanks to your impiety the ritual is spoiled. It must be resumed from the beginning at another time, with all the proprieties observed, to restore the link between mortals and the gods. At present, you may not be purified. For now you will be returned to the custody of the Minos and imprisoned. Guards, get them out of my sight!"

The guards hastened to obey. As they were being hustled out, Jason caught the eye of the priestess beside the table with the knives. Even after what had just happened, her disappointment was palpable. Jason gave her the most irritating look he could manage.

They were almost to the door when Perseus broke free and stood before Zeus. He flung his arms wide and cried out in a voice that held desperation but no trace of pleading.

"Father Zeus! I can offer you no sacrifice, here in this place. But I swear that if you aid me I will forge a kingdom where only the New Gods are worshipped—and you will be acknowledged as chief among them! You will be the god of kings . . . and the king of gods!"

"Silence him!" shrieked the chief priestess.

Shaken as they were, the guards responded. A spear butt descended on the back of Perseus' head, and others smashed at him as he fell forward. Two guards grasped his arms and dragged him out. The others nudged Jason and Nagel out with spearpoints. As they went, they passed Zeus.

The Teloi had not reacted visibly to Perseus' plea. And he remained still, not meeting Jason's eye. But he wore an expression that Jason could have sworn was . . . interested.

CHAPTER EIGHTEEN

They took the Grand Staircase back down . . . and down, and down. It extended two stories below the level of the central court, into depths which had been dug away centuries earlier from the eastern slope of the ridge which the palace crowned—regions where the clerestory light was dim indeed, and the foundations showed in all their brutal and unornamented massiveness.

"The archaeologists have never been able to entirely sort this area out," Nagel murmured as they were prodded—or, in Perseus' case, dragged—through torch-lit corridors. Jason concentrated on observing, enabling his implant to supplement the floor plan. They finally reached a bronze-studded hardwood door.

"In, mainland trash!" said the guard captain in almost incomprehensible Achaean. They were shoved through, and the door crashed shut behind them.

They were in a surprisingly large but rather low-ceilinged chamber, lit by shallow windows—little more than slits—near the top of the opposite wall. Nagel ran to that wall and, by standing on tiptoes, was able to peer out the window.

"We're in the east wing, near the base of the outer wall—this window is just above ground level, which slopes away to the east. I can barely see the East Bastion, off to the left—it has always been regarded as the only means of egress or ingress on this side of the palace. And . . . yes! Down below is what has to be the bullring. I *knew* it! It's the only suitable area. They couldn't possibly have used the central courtyard for that purpose! Jason, come over here and look at it so it will be recorded."

"Later, Sidney," Jason sighed, sinking to the floor, resting his back against one of the wooden pillars that upheld the roof. The historian had clearly forgotten everything about their current situation, including the unlikelihood of their ever getting back to the world of scholarly publications. Jason's own chief concern about the windows was their potential as a means of escape—and they were far too shallow for any adult human body to pass through.

Deirdre had gone to her knees above the unconscious form of Perseus. She observed his eyes and satisfied herself that his breathing was regular, then went to a pile of dirty rags in one corner beside a hole in the floor over which they were presumably expected to perform their bodily functions. (Jason recalled the inside plumbing that had amazed Knossos' late-Victorian excavators.) She made a rough pillow for him out of one of the rags. Then, unable to do any more, she finally met Jason's eyes.

"Hi," he ventured, essaying a grin.

She responded with a weary smile. " 'Hi,' yourself. We've got some catching up to do, don't we?"

"You might say that. Starting when you fell into the water off Cape Taenarum."

"Right. After Oannes' sub surfaced, I was trying to get out of it when that particle beam hit. The concussion threw me, and I banged my head against a stanchion and lost consciousness. I must have slid out when the sub started to list."

"You sank like a stone. Perseus tried to save you. Afterwards, he really tore himself apart for failing."

"I know he did," she said softly. "But the Teloi must have fished me out of the water, because the next thing I remember is having salt water pumped out of me." Her eyes were haunted by the memory of that experience. "That was in the Teloi pocket universe."

Jason nodded. They must have taken her directly into the caverns by aircar, and through the portal, using some kind of artificial aid to keep her drowned body from crossing the threshold of death.

"Afterwards, they put me in something like a hospital recovery room. Hyperion and some others questioned me about the TRD. I told them the truth up to a point—that time travel isn't my specialty, and I couldn't help them with the theory. But then I used my imagination, and made up a story about how the TRD itself was what allowed us to travel in time, but only under the control of our masters uptime."

"Good work," Jason said with feeling. Judging from what Hyperion had told them, the disinformation had taken root.

"Thanks. Anyway, there was just the one interrogation session. After which," she added emotionlessly, "they did a biopsy. Then I was back in the recovery room . . . but only for a little while, before they opened the door and shoved Perseus in." She suddenly looked embarrassed.

"You and he . . . ?" Jason let the sentence trail off on a note on inquiry.

Her embarrassment wasn't entirely gone, but she met his eyes squarely. "Yes." She gave a quick, rueful half-smile-and-shrug combination that spoke volumes. "Anyway," she hurried on, "we were only together for a little while before they hustled us out, and we found out we were here in Crete. I guess they must have flown the portal device here."

"No, they didn't." Jason told her about the differential time rate in the Teloi's private dimension, and repeated what he had told Nagel about the consequences of their stay there.

He didn't expect hysterics—not from her. But she still surprised him with her stoicism. After a heartbeat's silence, all she said was: "How do you know about the time rate?"

He lowered his voice, even though he was certain there were no surveillance devices here. "Oannes told me."

"Oannes?"

"Yes. We met him on the beach after getting off the sub. How much did Perseus tell you about what we had been up to?"

"He told me Oannes led the three of you through the caverns of Hades, and into the realm of the dead, which is where he thinks we were. I wasn't sure what to make of it all."

"That account is close enough. Anyway, when they caught us Oannes avoided capture with an invisibility device he's got. He made contact with us just before you saw us—that was when he told me about the time effects. He also said he was going to try to slip out through the portal while it was open at Amnisos. I don't know whether he succeeded or not, or what he's up to if he did."

"I hope he succeeded. If so, we have one thing going for us."

"We may have another. Zeus is playing some kind of game I don't understand. For one thing, he kept the fact of Oannes' presence to himself after Perseus blurted it out to him."

"That's something, maybe . . . for whatever good it does, given what you've just told me." She managed a smile of sorts. "Maybe I'm better off than you and Sidney after all, with my TRD cut out of me."

"Don't think you're getting off that easily! We'll get yours back, and then you'll have to take your chances with the rest of us. When we fail to appear on the displacer stage on schedule, I guarantee Rutherford will call a halt to any further departures pending an investigation. Hopefully, the moratorium will last until we do reappear. Of course, he can't stop returns from the past that are already locked in. But he can and will hustle them off the stage as quickly as possible. It has to improve our chances."

"I suppose so." She looked a little more cheerful. But then a new thought seemed to occur to her. "Jason . . . just exactly how much time passed in the outside world while we were in that other dimension?"

"I can't answer that, Deirdre. Not even Oannes could answer it. All I know is that it's autumn now."

"Autumn?" Urgency awoke in her eyes, as it had not when her personal survival had been all that was at issue. "Do you understand what that means, Jason? Kalliste could blow at any time!"

His eyes fell, unable to meet hers. "Before we left Amnisos, I looked northward. I saw a curl of smoke on the horizon."

"Oh, God!" She could think of nothing more to say. Jason couldn't think of anything either. They sat in silence as Nagel babbled on about some new archaeological enigma he'd glimpsed.

Guards brought them barely edible food and stagnant water twice daily. Otherwise, they were ignored in a way that was more nerve-wracking than constant attention from their captors would have been. Which, Jason reflected, was perhaps not an altogether bad thing. Without the tension, it would have been easy to lose track of the days.

Perseus soon recovered—he had a very hard head—and afterwards he held up under the tedium better than any of them. His background hadn't predisposed him to expect continuous stimulation, or robbed him of the ability to wait. He could sit cross-legged for hours, armored in a kind of patience latter-day humanity was to lose. Deirdre was able to draw on his reserves of strength as she spent more and more time sitting with him, although touching hands was the most they could do in the utter absence of privacy.

Jason and Nagel could only peer out the slit of a window for distraction. They never saw any Teloi, but there were occasional ceremonies in the cleared area Nagel had spotted on the meadows at the foot of the east slope, toward the Kairatos River. On one of those occasions, Jason's computer implant played what he had seen back for him in enlarged form, and he saw teenaged boys and girls vaulting over a charging bull, like Arthur Evans' restored frescoes come to life. Afterwards, the bull was sacrificed with much pomp and even more gore. He started to congratulate Nagel on the confirmation of his theory that this was the bullring, but then thought better of it. Frustration at not being able to share Jason's close-up view was not something the historian needed at this juncture.

The end of their incarceration, when it came, was disorientingly sudden. With no more warning than a muffled sound of tramping feet in the passageway, the bronze-studded doors were flung open to admit a file of guards. They were herded into the corridor and marched back the way they had come, to the Grand Staircase and up two flights. They emerged into the central courtyard, where more guards were drawn up in the midafternoon sun, flanking an array of priestesses. Beyond them was the three-storied west façade, on whose upper loggias Jason spotted the deep-blue robe and golden headdress of the Minos. He seemed to be overseeing the proceedings, but from a distance. The prisoners were still under the jurisdiction of the chief priestess, who stepped forward and addressed them in a voice whose formality almost overlay its vindictiveness.

"We have word from the gods," she began, suggesting to Jason that the gods were physically elsewhere—on Kalliste or in their private dimension, he had no way of knowing which. "The ritual may begin anew—but under the sky, at the place of sacrifice. We are also permitted to punish any interruptions." This last was accompanied by a glare at Perseus. Out of the corner of his eye, Jason saw Deirdre lay a restraining hand on the Hero's arm. He also saw the priestess who had stood beside the table in the Hall of the Double Axe. A slave accompanied her, bearing a kind of tray over which was draped a cloth, presumably concealing the cutlery.

The guards formed up, boxing the prisoners in, and the procession wound its way through a narrow roofless passageway and through what Nagel muttered was the "North Entrance." After a brief observance by the chief priestess at a sunken lustral basin to the left, they turned right and made their way around the palace and along a pathway leading down the eastern slopes to the bullring.

The chief priestess evidently wished to expedite things, for the bull-vaulters were already performing. Even at this moment, Jason could only stare wonderingly at their athleticism and courage. One after another, they grabbed the horns of the charging bull, somersaulted onto its back as it tossed its head, then did a backwards somersault over its hindquarters, to be caught by the preceding boy or girl—it wasn't always easy to tell which was which, despite the fact that they all wore a girdle and nothing else, for they were so young, and had approximately one percent body fat overlaying their wiry muscularity. Completely impossible to determine was the sex of the one who was being dragged off the ring, leaving a trail of blood from the hideous wound the goring horn had left. Jason was glad he'd missed that.

The only unexpected thing was the sheer number of bull-vaulters. The frescoes had shown only one team in action. Here, they were operating in relays, for the object was to wear the bull down in a ritually acceptable way. This one was lathered, and visibly slowing. Soon he could move no more, and the priestesses' male assistants moved forward to take him in hand. They led him, panting and heaving, to where another priest waited with the bronze original of the symbolic double axe.

A small part of Jason appreciated the irony of the sympathy he found himself feeling for the magnificent beast, when he ought to be saving all his sympathy for himself.

The chief priestess stepped forward and intoned a litany in the old tongue. The priest raised his axe—

Something caught Jason's eye, rolling across the ground and bouncing to a halt only a few yards away. The chief priestess noticed it too. Her fury at the impious interruption seemed tempered by puzzlement at what the bumpy, pineapple-sized plastic sphere was.

Jason, however, was fairly sure he knew. It wasn't the same as the twenty-fourth century riot-suppression models he was used to, but—*"Close your eyes!"* he yelled, and, before the guards could react, spread his arms wide and shoved all three of his companions away from the odd little object.

Even through eyelids squeezed tightly shut, he was dazzled by the rapid, stroboscopic flashing of super-intense light. A pandemonium of screaming arose from those who had been blinded, those who had gone into seizures, and those who were merely in the grip of panic, almost as loud as the high-pitched bellowing of the bull.

After ten seconds, the horrible flashing ceased. Jason opened his eyes and looked around. They were alone, for everyone else was either fleeing, or thrashing about in the throes of symptoms not unlike those of epilepsy, or crawling about sightless. The chief priestess, who had been looking directly at the grenade, was one of the latter. Jason had no liking for her, but he couldn't bring himself to feel any satisfaction at her wails of despair as she clawed at the eyes she believed (inaccurately, she would later find) to be permanently blinded. He did feel satisfaction as he saw that the bull had broken free and was thundering away through the already panicked humans.

He was still watching when all at once the universe turned to blurry shades of gray, and the noise ceased.

"I was hoping you would recognize the weapon for what it was," Oannes said quietly.

Jason turned. The Nagom was removing a pair of goggles. He wore a bulky device strapped to his back.

"One of the 'area-effect' versions you mentioned before?" Jason queried, indicating the backpack.

"With a radius that can envelop all of us if we stay close together," Oannes affirmed. "And incorporating a sonic privacy field, so that we are inaudible as well as invisible. But further explanations must wait." The Nagom switched from Teloi to Achaean so that Deirdre and Perseus could understand. "Come quickly. There is a cave down by the river where we can hide. And I don't think anyone will be venturing in this direction before tomorrow."

Jason gestured to the others. Deirdre and Nagel were blinking away the constellations of novas still exploding before their eyes, but at least they weren't blinded. Neither was Perseus, who seemed able to function in the face of one more manifestation of the supernatural. They formed a tight group and hurried down the slopes, carefully avoiding the convulsing or moaning figures that littered the ground.

As was the case with all the rivers of Crete, "river" was too strong a word for the Kairatos. In summer it was little more than a trickle, and even now it was best described as a stream. Likewise, Oannes' use of the word "cave" gave too much credit to the overhanging rock outcropping to which he led them. There he eased his backpack to the ground and touched its controls. The world came back into focus.

"I must conserve the energy source," he explained. "And I have warning devices out, in case of any intruders."

"That's reassuring," Jason sighed. "And thanks are certainly in order. But about those 'further explanations' . . ."

"Ah, yes. As you will have gathered, I made good my escape through the portal at Amnisos. I immediately set out for Kalliste—"

"Across almost seventy miles of open sea?" Deirdre interrupted.

"Remember, my species is fully amphibious. And I carry food concentrates which keep the body going . . . without, unfortunately, appeasing the pangs of hunger. By great exertions, I was able to make the crossing in three days, even though"—a touch of vanity—"I'm not as young as I once was. There, I went to the cache I mentioned. It held, among other things, another undersea craft like the one we lost off Cape Taenarum. I returned here in only an hour or so, concealed the craft on the coast not far from Amnisos, and made my way here, where I have been awaiting an opportunity to free you."

Deirdre had obviously stopped listening after hearing where the Nagom had been. She spoke with tightly controlled urgency. "Oannes, when you were on Kalliste, what was happening there?"

"'Happening'? Well, I had neither the opportunity nor the time for observations. But my impression was that most of the 'Old Gods' are not currently present there. Presumably they are in—"

"No, no, no! I mean volcanic activity."

"Ah, yes. The smoke rising from the island made it quite easy for me to find! As I understand, that smoke has been endemic since an eruption some months ago, and there have been occasional rumblings. Considerable damage was done at the time, but the people returned and cleaned up. The inhabitants of this part of the planet tend to be somewhat fatalistic about that sort of thing."

Deirdre was no longer listening to him. "The preliminary eruption . . . yes. And several months ago . . ." She looked up, and her eyes were haunted. No words were needed.

She knows, Jason thought. *It's going to happen any time now—one of the most destructive natural events in the lifetime of the human race.*

Nagel hadn't spoken in some time. He wore a look of intense thought. Now, abruptly, he spoke up in the Teloi tongue. "Oannes . . . what would happen if the idol concealing the portal device was destroyed?"

Oannes' nictitating membranes fluttered with surprise, as though he'd never thought of that. "Destroyed? Well, it is of course the only one they have. Extremely restricted access is, after all, the whole point to their private pocket universe. If it were destroyed, that pocket universe would be inaccessible until such time as a new device was constructed. That last is a purely theoretical qualifier, you understand, as the technology to construct such a device does not exist on this world."

"And if the Teloi were inside the pocket universe at the time?"

"Well . . . they would, I suppose, be trapped there permanently. But this entire line of thought is purely academic. The device is *extremely* durable, for obvious reasons. And don't forget the self-repairing capability that has enabled the Teloi equipment to last all these millennia. Any damage that could be done with the tools of the local human culture would be only temporary. Nothing would serve short of total obliteration by some truly cataclysmic force!"

Nagel turned to Jason. They stared at each other.

"Sidney," Jason finally said, "are you thinking what I'm thinking?"

CHAPTER NINETEEN

In the ensuing silence, everyone but Jason and Nagel looked bewildered—Deirdre and Perseus more so than Oannes, because the Teloi language was gibberish to them.

"Perseus," said Jason in Achaean, "there is something you must know. The lady Deianeira has a limited gift of foreseeing the future."

That which no one of Jason's era could know awoke behind the Hero's eyes as he stared at Deirdre. "An . . . an oracle?" he stammered.

"No. It is only intermittently and unexpectedly that a god comes to her. But she has received a warning of an overwhelming punishment that the Fates hold in store for Keftiu, and for the Old Gods who are worshipped there." Jason turned to Deirdre, who was quite clearly wondering what he was up to. "Tell Oannes and Perseus what you have told us about what is going to happen to the island of Kalliste."

Deirdre was now frankly confused at the sudden reversal of every cautionary thing she'd ever heard from Jason about sharing information with non-time travelers. But she played along gamely, and proceeded to relate the tale she had told him one evening on a restaurant terrace overlooking the Santorini caldera . . . but in the future tense, and within the limitations of Achaean.

By the time she was finished, the sun was setting. Jason watched Oannes' face in the shadows—the alien face he flattered himself he'd learned to read. What he read there now was an amused realization of the kind of "magic" by which Deirdre knew what was going to come to pass . . . and an understanding of what Jason and Nagel had in mind.

But it was Perseus who broke the silence. "Poseidon Earthshaker must have brought this vision to you, Deianeira. Only he could alter the world in the way you have foreseen—and even he would need the help of Hephaestus, god of volcanoes. A whole island . . . !"

"Yes!" Jason plunged into the opening. "It can only be Poseidon. And he is one of the New Gods: brother to your father Zeus." Perseus nodded, to Jason's relief; he'd been hoping the relationship was recognized in this era as it would be in later Classical times. "Well, then, this surely is a . . . uh, sign that the Fates have completed the doom of the Old Gods. And," he pressed on, inventing freely and ignoring Deirdre's dropped jaw, "Deianeira has received a further vision that we ourselves are to be the instruments of their downfall. We must steal their idol from this place and take it to Kalliste, so that it may be consumed in the fires Deianeira has foretold!" He hoped this wasn't starting to sound more like Tolkien than Homer. Perseus' look of openmouthed awe encouraged him.

"Yes," Oannes intoned for Perseus' benefit. "I, too, see the Fates in this. I know of a . . . grotto on Kalliste where we can conceal the idol." He and Jason shared a surreptitious eye contact of shared understanding.

"Thank you, Oannes," said Perseus simply. "We will need all the help we can get."

"You certainly will," said Zeus.

Well, so much for Oannes' "warning devices," flashed through Jason's mind as they all whirled to stare at the eight-foot-tall figure standing beside the stream in the twilight. *The Teloi must have countermeasures.*

With a motion almost too swift to be seen, Oannes snatched what looked like a small weapon from his utility harness. At the same instant, Zeus leveled a "head of the Hydra" at him. Neither fired. They stood locked in a standoff and stared silently at each other over their weapons, these enemies in an ages-long war of extermination that had burned its genocidal way across the stars. None of the humans dared move.

The tension was like a drawn wire at its snapping point when Perseus finally spoke. "Father, I have asked for your help. I ask it again now. The sea god Oannes has already agreed to aid us."

Amusement lifted the corners of the Teloi's wide mouth, although his weapon hand didn't waver by a millimeter. " 'Sea god,' is it?" he said in his own language. "I can think of other terms for the Nagommo!"

"And yet," Jason ventured, "you didn't betray him when you had the chance."

"No," the Teloi admitted, without letting his eyes leave the Nagom's. "Any secret one possesses—including that of his presence—is a potential weapon. As such, I cannot afford to throw it away. Not at the present time."

"And I know why," said Oannes. "These humans don't understand the game you are playing. But I do . . . and I understand its urgency."

"Quiet, Nagom!" hissed the Teloi.

Oannes ignored him and addressed Jason. "Remember when we spoke of the two generations of Teloi on this world? I told you that obscure environmental factors prevented the second generation, such as this one, from having children. I did not mention at the time that there are other effects as well. In particular—"

"I said—!"

"If you were going to risk trying to shoot me," Oannes said serenely to his ancestral enemy, "you would already have done so." He turned back to Jason. "As I was saying, the Earth-born generation's lifespan is drastically curtailed. It is still long on my standards, and extremely long on yours. But they cannot expect to outlive their elders."

Zeus' expression made Jason wonder if Oannes' confidence in his self-restraint was misplaced. But then his face cleared with an abruptness beyond the normal capacity of humans.

"Very well," he said evenly. "There is no point in denying it. My contemporaries and I have little to look forward to. And we have . . . certain resentments. So much so that I am even willing to act in concert with a Nagom." He turned to the obviously stunned Oannes. "I will now put away my weapon if you are prepared to do the same."

For a moment, the two pairs of alien eyes remained locked. Then, slowly, the two weapons lowered. Jason knew he would never fully appreciate what that gesture must have cost Oannes and Zeus. He did know, without being told, that he was witnessing a moment unique in history.

Zeus turned to Perseus and spoke in Achaean. "Perseus, I have heard your appeal for help. And you are right: the day of Cronus and Rhea and the rest of the Old Gods is over. I and my brothers and sisters—Poseidon and Hera and Ares and the rest—will not allow them to vent their senile envy on you."

This is getting deeper, thought Jason cynically. But then he saw the look Zeus was giving Perseus, and wondered. *Hmm . . . Could it be that there's more to this than just a Teloi power play? And could it be that the parental instinct wasn't edited out of their genetic code quite so thoroughly after all? Do they need a substitute?*

Perseus met the Teloi's strange eyes. "Father, I swore to establish your worship. I will keep my word, if you will take me to Mycenae."

"Mycenae?" Nagel echoed.

"Yes! Deianeira has told us what will ensue from Poseidon's destruction of Kalliste: earthquakes, tidal waves like mountains, darkness overspreading the daytime sky! If even half of it comes to pass, Keftiu will be prostrate. A small band of raiders who know in advance what is going to happen, appearing in the wake of the gods' anger, will be able to seize Knossos, kill the Minos, and take control. There will be a new order among men, to match the new order among the immortals, with you, Father, recognized as the ruler of the heavens!"

All of them, even Zeus, simply stared at the Hero, whose eyes blazed like openings through which could be glimpsed a soul made of pure fire.

Nagel finally spoke, almost timidly. "Why Mycenae? Isn't it a small, unimportant site in this era?"

"That's the whole point," said Perseus, too excited to notice the historian's slip of the tongue. "I can't go to Argos or Tiryns—not yet. Acrisius or Proetus would kill me. But Mycenae is neutral ground between the two Danaid kingdoms. There, below the hill-fort, is the sacred ring where the descendants of Danaos are buried with their weapons and other possessions, lying together in death no matter how bitterly they feuded in life."

"Grave Circle B," Nagel breathed.

"I'll issue a call to the warriors of the Argolid," Perseus went on, "summoning them to a council at Mycenae. When they learn I arrived with you, Father, in your chariot, they'll come! Acrisius and Proetus will go mad with rage, but they won't dare to interfere. After the warriors have heard Deianeira's prophecy from her own lips, I'll have more would-be raiders than ships to carry them!" The Hero abruptly turned matter-of-fact. "Afterwards, when I've returned laden with the plunder of Keftiu, I'll rescue my mother from Polydectes of Seriphos. Then I'll settle accounts with Acrisius and Proetus, as I've sworn to do, and unify the entire Argolid." A new thought occurred to him. "To set the seal on that unity, I'll establish a new residence at Mycenae. And to mark the dawn of a new era for men and gods, I'll start a new sacred ring for myself and my descendants. Acrisius and Proetus are pigs, but they carry the blood of Danaos, so I'll let them and their sons be buried in the old one."

"Grave Circle A." Nagel's whisper held something close to ecstasy. "Overlapping in time with B, and containing grave goods from Crete. So *that's* it! Yes, it all fits. . . ."

"You seem to have it all figured out," Jason said to Perseus—inadequately.

"Except for one thing," said Zeus. "My chariot can only carry two, including the driver. I can take you to Mycenae, but not this woman. You will have to make her prophecy live for the warriors of the Argolid."

Perseus turned a stricken look on Deirdre. Her own features wavered . . . but for less than a heartbeat. Then she met his look with one of steadiness.

"Go, Perseus, and do what you must do. I'll remain with Jason and Synon, and we'll do what we must do: take the idol of the Old Gods to Kalliste."

"What?" exclaimed the Hero with bewildered indignation. "You must be joking, Deianeira! Leave you in danger? No!"

Deirdre's eyes were unblinking and her voice was level. "Perseus, in the glimpse of the future Poseidon granted me, I saw one other thing: I myself am going to survive what is about to happen. My fate isn't played out. So you see, there is no real danger. I will be waiting for you here on Keftiu, where I should be safe."

"I know of a place, away from the coast and at a high altitude," said Zeus. "Mount Ida, to the southwest of here, has a cave that is sacred to me. Any of the local people should be able to give you directions. And," he added to Jason, "I have reason to think you have . . . a special talent for finding your way through these lands."

"Yes, you might say that." Just to be on the safe side, Jason activated his display, and expanded the scale. Mount Ida showed clearly.

"Then it's settled," Deirdre said to Perseus with a smile. "That will be our meeting point. I'll be waiting for you, when you return as a conqueror."

Perseus' expression went from awe to fierce exultation. "Yes! And I'll find you!"

Well done, Deirdre, thought Jason. *That's the way to get him motivated.* But then he saw the look she was giving in return, and wondered if that was all there was to it.

"Well," he said, a little more gruffly than was perhaps strictly necessary, "while we're on the subject of getting the idol to Kalliste . . . Zeus, can you get us a chariot? One of the cargo-carrying ones I've seen?"

"No. I only have my own chariot. However, the idol is lighter than you might think. And the local priests have a frame for transporting it."

"Yes, we saw them use it at Amnisos."

"Well, using that, the four of you should be able to carry the idol to the coast. And they probably keep it close to the idol itself."

"Where is the idol, by the way?"

"In a hall where various sacred images are kept, at the northwest corner of the palace."

"The Sanctuary Hall," said Nagel automatically. "I remember now, it was from there that the priestesses entered the Great Hall on the day we arrived here. But that is on the second story. How can we gain access to it?"

"There is an outside entrance to the second story at that corner. Late at night, there should be no one about except a few guards. Using the Nagom's invisibility device, you should be able to approach unnoticed—especially tonight, when everything will still be in a state of disorganization after your escape."

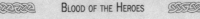

"What if the portal automatically opens while we've got it?" Jason demanded.

"I do not believe it is set to do so. But that is a chance you must take, if you dare." The Teloi turned to Perseus. "And now, let us be gone. My chariot is nearby. Come . . . my son."

Perseus swelled with pride. Then his face fell as he remembered Deirdre. He turned to her and grasped her by the arms. "Remember your promise, Deianeira. And be sure I will remember mine." He took her in the quick, hard embrace that was all he could do here in public, and then was gone, following the tall figure of his "father" into the dusk.

The antiglare goggles Oannes had used earlier also had a light-gathering setting, and there was a half moon in the clear sky. So even from within the cloak of refracted light, he was able to see his way through the night. The humans could only huddle together within the invisibility field and follow him.

They skirted the northern end of the palace, with the amphitheater to their right. Just around the northwestern corner, a couple of shallow flights of steps led up to a small propylon where a couple of nervous soldiers stood guard against whatever had hurled those horribly flashing bits of the sun at the bullring. Oannes picked them off with the weapon he'd pointed at Zeus—an electromagnetic disruptor, now on stunner setting—and deactivated the invisibility field. They slipped though the doorway, crossed a corridor, and entered a fifty-by-thirty-foot hall with two rows of three columns running down its long axis. Oil lamps dimly illuminated the objects set against the walls—crude stone god-figures that must date back to the Neolithic Age. But the place of honor, under a row of four windows at the western end of the hall, belonged to the Teloi's disguised portal device, seeming to loom larger than it really was in the flickering light.

A hasty search revealed the stretcherlike carrier—basically, two very stout wooden poles with several leather straps between them—folded on the floor behind the device. They maneuvered the idol onto the straps, finding that Zeus had spoken the truth: the artificial "stone" was lighter than the real thing. It must, Jason decided, add to the thing's uncanny quality in the eyes of the locals . . . and the slaves must surely be grateful for it. He knew he was, as they each took an end of a pole and bore it silently away.

The moonlight was enough for the humans to see by as they hurried northward, first along the road they'd taken and then cutting left across country under Oannes' direction. Then the moon set and they were entirely dependent on Oannes, with his light-gathering optics, to steer them across broken country. After several stumbles and near accidents, Oannes declared that it was almost dawn and that they must spend the day in concealment even though their goal was tantalizingly close. He found a secluded little field behind an orchard and they all sank gratefully to the ground beneath the dome of invisibility as the sun began to redden the eastern horizon.

"I'll take the first watch," said Jason. It was, he thought, the least he could do. Deirdre hadn't uttered a word of protest, but she was clearly close to collapse. Oannes was in little better case; he was bearing the backpack privacy field generator, and as he had been known to point out, he wasn't getting any younger. Nor was Nagel.

They spent the day napping in shifts and eating Oannes' food concentrates, which he assured them were harmless and fairly nutritious for humans, although lacking certain essentials whose absence would take a toll over the long term. Not that Jason could imagine subsisting on the stuff for the long term; Oannes hadn't exaggerated its lack of satiety value. At least they had water, fetched from a nearby stream by Oannes, using his personal invisibility unit.

Aside from making desultory conversation, their only amusement was watching through the distortion of the field as groups of soldiers passed by. Imagination failed at the hue and cry that must have gone up at Knossos when the idol turned up missing. Oannes held his weapon at the ready in case any of the patrols blundered through the boundaries of the field, but none did.

As soon as night fell, Oannes deactivated the field, about whose sustainability he was beginning to worry, and they resumed their trek in darkness. It didn't take long—although it seemed much longer—to cover the mile or so to a little indentation in the coast that didn't deserve the name "cove."

"Wait here," said the Nagom as they set their burden down on the pebbly beach. "I will bring my vessel." With the abrupt, sinuous movement that Jason still found unsettling, he slid into the water he must have missed beyond all telling. A remarkably short time passed before his submarine's illuminated bubble broke the surface.

The four of them took the idol out through the shallows. Jason was struck—not for the first time—with the sensation that they bore a genie's bottle, but with the "Old Gods" locked within.

"I say," groused Nagel as they manhandled the thing, "why can't we just sink it into the sea? Then, when the portal opens at whatever time it is scheduled to do so—"

"A delightful thought," Oannes agreed. "But they have naturally foreseen such a contingency. The instant that water comes rushing in through it, the portal automatically snaps shut. And there is always a Teloi aircar aloft, with a sensor which can detect the distinctive energy signature of the portal opening, so they will know where to locate it. No, you were right the first time. It must be destroyed."

The Nagom boarded the submarine and set up a kind of winch. The humans maneuvered the idol into a sling, and Oannes brought it aboard. He then backfilled, moving the submarine out of the dangerously shallow water.

"All right," said Jason, turning to his fellow time travelers in the knee-deep water. "We need to make some plans. Deirdre, I'm sure Oannes will leave you some of his food concentrates. You may have to last on them for a while, before things have quieted down enough for you to risk scrounging from the local peasants. At least we don't have to decide on a rendezvous; it may as well be this Mount Ida, where Perseus is going to meet you anyway. But we need to decide on—"

"What the *hell* are you talking about?" Even in the moonlight, Deirdre's eyes could be seen to flash. "I'm coming with you!"

"But you told Perseus you'd wait for him here on Crete."

"I *had* to tell him that! Otherwise he wouldn't have gone with Zeus. It's just the way he thinks, where women are concerned. He can't help it. You, on the other hand, aren't *supposed* to have a Bronze Age mentality!"

"But, Deirdre, we're going to Kalliste. You said yourself it can explode at any time."

"Yes, that's the whole point!" Her voice held something like exultation. "Do you think I'd miss this last chance to see the island as it was before the event?"

And I thought Nagel was bad! Jason kept his voice down with an effort. "Deirdre, we're not exactly going there for sightseeing. Kalliste is also the Teloi's center of operations. This is going to be dangerous in ways beyond the chance of being vaporized by superheated volcanic gas!"

"Oh. And I suppose just because I'm a woman—"

Sheer exasperation made Jason forget the need for quiet. "That is *not* the issue, and you know it!"

"Ahem!" interjected Nagel hesitantly. "Perhaps this is not the best possible time to—"

Neither of them heard him. "It is *so* the issue!" Deirdre declared.

"Only on your backwater planet! You're still fighting a war that nobody else even remembers."

"Then why is it that you see nothing wrong with taking Nagel, who has no qualifications in geology or vulcanology but who does have a penis?"

"I *beg* your pardon!" blurted the historian, his out-of-character attempt at peacemaking forgotten.

All three were gathering their forces for crushing retorts when the soldiers appeared on the shore.

They were without shields—doubtless considered unnecessary for dealing with unarmed fugitives anyway—

so that they might carry torches. Jason had only a split second to realize that he might have noticed the approaching glow of those torches, had he not let himself be drawn into a contest of petulance. Then there was no time for self-reproach, as the commander barked a command in the tongue of Keftiu. The soldiers plunged into the water, torches borne high in their left hands while their right hands held spears in an underhand grip suitable for jabbing or throwing.

"Run for it!" yelled Jason, with no particular confidence that he would be obeyed. At the same instant, he dropped into the shallows, breaking his fall with both hands and bringing his feet up and around in a sweeping motion that cut the foremost soldier's legs out from under him. As the man fell face-forward in the water, Jason grasped him around the neck from above and gave a quick neck-breaking twist. Then he allowed himself a quick look around. To his surprise, Nagel was actually following orders and splashing toward the submarine. Deirdre, however, couldn't have complied even if she'd wanted to; as it happened, she was closest to the main body of onrushing soldiers. She gave one of them a doubtless deeply satisfying kick to the crotch, then ducked a jabbing spear, grabbed the arm holding it, and sent the man flying forward with a very serviceable approximation of judo. The soldiers halted for a moment, stunned by this behavior. Then one of them collapsed, stunned in a very literal sense by Oannes' neural disruptor.

Jason looked behind him. The sub was heading straight toward him, coming in recklessly close. Oannes was pointing his weapon from above the windshield cowling.

"Get aboard!" Oannes called, as he dropped another

of Deirdre's assailants. Jason saw the sense in it. He splashed toward the approaching craft.

"Keep stunning them!" he called. Soon they'd break, leaving Deirdre free. . . .

But then one of them grasped Deirdre from behind, around the waist, and swung her frantically struggling form between himself and the malevolent sea demon who rendered men unconscious from afar. Oannes' aim wavered as he saw the impossibility of a clear shot in this light.

The other soldiers, sensing safety, clustered behind the human shield and began hurling their spears. One of them glanced off the curved surface of the sub, just below the cowling, and sliced through the flesh and muscle of the Nagom's left arm.

"Get aboard," repeated Oannes in a voice thick with pain.

Jason had reached the vessel, and only now saw the impossibility of going back for Deirdre, even if he'd felt inclined to take on a squad of soldiers.

"Go!" Deirdre yelled.

Not clearly aware of what was happening, Jason let Nagel pull him over the side amid the clatter of other thrown spears. Oannes, one-handed, brought the sub around a hundred and eighty degrees and headed for the open sea, with the bubble closing above them. Then they all collapsed as the vessel's artificial brain took over, submerging and proceeding on its preset course for Kalliste.

After a time, Jason felt Nagel's hesitant hand on his shoulder. "She'll be all right," the historian assured him. "Remember, Hyperion made clear that he wants her unharmed. They won't dare do anything to her."

"Right," said Jason emphatically. He took Nagel's hand in a quick squeeze to show he appreciated the historian's attempt—including his omission of the fact that Deirdre's usefulness to the Old Gods was as breeding stock with Perseus, whom they no longer had.

Then they got busy attending to Oannes' wound, and there was mercifully little time to brood.

CHAPTER TWENTY

For a seventy-mile trip, the main limiting factor on a supercavitating submarine's travel time was the need to slow down to a halt at the end. It was still pitch dark when Kalliste loomed ahead, a mountainous mass against the star-filled sky. The only illumination was the glow at the top of the mountain, which gave the rising smoke a sinister ruddy tint.

Jason, watching it in the surface-view screen, reflected that Deirdre would have been disappointed at how little could be seen. But then he looked at the scrolling electronic map of the roughly circular island. It was about a dozen miles across, partly filled with a lagoonlike embayment from whose edge the volcanic mountain rose, and whose shore held a city which dwarfed the coastal town of Akrotiri to the south which the archaeologists would one day dig up. He tried to imagine what she would have given to see it. The thought didn't help with the guilty self-reproach he was already feeling. He now admitted to himself that she'd had a right to come, and for a reason she hadn't even raised: they were in search of her TRD, and no one had a greater stake in that.

So he consoled himself with the thought that his implant was recording it all, for her to see when it was downloaded and played back—on the cheerful assumption that it ever was. And he occupied his mind by watching closely as Oannes manipulated the controls, doing his best to memorize what he saw. He also noted a flashing violet light on the map display. Their projected course led to it.

"Is that the Nagommo cache, Oannes?" he asked.

"Yes," said Oannes without taking his eyes off the control board. "My thought is that we should take the portal device there, where it will be well concealed. The Teloi currently operating in the normal universe cannot detect it with instruments unless the portal is activated."

"Seems sensible," Jason agreed absently. Most of his mind was elsewhere, worrying, for the Nagom had inadvertently reminded him of a fundamental flaw in the entire plan—one he hadn't mentioned to anyone, least of all Deirdre, and in fact had done his best to conceal from himself. If the Teloi came upon them and opened the portal, the basic idea was scotched. But if the portal remained closed, how were they to even attempt recovering Deirdre's TRD?

"By the way, there is one other thing," said Oannes. His eyes were still fixed on his readouts and therefore not meeting Jason's. And his voice held a kind of controlled tension which brought Jason out of his dismal reflections and into full alert status. "Just before the fight on the beach, while I was maneuvering this vessel, I could not help overhearing your . . . discussion with Deirdre. Most of it was fairly meaningless to one of my race, for obvious reasons. But one turn of phrase struck me." The Nagom was now speaking like an automaton, and staring fixedly ahead. "You intimated that her attitudes were rooted in the peculiarities of her native *planet*."

Silence fell in layers.

"Uh, I think you may be reading too much into a, uh, figure of speech," Jason floundered.

Oannes finally turned to face him. "You led me to believe that your society did not have the secret of interstellar travel, Jason." His tone wasn't even particularly reproachful or accusatory. That might have been easier to take.

"I never actually *told* you that we didn't," Jason began . . . but his attempt at pettifoggery died under the gaze of those huge, unblinking eyes, and his own eyes fell. "All right. I haven't been entirely honest with you. But you must believe this: I *was* telling you the truth when I said the Teloi are forgotten in our era. And we've found no trace of them anywhere we've wandered among the stars."

Oannes' grave serenity wavered. "Yes, yes, I believe you. But . . . you must know of my race!"

And so the moment Jason had dreaded arrived. *What do I tell him? He's earned our honesty as well as our gratitude. I will not lie to him. I cannot.*

But to tell him the whole truth—the hell his planet has become, peopled by obscene travesties of the Nagommo of old, the legacy of what the Nagommo did to themselves. . . .

"No," was all he said.

Oannes took it better than a human would have. A human would have demanded more. Oannes merely met Jason's eyes, and knew that Jason's reticence was founded in kindness. And he received that kindness with a bleak calm that held no room for angry denial.

"Well," the Nagom finally said . . . and could not continue. Another long moment's silence passed before he resumed. "Well, I myself still live. And I have one thing left that I can do." He turned back to the controls, businesslike. "Let us proceed to the cache."

"Yes, let's," Jason echoed.

They didn't enter the lagoon. The Nagommo had avoided those densely populated inner shores when they had established their cache. Oannes, taking over from the computer, steered them into a tunnel beneath the low cliffs that fronted Kalliste's southwestward coast.

"This isn't altogether artificial," the Nagom explained as their craft glided slowly through a passage that accommodated it with suspicious exactness. "We widened it a bit. But it always led to . . . this," he finished, as they emerged into a subterranean pool. They surfaced under a rocky dome whose extent did not become apparent until Oannes touched his controls and light flooded it.

Oannes brought the submersible around and backed it into a kind of cradle that was the only work of obvious artificiality under the dome. He gestured at a cave mouth off to the side. "I suggest that we take the device into the inner cavern, for maximum security."

It was easier said than done, even after they maneuvered the *faux* idol into the carrying sling. Jason took the front ends of both poles, one in each hand, while Nagel and Oannes, with his injured arm, each took one of the rear ends. Carefully, to avoid stumbling, they carried it through the opening and along a short passageway. It didn't help that the ground occasionally shivered, and a rumbling could be felt as much as heard. But soon the passageway opened into another large, illuminated cavern, whose floor lay below a ridge.

Here, in the glow of the lights, Jason saw spread out before him the wonders the Nagommo had stored here against their hour of need. He couldn't take it all in. He could only wonder how much of the technology was duplicated by what his own culture could produce. Most of it, probably; little of what he had seen Oannes use was beyond the twenty-fourth century's horizons. But surely some of it . . . he couldn't let himself dwell on that as they maneuvered their burden over the ridge and across a floor that had clearly been leveled but was still unfinished enough to require care in where they stepped. Finally, they set the idol down against the far rock wall.

Oannes walked to a nearby control console. "I must activate certain special security measures that are currently dormant. The two of you may as well start back to the submersible."

"Right," Jason nodded. "Come on, Sidney."

They had topped the ridge and were about to enter the tunnel when Jason suddenly knew that something was not right. Or, rather he *felt* it with his entire being, on a level deeper than that of conscious intellect. Something profoundly unnatural was happening behind him.

"Fall down!" he snapped at Nagel, without pausing for anything, including thought.

The historian stood frozen in shock. Jason grabbed his arm and pulled him down. Only after they were both flat on their stomachs did he crawl to the ridge and peer over it.

Beside the idol, the portal was forming.

Zeus assured us that he didn't think it was scheduled for one of its periodic openings, thought Jason, oddly calm. *Some god!*

And here he lay, unarmed even with what passed for weapons in this era, too far away to do anything except watch as Oannes, who had also become aware of what was happening behind him, whirled around just as the dimensional opening stabilized, and faced a Teloi.

The Teloi looked startled—as well he might, having expected to find himself in the Sanctuary Hall at Knossos—but he already had a weapon in his hand, doubtless as a routine precaution. This was no "head of the Hydra." It was smaller and somehow uglier . . . and before Oannes could draw his own weapon from his utility harness it speared the Nagom with a dazzling line of ionization. A fraction of a second later, Jason heard the unmistakable crack of air snapping back into the tunnel of vacuum drilled through it by a weapon-grade laser.

A puff of pink steam exploded from Oannes' body where the beam touched it, and the knockback effect of energy transfer sent him staggering back before he fell and lay still.

The Teloi stepped forward, emerging from the portal, and stared down at the alien corpse. Then he stared around him, while Jason looked on, suspended in horror. *Not a damned thing I can do*, he thought over and over.

The Teloi finally pulled himself together and spoke into a wrist communicator. The acoustics of the cavern were such that Jason could hear his voice across the distance. But the rapid-fire Teloi, mumbled into the communicator, was unintelligible. Almost immediately, more Teloi emerged, to stand gawking. Then they came to positions of respectful attention when a new group arrived. Jason recognized Hyperion and Rhea. But the chief focus of deference was a male Jason hadn't seen before, and who for some indefinable reason seemed older than the others, even though he bore the usual indicia of agelessness. He walked over to that which had been Oannes. He looked down on it with eyes empty of pity or any other emotion save satisfaction.

"So," he said after a moment. "*This* one. We've wanted it for a very long time." Jason took a second to realize that the neuter pronoun referred to Oannes. The Teloi turned to Rhea. "Have you ascertained just where we are?"

"Yes, Cronus," Rhea replied, following a custom Jason had noted before among the Teloi, of using the names by which they were known locally. He wondered what she would have called the leader if they had been in Ireland, or northern India. Did they even remember the names they'd been born with? "Our positioning system has had time to orient itself. We are on the southwest coast of Kalliste."

"Kalliste! So the Nagom stole the portal device from Knossos only to bring it to the very center of our worship in this region—specifically, of *your* worship. For what conceivable reason would it do that?"

"I have no idea." Rhea shot a venomous glance at the Teloi who had killed Oannes. "And we will never find out, will we? We have no prisoner to interrogate, thanks to Tethys. What game is he playing, I wonder?"

"What was I supposed to do?" Tethys demanded indignantly. "Let it shoot me, as it was about to do?"

"Small loss," Rhea sneered.

Even across the distance, Jason could see Tethys stiffen with controlled rage. "I find myself wondering why are *you* so concerned over the death of a Nagom!"

"Enough of your bickering!" roared Cronus with a hundred thousand years' worth of exasperation.

"I quite agree," Hyperion put in smoothly. In any other circumstances, Jason would have found something amusing about the imperious Teloi in the role of sycophantic flunky. "Instead of exchanging recriminations, we should be congratulating ourselves on our good fortune. We have been presented with one of the equipment caches of the Nagommo vermin." There was a general noise of agreement, and everyone's wounded feelings seemed to subside.

"Furthermore," Hyperion continued, "there is something else we need to consider." He indicated the carrying sling, lying where it had been dropped behind the idol. "The Nagom could hardly have used this alone. It must have had help."

"Yes!" exclaimed Rhea. "And that help could not have come from the few remaining members of its odious race; we know in general where *they* are. The human time travelers must be involved."

"Ah, yes," Cronus nodded. "The ones you told me about. They must be recaptured; the possibilities they open up are fascinating. And," he added with a glare at Hyperion, "your attempts to investigate the workings of the device that was removed from the female have been unavailing, as has your study of the biological samples removed from her."

"A temporary setback only, Cronus. And," Hyperion continued, in what Jason recognized as the tone of an underling coming as close as he dared to criticism of policy directives from above, "we have been hampered by the requirement that the implant be undamaged."

Jason's heart lifted. He had almost forgotten the sensation.

"No doubt," said Cronus absently. "But in the meantime, there is work to be done! Alert those who are now airborne; their detection of the portal opening may have been delayed by surprise at its location, as they were expecting it to take place at Knossos. And determine the precise whereabouts of Zeus and the rest of his faction of malcontents. Eurymedon, I leave this matter in your hands—and I expect a prompt report."

"Yes, Cronus," cringed a Teloi Jason recognized as the first one he had ever seen, the one who had appeared above the road to Lerna.

"In the meantime," Cronus resumed, "we must search this Nagommo cache. It is the logical starting place for locating the time-traveling feral humans."

With a rumble of acknowledgment, the Teloi dispersed. Some of them reentered the portal. Others, including Cronus and Hyperion, remained in the cavern, examining the Nagommo artifacts curiously.

"That tears it, Sidney," Jason whispered to Nagel. "As soon as they get themselves organized, they're going to explore through this passageway. Very carefully, let's get back to the sub and . . . Sidney? *Sidney?*"

The historian wasn't listening. He was staring at the scene below, with an expression Jason could not interpret. "Yes," he whispered to himself, "they must return through the portal, and close it." Then, all at once, he seemed to come into focus. "Listen, Jason, this is important. We have the key to most of the riddles now. The idea of a Greek conquest of Crete in the seventeenth century B.C. was always a minority view. But now we know that it's going to happen; Perseus will lead it. And given that, everything else falls into place—"

"Sidney!" Jason rasped, holding his voice down. "This is not the time for—"

"Listen to me! This is *important!*" Nagel's whisper held an urgency, and his eyes a fiery intensity, that stopped Jason in mid-sentence. "You *must* get back with this data! And . . . you must get back to Crete. Deirdre is in danger there. She needs you."

"Why . . . of course, Sidney. That's what I'm saying. We need to hurry and get back to the sub. Let's go, and—"

Before Jason realized what was happening, Nagel scrambled over the ridge and was stumbling down the slope toward the Teloi.

Sheer, stunned surprise held Jason immobilized. That, and his realization that there was absolutely nothing he could do except be captured or killed himself, held him flat against the rock floor, peering over the ridgetop as the Teloi saw the historian and raised their weapons.

"No! Don't shoot!" cried Nagel in their own language. "I'm unarmed. I wish to surrender."

Two of the more junior Teloi converged on Nagel, seized him by the arms, and shoved him in front of Cronus and Hyperion. The latter gazed down at him. "One of the time travelers," he informed Cronus.

"Yes!" Nagel nodded frantically. "Our leader ran off and left me when your portal opened. He's always hated me. He's consumed with envy of my academic eminence. You remember the time he attacked me, don't you?" he asked Hyperion eagerly. "Tell him!"

"I do recall such an incident from their earlier captivity," Hyperion admitted.

Cronus was clearly uninterested. He looked down at Nagel with contemptuous distaste, then turned to Hyperion. "Kill him."

"No! Please, lord! I can help you! I overheard you to say you hadn't made any headway in puzzling out a device you had removed from the woman in our party. Well, I am a specialist in the field of time travel."

Cronus had started to turn away, the feral human already forgotten. Now he paused and turned back, looking thoughtful.

"Perhaps . . ." Hyperion began.

"Yes!" said Nagel avidly. "I can be useful! You'll see. But first I need to examine that implant you spoke of. I'm somewhat puzzled about that."

Cronus considered for a moment. Then he gestured to an underling, who spoke into one of the wrist communicators. For a minute or so, they all stood, waiting, while Jason watched and struggled to understand.

Presently a Teloi appeared in the portal. He bore the small plastic case Jason had first seen in Proetus' courtyard. Cronus took it, opened it, and handed it to Nagel.

"Well?" he demanded.

Nagel took the TRD between thumb and forefinger and made a great show of studying it. Then he looked up, and his face wore the supercilious look that came naturally to it.

"Oh, *this!*" He put the tiny object back in the case and

closed it with a snap. "I remember now: you chopped it out of her at Tiryns. It is merely a homing device used by our leader to monitor our movements. It has nothing to do with time travel."

"But the woman told us—" Hyperion began.

"Of course she did," sneered the historian. "Don't you see? She was trying to put you on a false scent—not without success, it would seem. And she had an additional motivation: avoiding any further removal of samples from her body. Because *that* is where the true secret lies."

He now had his listeners' rapt attention, as he launched into the condescending lecture style that was pure Nagel, but with an inventiveness Jason had never dreamed he possessed.

"We time travelers," he began, "are a special class—a subspecies, actually. The capability of temporal displacement is a psionic talent that has been engineered into us, using artificially created genetic material—the trait does not occur in the natural human genotype. We activate it by direct neural induction, with the help of an implant in the brain. I thought *that* was what you were referring to." A sardonic chuckle. "I was wondering how you'd gotten it out of the woman without killing her."

"Do you mean to say," Hyperion demanded, "that you can travel in time simply by *willing* it?"

"Only under certain highly restricted circumstances," Nagel cautioned. "It requires a great deal of training. And only at certain times is the temporal 'fabric' weak enough to permit it. The physics is rather too complex to go into just now. This is why we've been unable to return to our own era."

Looking at the Teloi's faces, Jason could tell they had

accepted Nagel's fantasy. And he understood why. Fitting in so well with their own background, it was more believable than the truth would have been.

"Fortunately," Nagel continued, "you have biological samples from the woman. *Those* are what you need to study, on the genetic level. Using samples from ordinary humans as a 'control,' you should have no difficulty isolating the trait. But *this*—" he held up the little plastic case "—is valueless." With an offhand flick of his wrist, he tossed it over his shoulder, in Jason's direction, to land with a clatter on the cavern floor.

All at once, Jason understood. And he tried to comprehend the magnitude of the courage he was witnessing.

"So," Cronus said after a moment. "When you say that we 'should have no difficulty,' do I take it to mean that you yourself are not qualified to assist in the genetic testing?"

"That is correct. I am no geneticist."

"I thought not. And I find your attitude insufficiently respectful—quite objectionable, in fact." Cronus nodded to Hyperion, who raised one of the small laser weapons.

Jason closed his eyes and bit down on his tongue hard enough to draw blood, so as not to cry out when he heard the crack.

When he looked again, the Teloi were deep in conversation. "The exploration of this cache can wait," Cronus declared. "This is more important." He turned toward the portal.

"Also," Hyperion suggested, indicating the pathetic, crumpled body, "we should bring that, and remove the brain implant."

"Definitely. See to it." Cronus passed through the portal.

Hyperion turned to the remaining Teloi and gave orders. Two of them picked up that which had been Sidney Nagel, Ph.D., and they all filed through the portal. A few moments passed. The portal vanished. The idol stood dormant.

Jason waited a few cautious moments. Then he rose and walked down the slope. He scooped up the plastic case that Nagel had died to leave there. He tore a strip of cloth off his ruined tunic, and used it to tie the case to his arm, almost tourniquet-tight. He paused for a moment beside the body of Oannes. There were no eyelids to close, and the appropriate rites lay beyond his knowledge. He departed the cavern and started down the tunnel, toward the submersible for which the Teloi hadn't yet gotten around to searching.

As he went, a realization penetrated the swirling chaos of his thoughts. The rock floor was steady under his feet. For some time, there had been no tremors and no rumbling.

Deirdre, he was sure, would have been able to tell him what that portended.

CHAPTER TWENTY-ONE

Jason had been aboard the submarine, or its sister ship, on two occasions when it had submerged. But the frantic desperation of both those occasions hadn't left him with enough time to watch Oannes manipulate the controls. So he still had no idea how to do everything.

Which, he reflected, was probably just as well since he also didn't know how to close the bubble canopy.

He did know how to activate and control the drive. And he knew how to steer the thing . . . or thought he did. After his first few attempts to back away from the mooring, he began to wonder. But he finally got it started down the subterranean channel, and his steering grew surer and more confident.

The eastern sky was paling with dawn when he emerged into the open sea. He activated the map display and set course for Crete, putting Kalliste behind him.

It soon became painfully obvious that the submarine was not designed for surface cruising. Jason estimated that he was struggling along at five or six knots at most. Twelve hours or so to Crete, then—twelve hours continuously at the controls, given his inability to set the automatic pilot. And he was starting out hungry, sleepless and emotionally drained.

He grimly kept on course, alone save for the dolphins that doubtless found this craft a novelty. As the sun rose higher in the sky, Kalliste gradually fell astern until nothing was visible above the horizon save the upper cone of the central mountain. More and more, as steering came to be second nature and his concentration wavered, he found himself watching the antics of the dolphins, just to stay awake.

He was watching as one of those sleek shapes came cavorting alongside and then swerved away. He turned with a wan smile to watch it go.

That turning motion, along with a subliminal sense that something *wrong* had occurred, caused him to turn around and look behind him.

The cone of the volcanic mountain wasn't there anymore. Instead, there was a region of night, spreading more rapidly than anything had a right to.

Even as he watched that blackness expand to blot out more and more of the blue Mediterranean midmorning sky, a calm corner of his mind felt irrationally disappointed. *Is this* it? *Surely there should be some noise, or something.*

Then, less than a second later: *Oh, yes, of course, you ninny! Light moves a lot faster than atmospheric vibrations, including sound. Naturally you can see it before—*

That was when the shock wave hit him, blasted him over, and smashed him down against the control panel with a pain that he didn't even feel because at the same instant the sound arrived. Except that it wasn't sound, it was a . . . words like *roar* or *bellow* or *thunder* were too feeble. It was a *thing* that transcended sound. Jason didn't hear it; he felt it.

At the same instant, the spreading darkness engulfed him, extinguishing the sun and enveloping his entire world . . . except that it wasn't altogether darkness. It was riven with blinding sheets of lightning whose accompanying blasts of thunder rose even above the general background noise, until they could be heard not just with the ears but with every suffering cell of the body. The universe was a drum, and he was inside it.

Jason forced himself to stand, and righted the staggering hull. As he did, he glimpsed what seemed to be shooting stars, far above in the evil blackness. But then they began to curve downward, and he knew they were really red-hot boulders, spewed forth by dying Kalliste. With horrified fascination, he watched one as it began to fall. It grew—gradually at first, then with soul-shaking rapidity—and he knew it was bigger than his craft, bigger than a house . . . and it was headed for him.

It struck less than a mile away. The water simply exploded on impact, then crashed back down into a wave that swept toward him. He managed to turn bow-on into it before it crashed over him, and held on grimly as his clumsy craft pitched and heaved. He didn't even have time to give thanks for his lifelong freedom from motion sickness.

The wallowing craft righted itself, largely from the

inertia of the water sloshing in its bilge, and he had a moment to look around. Other burning stones were striking the sea, sending gouts of steam skyward. But they were smaller, and at greater distances. He felt a strange fatalism. If one of them struck him, he was dead, and that was all there was to it. But none did. What did begin to fall on him was fine and gray-white in the blackness. For an idiotic split second he thought: *Snow?* But it was ash. And then the rain began. Not a cleansing rain, as rain was meant to be. It reeked, and stuck, and stung.

Acid rain, he thought with a clinging remanent of rationality. But the rest of him knew that all such thoughts were vain. *Deirdre was wrong. This is the end of the world.*

Only, insisted the stubborn remnant, *if the world ends now, in 1628 B.C. . . . then where did* I *come from?*

The thought steadied him. He made himself concentrate on the glowing control-board display, and steered by that, ignoring the pain and the din and the lightning-shot darkness. He even ignored the water—mud, really, mixed as it was with volcanic ash—that was now up to his ankles, and rising. He couldn't let himself contemplate the unlikelihood that his vessel would stay afloat long enough to reach Crete. He didn't even have a bucket to bail with.

He had no way of measuring time in this continuum of horror. Bur sooner than he had dared hope, the sun became visible as a dull-red disc in a slate sky. The blackness, rumbling with thunder and flickering lightning, loomed astern, to the north where Kalliste lay. *No, not any more,* he corrected himself. *Not Kalliste. Santorini, now.* The black rain finally stopped, leaving him grimed with its sooty, tarry residue, but the sludge was now up to his knees.

Then, by the dim light of the rust-red sun, he saw the cliffs of Crete ahead.

At first, his mind couldn't accept the impossible input of his eyes. *It can't be—not already. There hasn't been enough time.* But then understanding dawned.

He had ridden a tsunami.

Out at sea, there had been no way to tell the sea was rising beneath him, lifting his craft and carrying it along at astonishing velocity. Only when it met a shore did that mountain of water become a monster of destruction . . . which it wasn't through doing, for even at this distance through the gloom Jason could see the raging surf that battered the coast.

He frantically brought the vessel around, fighting to stay off the rocks ahead until he could find a break in the cliffs. There was no point in even trying to find Amnisos; it would be a mass of half-submerged, mud-choked wreckage. He struggled against the insane currents, fighting to keep offshore as long as possible while stealing glances at the scrolling map.

He finally located a cove of sorts—it might have even been the same one they'd departed from, but it was hard to be sure in his hunger and exhaustion, trying to breathe the foul, stinking air. He could barely concentrate on trying to bring the craft in between waves.

He almost made it. He was nearing the shore when the hissing roar of another wave grew behind him. He started to abandon ship, stepping up onto the rail. He lost his balance, and came down with his left foot turned inward. He felt a sharp pain, and knew with sinking despair that he'd broken a bone on the outer edge of the foot. At that moment when the wave hit, tumbling the submersible over and smashing it down in the shallows. Jason himself was thrown free, and then sucked under the black, filthy water. He held his breath grimly, enduring the agony of suffocation as he clawed against the irresistible strength of the undertow. His lungs hadn't quite burst when he finally broke the surface and took deep, gulping breaths of the thick, dust-filled air.

He was in waist-high water. It wasn't far to shore, but it took him a long time to struggle through the surf. When he took his first step on land, the pain in his foot made him gasp.

He looked around. Oannes' submarine lay capsized among the rocks, where it would be pounded to pieces and washed out to sea. A short distance away was the wreckage of a local boat that had been swept ashore by the tsunami. He crawled to it on hands and knees, and found a broken plank that he could use as a clumsy crutch. He also tore some fabric from the clothing of a dead sailor—his own tunic was reduced to tatters—and bound his left foot as tightly as he could stand. Then he spotted a half-empty wineskin that had miraculously survived. He squeezed the contents down his throat without pausing for breath, heedless of the impact of the alcohol hitting his empty stomach. At least it deadened the pain of his foot.

Finally, he looked down at his arm. The plastic case containing Deirdre's TRD was still tied to it. He activated his map display. The red dot of that TRD showed him where he was—a little west of Amnisos as he'd thought. He expanded the scale so that it included Mount Ida.

There was no point in delay. Indeed, if he sat for much longer he would never be able to force himself to get up, for it would be so much easier to lie down and die. He used the plank to lever himself up onto his right foot, and began to hobble off.

Jason's brain implant held the archaeologists' deductions about the Minoan roads and trails. So he was able to find the one that led west. He wanted to avoid the southbound route to Knossos, which must be in a chaos he was in no shape to cope with. He was also in no shape to help Deirdre escape if she was still there. He could only hope she had been able to get away in the aftermath of the cataclysm. If so, he knew where she would be heading.

So he struggled southwestward, joining the human flotsam of refugees from the coast, trudging through the stormy weather as the atmosphere righted itself after what had been done to it. He was unmolested, unlike those who had anything worth stealing. Once, he even fell in with a group whose leader, a deserted soldier called Koza, was able to get by in Achaean despite his quintessentially Cretan name. He was good-natured in his brutal way, and shared a windfall of food they'd obtained from a wealthy villa. (Jason was in no position to quibble about how they'd gone about obtaining it.) But their hospitality didn't extend to letting him slow them down. They pressed on, leaving him to forage from abandoned peasants' hovels for food, and for cloth to wrap around himself against the increasingly cold nights.

He lost track of time as he limped slowly across the landscape of Hell. After a while, he found he was able to walk on his broken foot, with the aid of a walking stick. It was painful, and he knew it wasn't doing the fracture any good in the long run. But it was a little faster, and that was the only factor he could let himself consider just now.

He was on the road for only about ten miles, but it seemed ten times that. Then he turned due south, toward the looming mass of Ida, and the hard part of his journey began.

The distance he had to cover was only about seven miles as the crow flies—but such distances had ceased to have any meaning for him. The trek was an eternity of trails suitable for donkeys but not for a half-lamed man, over what his neurally displayed map called the Kouloukounas Range (with a subscript indicating that it had been called the Tallaion in Classical times—God knew what it was called currently) and into the Mylopotamos Valley. He avoided a town called Anogeia (subscript: Axos) because it was choked with refugees from the coast. Then it was upward again, every step a pain-filled struggle.

By now he was in regions not directly affected by the tsunami. And the clouds were thinning out, gradually dispersed by the winds that would carry the volcanic ash around and around the planet, west to east, until everyone in the north temperate zone had breathed atoms of Kalliste . . . and of the Teloi portal device. And of Oannes.

Of course, the "temperate zones" aren't going to be so temperate for a couple of years, are they? he thought to himself, because it was important to keep thinking of things other than the fatigue and hunger and pain that might otherwise break down the barrier behind which lurked despair. *It's going to be like the "nuclear winter" people were worried about back in the late twentieth century, when atomic energy had arrived a few decades before the Age of Totalitarianism ended, and things looked scary for a while. Deirdre said there are going to be two bad growth years—the puny tree-growth rings will show that, four thousand years from now.*

The thought of Deirdre quickened his pace a little. He continued southward, along trails through slopes whose maple, oak, pine and cypress were coated with an ominous dusting of ash, until he had reached the upland plain of Nidha. The local shepherds fled at his approach—they were probably wary of strangers at the best of times, and times had ceased to be the best when the heavens had filled with soot and strangers from the coast had begun to flee into the highlands to escape the fury of Poseidon.

Here, his brain implant told him, he was five thousand feet above sea level. The snow-capped peak of Mount Ida, in front of him, towered another three thousand feet.

He didn't need to go that high, though. Instead, he worked his way around the mountain toward the southeast until, just above the plain, was his destination: a cave mouth that glowered forth from under a beetling shelf of rock.

The later Greeks, his orientation had told him, believed that cave to have been the nursery of Zeus—and also his birthplace, according to some traditions, although there were other claimants to that honor among Crete's caves. He didn't know the current inhabitants' position on the question. But Zeus had indicated that they regarded it as sacred to him in some way, and that Deirdre could hope for some sort of sanctuary there. Jason's experience in history's unsettled epochs made him skeptical of the value of such assurances in such times—and it was hard to imagine a time more unsettled than this one had suddenly become.

But he could only press on, hoping against hope. The sun was low in the ashen-streaked sky when he topped the lip of the cave and peered within. Someone had been in residence, for the embers of a dead fire glowed in the dark recesses. . . .

A split-second danger instinct made him twist aside and duck. The heavy tree limb, swung from behind, swooshed over his head. He automatically reached up to grab the cudgel with one hand and one of the arms holding it with the other, simultaneously pulling forward, using the attacker's own momentum to bring him around, off balance. But he forgot about the dull ache to which he'd become accustomed, and let his entire weight fall on his left foot. Sickening pain tore through him, and he lost his grip and his balance. Collapsing, he pulled the attacker down atop his back. An arm went around his neck. He managed to break the hold, and a moment's clumsy wrestling ensued. It ended abruptly when one of his opponent's knees, by accident rather than design, came down on his left foot. The agony took his breath away, and he found himself on his back, looking up into a face that could barely be seen amid a tangle of long dark-auburn hair.

"Hey," he gasped, "do you always pick on cripples?"

Deirdre's green eyes widened, and she fell on top of him with a laugh.

"Jason!" she finally gasped. She raised herself back up with her arms and looked down at him. "It's really you! But you're hurt. And where's Sidney? And Oannes?" Then, abruptly, she grew silent. Jason's face gave her all the answer she needed. She got to her feet and helped him up to a sitting position.

"Tell me about it," she said quietly, "while I get the fire going again."

Jason related everything that had happened, pausing only to take bites of the cheese she brought him, and sips from a wineskin. By the time he was done, the sun had set in a blaze of red and orange. With all the particles in the atmosphere, this part of the world should have some spectacular sunsets for a while. Jason wondered if the people would appreciate the sight, busy as they were trying to find enough to eat.

"And so," he concluded, "you can thank Sidney for the fact that we finally have this back." He untied the little plastic case from his upper arm and handed it to her with great solemnity, like an offering. She took it from him the same way.

He wasn't sure what he had expected in the way of a reaction. She held the case for a moment, then opened it and stared down at the nondescript little sphere with an expression that was . . . what? Serious, certainly. But there was something beyond that. Sorrowful, perhaps?

"So Sidney died for this," she finally said. She did not meet his eyes.

"Not just for this," he reminded her. "He also made certain that Cronus and the rest of the first-generation Teloi—except for whoever was aloft at the time, as per their standard operating procedure—were in the pocket universe at the time the portal device was destroyed. Which means the genies are inside the lamp . . . only the lamp isn't there to get rubbed anymore. They're in for life." He grinned wolfishly. "I wonder how long those lives will be, trapped there with each other?"

"It's just as well Sidney was already dead when he went through the portal with them."

"Good point." Jason shivered. "I wonder if he thought of that, and deliberately provoked them into killing him?" He shook his head. "I never would have thought it of him.

But then, I never would have thought *any* of it of him."

"I suppose we never really know each other until we're forced to make extreme decisions, do we?" She continued to avoid his eyes.

"I guess not. But what about you? What happened to you after your capture?"

"Oh, they took me back to Knossos," she said briskly, as though grateful for the change of subject. "The palace was still in an uproar over the disappearance of the idol. The chief priestess was out of her mind with rage. I don't know what they would have done to me. But then, before they could make up their minds, the sky darkened, and the tsunami hit the coast. Knossos was too far inland for that. But the secondary quakes did a lot of damage, and fires started when all those oil lamps got knocked over. The wind whipped those fires into something resembling a firestorm. Everything collapsed into panic. I was able to get away in the confusion.

"Afterwards, hiding out in the countryside, I met an escaped slave who spoke Achaean. He knew about this cave. It seems there's a cult of Zeus among the slaves from the mainland; it makes you wonder how long he's been laying the groundwork for his little power play. Anyway, this slave gave me directions. It's not far."

"Not if you have two good feet," Jason remarked pointedly.

"Oh, yes! Let me see that." She carefully removed the filthy bindings from his left foot and wrapped it anew, muttering apologies for her lack of anything cold to put on it, while continuing with her story. "After I got here and settled into this cave, the local shepherds thought I must be some kind or priestess or wise-woman. I didn't do anything to discourage that impression," she added primly. "I was able to do some healing that they found impressive—I have experience in twenty-fourth-century first aid from my field work on Mithras, in addition to the course the Temporal Regulatory Authority put me through. In return, they've kept me supplied with food."

"Not bad cheese," Jason commented, taking another sample.

"Now, though, they're staying away. They're getting more and more of a worse class of refugees from the north."

"Yes—I spent a little time with some of those."

"So you can understand why these people have taken themselves—and their sheep, and their daughters—into hiding. You can also understand why, when I saw you . . ." She looked embarrassed in the firelight. "Well, I didn't recognize you, and—"

"I guess I do look a little savage," Jason acknowledged with a smile.

She smiled back, then looked at him levelly. "So what are we going to do now?"

"We're going to wait. It wouldn't do us any good to go anywhere else on Crete even if I was up to it. We can forage for food—*I* can even forage for food if I don't have to do it fast."

"Yes," she nodded. "You're right. This is where Perseus will be looking for us."

"Well, yes. And it's going to be important to get you set up somewhere, to wait until you snap back to the linear present. You see, you're going to have to wait in this era without me for a while."

"What?"

"You were in that pocket universe, with its distorted time, longer than Sidney and I were," Jason explained. "More to the point, your TRD was there a lot longer than ours. It turns out that I wasn't there very long after all; I can bring up the countdown on my optical display, and I'm due for retrieval before too much longer. But I have no idea when *you* are, and I have no way of finding out. The timer in my brain implant is linked to my own TRD and its atomic 'clock.' Nobody ever dreamed that the members of an expedition wouldn't all return at the same time—it's unprecedented in the history of the Temporal Regulatory Authority. In fact, it's unprecedented to have *any* of them return behind schedule. When I appear on the displacer stage, late and alone, it's going to be two firsts. Rutherford is probably going to have a stroke when he finds out he's going to have to keep the stage clear for some indefinite time, until you appear!" He chuckled evilly at the thought, then sobered. "It means you'll have to keep your TRD with you at all times. It also means you'll have no advance notice of your retrieval. One fine day, without warning, this world will vanish and you'll be in the dome in Australia. I'm sorry, but there's no help for it."

"I see," Deirdre nodded. It was, Jason decided, only natural that she looked so very thoughtful.

The days passed, with their breathtaking sunsets and cold nights. Jason's broken bone gradually knitted itself together, and he was able to venture further and further afield, gathering firewood and seeking out food. He fashioned a crude bow and managed a little light hunting for the wild goats and tiny deer that roamed the mountainside.

It was a tedious and still-painful effort for a small yield, but it was necessary to supplement their food supply. The shepherds of the Nidha plain were still mostly in hiding from the runaway slaves and other fugitives who had, for whatever reasons, found it advisable to remove themselves to this remote district.

After a while, the locals crept out again and began coming back to the sacred cave and the strange but kindly woman who dwelt there. But then the visits became less frequent, and those who did come acted frightened. Since none of them spoke Achaean, Jason and Deirdre were unable to ascertain the source of their fear.

They found out a few nights later.

Jason awoke to a kick in his side, a flare of torches, and Deirdre's screams.

He reached out, grabbed a hairy ankle, and pulled, sending the man sprawling. Then he sprang to his feet, forgetting his still-not-altogether-healed fracture. The pain made him stagger, and he was grasped from behind by two pairs of hands. He saw Deirdre, being held in the same way by one ragged man and being groped by a couple of others, while a half-dozen others stood around making comments. They were mostly armed with knives and cudgels, although a few had spears. He had barely had time to take it all in when a face came into his line of sight at close range. The puzzlement on that face gave way to recognition, and then to a laugh whose joviality would have been easier to appreciate if Koza's breath hadn't been so bad.

"Jason! By Rhea's tits, you made it this far—and on that foot! And then you ended up with *her!*" Koza jerked a thumb in Deirdre's direction and laughed again. "What a man! Let him go, you turd-eaters!" Jason's arms were released, but he noted that his erstwhile captors were still eyeing him watchfully. Koza flung a brawny arm around his shoulder and spoke in what passed with him for a quiet voice.

"See here, Jason, we've been on the run—a little trouble down by the coast—and since we've come up here the locals have kept themselves and their women hidden. And sheep are no substitute. Now, I don't begrudge you your good luck in catching this piece. But the fact is, you've already had the use of her for a while, and we're a little hard up, if you take my meaning. Don't get upset—you can still share her. But you ought to let your old friends have her first. Don't you think that's fair?" His tone was ingratiating, but left no doubt as to the basic unimportance of what Jason thought was fair.

Jason assumed his best raffish smile. "Sure. Seems reasonable to me. I just hope you like it, after . . ." He launched into a detailed and boastful explanation of why they might not find Deirdre altogether satisfying after her time with him. Koza roared with laughter, and the vigilance of the two men flanking Jason seemed to ease.

"Is that so?" Koza finally bellowed. "Well, we'll see about that!" He turned toward Deirdre and started to remove his tunic. "Spread her!" he ordered his underlings. Everyone else relaxed to enjoy the show.

Koza had his tunic up over his head, temporarily confining his arms, when Jason pivoted on his good foot and brought his left leg around a sweeping kick that knocked a spear-carrying bandit's legs out from under him. As the man lost his balance, Jason grasped the spear and rammed its butt into another man's side. Then, as swiftly as his bad foot permitted, he sprang for Koza.

He almost made it before Koza's tunic came completely off. But at the sudden tumult, the bandit leader threw it off, whirled around, and with the unerring instinct of a veteran brawler, stamped on Jason's left foot.

For an instant, pain was all that Jason knew, or could know, and he collapsed. The naked Koza snatched a cudgel from one of his men and raised it two-handed over his head as he advanced, his face a mask of rage.

He had almost reached Jason when his expression turned to one of blank surprise, and a spearpoint protruded from his chest. Already dead, he toppled over forward, revealing the shield-bearing, helmeted figure in the cave mouth who had hurled the spear.

Other similarly equipped warriors rushed in past him. It wasn't so much a fight as a massacre of the trapped bandits. Jason barely noticed the slaughter, for he recognized the spearman even before he removed his boar's-tusk helmet. He had seen a spear-cast like that once before, on the road between Tiryns and Lerna.

"Perseus!" he called, rising awkwardly to his feet.

Before the Hero could reply, Deirdre had rushed past Jason and flung herself into his arms with what sounded very much like a sob.

CHAPTER TWENTY-TWO

To Jason's delight, they sailed from Crete aboard Sotades' ship.

"Yes," said the grizzled old mariner—as Jason still couldn't help thinking of him, even though he would have been considered no more than middle-aged in Jason's world. "We were in Lerna when Poseidon made his anger felt. The coast gave us some shelter—unlike a lot of places, including practically all the islands. Thank Zeus I wasn't home on Seriphos!" He spat over the rail with the expressiveness Jason remembered. "But we survived. And when Perseus and his warriors came down to the coast from Mycenae looking for ships . . . well, I would have joined even if it had been somebody besides Perseus."

"So you were willing to put to sea after . . . what had

happened? When this isn't the sailing season even in normal times?"

"Of course." Sotades looked surprised that the question had even been asked. "All the shipmasters wanted to join Perseus' great raid on Keftiu, just like all the warriors of the Argolid. Everybody knew he enjoyed the favor of the gods. First he appeared at Mycenae in Zeus' chariot. And then, just as he was telling the warriors what was going to happen—it actually happened!" Sotades gave a smiling headshake of quasi-fatherly pride. "That Perseus!"

"Yes, I can imagine the effect that must have had," said Jason absently. They were standing in the stern, with Jason leaning on a crutch and Sotades gripping the helm against the still-treacherous currents and blustery winds. Behind them, the cliffs of Crete were dropping below the horizon. There, various adventurers who had elected to stay behind were already starting to squabble over Knossos. Perseus was leaving them to their squabbling. There would be no empire of the mainland and the islands; such a thing was beyond the scope of people at the Achaeans' level of political evolution. Perseus would return to Mycenae—their current destination—and content himself with the Argolid.

And as for Zeus . . .

"So," he said in what he hoped was the right tone of voice, "you're certainly right about Perseus being favored by the gods—or at least by Zeus and Poseidon and the rest of the younger gods. And I suppose that what Poseidon did to Kalliste, which was sacred to Rhea, proves . . ." He let his voice trail off and gave Sotades a quizzical glance.

"I don't really know anything about these deep

matters," growled the skipper. It was a quiet growl, accompanied by an anxious glance over his shoulder. Like any sensible man, Sotades was hedging his bets. "But some say that the gods have a new king—that Zeus has taken over from Cronus, his father, and imprisoned the Old Gods in Tartarus!"

Close enough, thought Jason. *Except that it wasn't Zeus who did it.*

"Well," he remarked aloud, "it does seem to stand to reason that the Old Gods would punish such talk if they still could."

"Hmm . . . You know, you may have something there." This seemed to resolve Sotades' theological perplexities, such as they were. "And anyway, who will defy the power of the younger gods now?" He gestured toward the starboard bow and beyond it, to the northeast where Kalliste had been. A black cloud still hung over the horizon.

Following his gesture, Jason noticed Perseus and Deirdre standing in the bows, arm in arm. As usual.

Sidney, Jason thought with a touch of sadness, would have felt vindicated by Mycenae. Not that there had ever really been any controversy about the great cyclopean stone walls that still stood in the twenty-fourth century. Everyone agreed that they dated to the fourteenth century B.C., with the extension that included the Lion Gate to be added a century later. In this era, the hillock overlooking the Plain of Argos was surmounted only by a wooden stockade—and not much of a stockade, for this was a politically powerless neutral ground between Argos and Tiryns.

That all began to change almost the instant they arrived. Perseus was a man in a hurry, and a stronger stockade began to go up. Nobody denied his right to establish himself here; his earlier spectacular arrival and accurate prophecy gave him a certain local clout. Not that he was ignoring the real basis of royal power in Achaean society: the giving of rich gifts to the warrior nobles, thus placing them under an obligation that wasn't formal enough to be called "vassalage" but was nonetheless real. His Cretan plunder gave him the wherewithal to do this on an unprecedented scale. Acrisius and Proetus still sat in Argos and Tiryns respectively, but if legendry was any guide their "accidental" demise was only a matter of time.

Loot wasn't the only thing Perseus had brought back from Crete to cement his power. Jason had noticed some Cretans in the ships who looked a cut above the general run of captured slaves.

Perseus chatted with him about it one day, as they stood on the summit where the new megaron was being built, looking out over the entire citadel—the perfect spot from which to survey the work on the new stockade. It would, thought Jason, have been a crushing disappointment to classicists and romanticists. It looked like any other construction site, only very low-tech.

"Yes," the Hero was saying, "I had never really thought about these things before. But while we were on Keftiu, I began to wonder if there might be something to be said for being able to . . . well, you know, keep track of things, the way the Minos had always done for the Old Gods and their priestesses. So I thought I'd bring in some of their scribes to do it for me."

"But," Jason asked, "how will you know they're not taking a cut for themselves?"

"Oh, of course they'll do that. They always did on

Keftiu. But I see what you mean: how will I know they're not cheating *me*? Well, it will help that their language is so close to the one I grew up with on Seriphos. Early on, I'll let them know I can understand what they're saying among themselves."

"That should help," Jason agreed. "Still . . . wouldn't it be even better if they were keeping their records in your own language? And if you had people you knew you could trust who could read those records?"

Perseus stared at him uncomprehendingly, as though he had spoken a *non sequitur*—which, Jason knew, he had, from Perseus' standpoint.

He described the exchange to Deirdre a few days later. It was sunset—yet another sunset of sinister beauty. They were standing beside the circular area Perseus was laying out just beyond the main gate of the stockade to hold the remains of himself and his descendants—"Grave Circle A," as the archaeologists would one day name it. Heinrich Schliemann, believing that "I have gazed upon the face of Agamemnon," would never dream of the true identity of the man whose gold death mask he had set eyes on—the first to do so in thirty-four centuries.

And as for me, thought Jason, remembering that famous death mask, *now I finally know why Perseus looked strangely familiar when I first saw him. And I also know how he's going to look in middle age, with a beard.*

"Of course Perseus didn't have the slightest idea what I was talking about," he finished. "In his world, writing is, by definition, linked with the language of Keftiu. So naturally the scribes he brought back must do their record-keeping in that language, and in their own script—Linear A, as it will one day be known. The idea that *any* language can be written down—including Achaean Greek—is beyond him."

"But somebody will think of it eventually," Deirdre predicted. "And then the Cretan scribes will be out of a job."

"Right. Some genius will get the idea of adapting Linear A to the sounds of Achaean, much like Saint Cyril will adapt the Greek alphabet to Slavic two and a half millennia from now. The result will be Linear B. Then a later wave of mainland Greek conquerors will carry it to Crete with them. And that's the answer to a riddle that's going to support innumerable academic careers, starting in the twentieth century."

"Sidney realized that, at the last, didn't he?" Deirdre asked softly.

"Yes." Jason sat down on the low stone wall surrounding the grave-circle-to-be, for all at once his left foot was giving him renewed pain. "He understood all sorts of things—like the artistic flowering of Crete in 'Late Palaces' period. We're seeing the start of that. One of the Achaean warlords there will win out in the end—and probably take the name 'Minos' and all the prestige that goes with it. The Cretan artists will be working for Achaean patrons, and from that cross-fertilization will emerge the synthesis our age thinks of as 'Minoan.' "

"So," said Deirdre after a while, not meeting his eyes, "Sidney knew all this—the fulfillment of a lifetime for him—and still he . . . did what he did." With an unconscious motion, she touched the little plastic case she wore tied to her arm.

"You have to understand him. I think I do, now. What was important to him was the knowledge itself. Of course, the fact that it tended to validate his theories didn't hurt!

But the point is that what we now know—the final solution to all the mysteries and controversies—will be brought back to our time. You and I will bring it. That will be his legacy."

"Yes," she said, almost too quietly to be heard, still staring into the lurid sunset.

Winter approached, and so did Jason's departure.

He could summon up the digital countdown any time he wished. He knew it would happen in the predawn darkness. That would be around noon, Australian time, so it worked out nicely all around. He could simply make sure he was unobserved—no trick, at that time of day—and that would be that.

He came to the realization that he didn't want to do it that way. Perseus deserved better . . . and even a lie was better than an unexplained disappearance.

"I find I must return home to Aetolia," he told Perseus in private one day.

"But why, Jason?" The Hero looked genuinely stricken. "Your foot isn't healed."

"I can walk well enough, if I don't have to do it very fast. And as you know, Synon was distant kin to me. It is my obligation to tell our kindred what happened to him, so that his memory may be properly honored, even though his remains are, of course, lost to us."

Perseus nodded. He had been given a suitably edited account of how Nagel had died on Kalliste. "Yes, I understand. But as unsettled as things are these days, let me send an escort with you."

"Thank you. But I'll be all right alone. I'll just leave very early, before sunrise, to get a good start."

"But, Jason—"

"Don't worry about me, Perseus. I'll be all right. And now I don't have to protect the lady Deianeira. I know she's safe, here with you."

"Yes." Perseus brightened. "She'll always be under my protection—and that of my father, Zeus."

"Of course," Jason nodded piously. "By the way, have you seen him lately?"

"No. He hasn't appeared since Poseidon's destruction of Kalliste. Neither have any of the other gods."

Probably making sure to consolidate their power in the other areas of the world where they operate, Jason speculated. Zeus and his allies had paid a price for their little coup. The Teloi pocket universe and everything in it was lost to them forever. Their only resources were whatever advanced equipment was already deployed at the time the portal device ceased to exist. That, and the awe in which humans held them.

From now on, they'll have to run a bluff, thought Jason with satisfaction. *And, as Oannes said, their lifespans are limited. Sooner or later, there'll be no more gods except in people's memories, and in the stories they'll make up.*

"Well, Jason, do as you must. Will I ever see you again?"

"Perhaps," Jason made himself say.

In theory, there was no reason for Deirdre to keep vigil with Jason in the predawn darkness as he waited for the time to wind down. But the possibility of her not doing so never even occurred to either of them.

When she entered his room, her dark-auburn hair made ruddier by the light of the oil lamp, he felt no surprise at all. He did, however, feel gratitude. He needed company, if only to fend off the gnawing worry that he had put out of his mind for so long. Admittedly, the chances of there being anything—or anyone—on the displacer stage at the moment he materialized there were slim to the point of statistical insignificance. But it still didn't bear thinking about.

Because of his preoccupation, he failed to notice the look on her face. It was the look of someone who had something difficult to say.

"Now," he began, making conversation, "just remember what I told you about your retrieval. It will be completely without warning. It could happen while you're asleep. Unfortunately, it could also happen when somebody is watching."

"Jason—"

"But I'm not too worried about that. People at this cultural level are matter-of-fact about the supernatural. A disappearing woman would be nothing compared to some of the things they take for granted!"

"Jason—!"

"There's something else we've both been avoiding talking about. But I want you to try not to worry about it. I'll explain the situation to Rutherford, and he'll keep the stage clear until you reappear, no matter how long as it takes."

"Jason—!"

"The most important thing, though, is that you keep that case holding your TRD tied to you at *all* times, no matter where you are or what you're doing. If it's out of contact with you at the moment the TRD activates, then—"

"JASON!" Deirdre took a deep, unsteady breath and, in the midst of the sudden silence, she untied the plastic

case and held it out to him. "I've been trying to tell you, Jason: I'm not going back."

The silence returned. Jason stared at her outstretched hand which held the entire world she'd known. And in that compartment of his mind where he never lied to himself, he knew he wasn't really surprised. And *that* surprised him.

"Not coming back?" he finally managed.

She nodded.

"Perseus?"

She nodded again.

Not the most scintillating conversation on record, gibed another part of his mind—the part whose function was to gibe. He dismissed it, and took the case from her hand.

"You know, don't you, that this part of the world is facing a difficult time? But of course you do. You were the one who told me about those two hard winters."

"Yes, I know. That's part of the reason I'm staying. I may be able to help."

"With no equipment or supplies? No access to high technology?"

"I will have knowledge. I never realized how much difference that can make, in a society this far behind ours, until the time I spent in that cave on Mount Ida. I know I can help these people through what's coming."

"I'm sure you're right. But that's not the real reason." He didn't even say it as a question. Nor did she answer. There was no need. After a time, he shook his head and gave a resigned sigh.

"Well," he said, "if you're going to make a crazy decision, you might as well make it for someone who's worthy of it. And I can't deny that Perseus is."

"He really is going to live in legend, isn't he?" she asked softly.

"Oh, yes. Of course, the mythmakers will get things confused, as always. They'll get his family relationships right; Sidney once told me that was the one part they *had* to get right, to earn their keep. And they'll remember—and elaborate—the part about the 'head of the gorgon.' But everything else they'll misinterpret and confuse. In particular, I can already see how they'll get his legend mixed up with that of Hercules." *Including the name "Deianeira,"* he added silently. *And may the God in whom I do not believe grant you a better fate than hers. But of course I'll never know, will I?* He shook off the thought and managed to smile. "Yes, they'll attach all sorts of monster stories and fairy tales to his name, while leaving out everything he should be remembered for. But, as I say, that's typical. And I don't suppose we should complain. At least the people who ought to be remembered sometimes do get remembered, if only for the wrong reasons."

She smiled tremulously. And he understood that she had asked for a kind of blessing from him, and had received it. He wondered if she understood that herself.

But she seemed happy. That was enough.

Out of habit, be summoned up his neural display. "Hey! I lost track of time. I'm almost down to the short count now." He stood up, having no desire to arrive in the twenty-fourth century with a pratfall from a couch that was no longer there. Then, on a sudden impulse, he extended his hand that held the plastic case.

"Deirdre, I want you to do one thing for me: keep this." He hastened on as she started to open her mouth. "If you don't want to use it, nothing could be simpler; just put it on your end table or something, and one fine day it will be gone. But just in case you have second thoughts before that happens . . . well, this way you'll still have the option."

"All right," she said, and took it from him.

They stood facing each other. The digital count worked its inexorable way down.

"Goodbye, Deirdre," he said when the count was almost at zero.

"Goodbye. Oh, and . . . one more thing, Jason."

"Yes?"

With a lightninglike flick of her wrist, she tossed the plastic case to him.

By sheer reflex action, he caught it.

At that instant, reality dissolved in the way Jason remembered so well. The Bronze Age was gone.

For the barest instant, Deirdre's green eyes, like the smile of the Cheshire cat, remained in the swirling chaos. . . .

And then he was under the dome of the temporal displacer installation in twenty-fourth century Australia.

The sudden change from the dim glow of the oil lamps to the glaring electric lights blinded him, and the disorientation of temporal displacement hit him harder than it should have—harder than it had since his first time. He fell to his knees, clutching the plastic case tightly.

Before he could see again, he could hear the uproar in the dome. He got slowly to his feet, blinked away the constellations of exploding stars, and looked around at the banks and tiers of control panels, from which people were streaming toward him from all sides.

In their midst was Kyle Rutherford. He must have been

in the dome at this particular moment by sheer chance. It occurred to Jason to wonder how much of his time he'd been spending here since the day the stage had remained inexplicably empty at the moment of their scheduled retrieval.

In a way, it must be even worse for him now, with just me here, Jason reflected. *Instead of a solution, another mystery.*

He stepped off the stage with the limp he still hadn't altogether lost, and advanced to meet Rutherford. The latter looked as though he had been missing a lot of sleep.

"Where—?" Rutherford began . . . and could get no further, having exhausted the subject with that one word.

"Dr. Nagel is dead. He died . . . heroically."

"But . . ." Bewildered, Rutherford gestured at the stage where the historian's remains should have been.

"His corpse, and his TRD, are in another universe—a small, artificial universe. Permanently."

"And Ms. Sadaka-Ramirez . . . ?" Rutherford finally managed after an interval of silence.

"She was alive when I left her. But she won't be coming back either." Jason held out the plastic case. Rutherford took it, opened it, and stared at the tiny object it contained.

"Hers," Jason nodded in confirmation. Had he only known it, his smile seemed strangely inappropriate. "It got cut out of her. It's only here because I was carrying it. At some point, it will disappear from wherever you decide to put it, and you'll find it lying here on the stage. I can't say precisely when that will be."

Rutherford struggled to form words in the face of yet

another manifest impossibility. Finally, as people often do when faced with a surfeit of mysteries, he opted for the lesser one. "But if she was alive—?"

"Oh, yes. She could have kept it. She really could have, you know. In fact, I wanted her to. But she didn't."

"Why didn't she?" breathed Rutherford.

For a time, he thought Jason hadn't heard him.

"To simplify her life," Jason finally said. "She was afraid that if she had the option, she might not be able to resist using it. You see, she didn't trust herself. She knew herself too well."

After another interval of silence, Rutherford pulled himself together and spoke in quite his old style. "Clearly, you have quite a lot to tell me!"

"Yes, I suppose you might say that. I also have quite a lot to show you, once my brain implant is downloaded. You, and others as well, are going to have to adjust a lot of your ideas. And you may want to reconsider the notion of any more expeditions into the distant past."

Rutherford started to open his mouth, then closed it, and finally contented himself with a simple "Come with me." They started to leave. But then Jason paused.

"Kyle, could I ask one favor?"

"Certainly."

"Can I keep Deirdre's TRD?"

Rutherford's eyebrows rose into arches of inquiry.

"When it vanishes," Jason explained, "that will be a kind of . . . closure. Don't ask me why I feel that way, but I do."

"You realize, of course," Rutherford reminded him, "that if you take it back to Hesperia with you before that happens, it will *never* happen."

"I hadn't thought of that."

"Well, then: would you want it as a permanent souvenir?"

"I might, at that. You see . . ." A moment passed before he could continue. "We went through a lot to get it back."

Jason expected something supercilious from Rutherford. But the older man simply handed the plastic case to him without a word. They departed the dome, and the crowd of curious technicians parted for them like the Red Sea.

PRAISE FOR STEVE WHITE

"Exciting extraterrestrial battle scenes served up with a measure of thought and science."—*Kliatt*

"White offers fast action and historically informed world-building."—*Publishers Weekly*

"White perfectly blends background information, technical and historical details, vivid battle scenes and well-written characters. . . . a great package."—*Starlog*

BLOOD OF THE HEROES

1-4165-0924-0 • $24.00 • HC

Jason Thanoi of the Temporal Regulatory Authority was nurse-maiding an academic mission to ancient Greece to view one of the biggest volcanoes at the dawn of human history. He and his charges were about to find that there was more to those old legends of gods and heroes than anyone had imagined. . .

DEMON'S GATE

0-7434-7176-8 • $24.00 • HC

1-4165-0922-4 • $7.99 • PB

Long ago, demons ruled the world, until they were exiled to the nether realm. Now, someone is trying to reopen the gate to that realm. Unless Prince Valdar can stop them, darkness will rule the world forever.

FORGE OF THE TITANS

0-7434-3611-3 • $22.00 • HC

0-7434-9895-X •* $7.99 • PB

The old gods—actually extra-dimensional aliens with awesome powers—have returned, requesting human help against the evil Titans. But, judging from mythology, how much can you actually trust a god?

Flag in Exile 0-7434-3575-3 • $7.99

"Packs enough punch to smash a starship to smithereens."—*Publishers Weekly*

Honor Among Enemies 0-671-87723-2 • $21.00
0-671-87783-6 • $7.99

"Star Wars as it might have been written by C.S. Forester...fast-paced entertainment."–*Booklist*

In Enemy Hands 0-671-87793-3 • $22.00
0-671-57770-0 • $7.99

After being ambushed, Honor finds herself aboard an enemy cruiser, bound for her scheduled execution. But one lesson Honor has never learned is how to give up!

Echoes of Honor 0-671-87892-1 • $24.00
0-671-57833-2 • $7.99

"Brilliant! Brilliant! Brilliant!"—Anne McCaffrey

Ashes of Victory 0-671-57854-5 • $25.00
0-671-31977-9 • $7.99

Honor has escaped from the prison planet called Hell and returned to the Manticoran Alliance, to the heart of a furnace of new weapons, new strategies, new tactics, spies, diplomacy, and assassination.

War of Honor 0-7434-3545-1 • $26.00
0-7434-7167-9 • $7.99

No one wanted another war. Neither the Republic of Haven, nor Manticore—and certainly not Honor Harrington. Unfortunately, what they wanted didn't matter.

At All Costs 1-4165-0911-9 • $26.00

The war with the Republic of Haven has resumed...disastrously for the Star Kingdom of Manticore. The alternative to victory is total defeat, yet this time the cost of victory will be agonizingly high.

HONORVERSE VOLUMES:

Crown of Slaves (with Eric Flint) 0-7434-9899-2 • $7.99
Sent on a mission to keep Erewhon from breaking with Manticore, the Star Kingdom's most able agent and the Queen's niece may not even be able to escape with their lives....

The Shadow of Saganami 0-7434-8852-0 • $26.00
1-4165-0929-1 • $7.99
A new generation of officers, trained by Honor Harrington, are ready to hit the front lines as war erupts again.

ANTHOLOGIES EDITED BY DAVID WEBER:

More Than Honor 0-671-87857-3 • $6.99

Worlds of Honor 0-671-57855-3 • $7.99

Changer of Worlds 0-7434-3520-6 • $7.99

The Service of the Sword 0-7434-8836-9 • $7.99

THE DAHAK SERIES:

Mutineers' Moon 0-671-72085-6 • $7.99

The Armageddon Inheritance 0-671-72197-6 • $6.99

Heirs of Empire 0-671-87707-0 • $7.99

Empire from the Ashes trade pb • 1-4165-0993-X • $15.00
Contains *Mutineers' Moon, The Armageddon Inheritance* and *Heirs of Empire* in one volume.

THE BAHZELL SAGA:

Oath of Swords 0-671-87642-2 • $7.99

The War God's Own hc • 0-671-87873-5 • $22.00
pb • 0-671-57792-1 • $7.99

Wind Rider's Oath hc • 0-7434-8821-0 • $26.00
pb • 1-4165-0895-3 • $7.99

Bahzell Bahnakson of the hradani is no knight in shining armor and doesn't want to deal with anybody else's problems, let alone the War God's. The War God thinks otherwise.

BOLO VOLUMES:

Bolo! hc • 0-7434-9872-0 • $25.00
pb • 1-4165-2062-7 • $7.99

Keith Laumer's popular saga of the Bolos continues.

Old Soldiers hc • 1-4165-0898-8 • $26.00
pb • 1-4165-2104-6 • $7.99

A new Bolo novel.

OTHER NOVELS:

The Excalibur Alternative hc • 0-671-31860-8 • $21.00
pb • 0-7434-3584-2 • $7.99

An English knight and an alien dragon join forces to overthrow the alien slavers who captured them. Set in the world of David Drake's *Ranks of Bronze.*

In Fury Born 1-4165-2054-6 • $27.00

A greatly expanded new version of *Path of the Fury*, with almost twice the original wordage.

1633 with Eric Flint hc • 0-7434-3542-7 • $26.00
pb • 0-7434-7155-5 • $7.99

1634: The Baltic War with Eric Flint hc • 1-4165-2102-X • $26.00

American freedom and justice versus the tyrannies of the 17th century. Set in Flint's *1632* universe.

THE STARFIRE SERIES WITH STEVE WHITE:

The Stars at War I 0-7434-8841-5 • $25.00

Rewritten *Insurrection* and *In Death Ground* in one massive volume.

The Stars at War II 0-7434-9912-3 • $27.00

The Shiva Option and *Crusade* in one massive volume.

PRINCE ROGER NOVELS WITH JOHN RINGO:

March Upcountry 0-7434-3538-9 • $7.99

March to the Sea 0-7434-3580-X • $7.99

March to the Stars 0-7434-8818-0 • $7.99

We Few 1-4165-2084-8 • $7.99

"This is as good as military sf gets." —*Booklist*

Available in bookstores everywhere.
Or order online at our secure, easy to use website:
www.baen.com